Mainline

Mainline

(Based on some real shit)

Joseph McCarty

authorHOUSE®

AuthorHouse™
1663 Liberty Drive
Bloomington, IN 47403
www.authorhouse.com
Phone: 1-800-839-8640

First published by AuthorHouse   06/25/2011

ISBN: 978-1-4634-1323-1 (sc)
ISBN: 978-1-4634-1333-0 (ebk)

Printed in the United States of America

To: Jerry Brown, California Governor
From: Trident
Subject: RICAP Investigation
Date: January 26, 2011

Arnold Schwarzenegger was governor of California in 2005 when he approved the RICAP Program (Research and Investigation for California's Administration of Prisons). To say California State Prisons are out of control would understate the problem. The institutions suffer from massive riots, from violence against inmates as well as violence against staff, and from a massive influx of narcotics and other contraband. These prisons nurture an absolute form of racism and do little to correct criminal behavior. We lead the nation in recidivism rate; reoffending is the expected norm and rehabilitation a rarely seen exception. Overcrowding left inmates sleeping on the floors of gymnasiums until a recent court ruling declared such housing conditions improper. The Department's current budget is unsustainable, and even with generous spending we are unable to give each inmate appropriate medical attention.

Recent Investigation has produced meager results. California's legislature, since 1989, has orchestrated numerous investigations and inquiries in an attempt to better understand the causes that lurk behind such dismal returns. We sent investigators from within the State's own Department of Corrections and Rehabilitation (CDCR), investigators from other State departments, and we have initiated investigation from private firms and State universities. Findings are detailed, but shallow. Each report included the same footnote, the same excuse for its lack of valuable data. Prisons are a large social institution. Even most inmates require years inside before they fully understand the nature or governing principles that underlie its dynamic and complex social structure, and our investigators spend much less time there than the inmates. We expect our analysts to produce results when they barely understand their subject matter.

The RICAP Program responds to prison's complexity by embedding its agents directly into the institutions they investigate. RICAP Investigative Personnel (RIPs) work undercover. The program coordinates with individual State courts to plausibly arrest and sentence these men (and woman—one of our investigators is female, stationed at Central California Women's Facility), so that no member of CDCR should treat that person differently. Each RIP is essentially an inmate.

Understandably, RICAP encountered some difficulty staffing its program. Qualified investigators were reluctant to surrender comfortable family life in exchange for a prison cell. For help solving this dilemma, the State turned to the Federal government, who in turn directed them to the United States Military. The Army, the Navy, and especially the Marine Corps suggested RICAP would have little trouble finding young, unmarried servicemen looking for a dangerous job.

The RIP's assignment is indeed dangerous. Where those investigators will live, tattling once is often punishable by death. The program is under no delusions about what might happen to its agents if they are discovered. Precautions have been taken. Only the RIP's immediate family learns of the nature of this assignment, and only after being counseled on the importance of maintaining secrecy. Any disclosure could jeopardize the RIP's safety. In addition, the warden (and only the warden) of each prison is informed that one of the inmates at that facility is an agent for the State of California. If at any time the warden receives a specified password, he or she will immediately contact program directors so the RIP can be withdrawn.

My Involvement with the RICAP program began just months after I joined the US Navy. During recruit training in Great Lakes, I persuaded my RDC to sign me up for SEAL training. At eighteen years old, I believed I would become the youngest sailor in our nation's history to earn his trident. I was at Coronado Island three days before I washed out—one of the first in my division to quit. Many have heard the rumor that SEAL applicants can only fail if they voluntarily resign. That's not true. If you physically cannot carry the hundred-pound pack across the five-mile-long obstacle course in the time allotted, then you quit, whether you want to or not.

I was disgusted with myself, frustrated with my own shortcomings and emotionally upset. While awaiting reassignment, I was invited to lunch by two civilian doctors who I later learned were program directors for RICAP. They asked me if I were still interested in doing something exciting and useful for my country. I signed before they finished speaking.

The RICAP training was extensive but quick, condensed down into ten eighteen hour days. Most of my time was spent with ex-cons. I met one old criminal after another, sometimes I sat with all of them at the same time. I ate meals with them, I used the bathroom in front of them, they taught me some prison card games. Always they spoke; always I listened.

After training I was directed to arrive on foot at a home in an affluent neighborhood in my own home town. I entered the residence, I shook hands with Program Director Roland, then I shook hands with a member of the Modesto Police Department. The officer placed me in hand restraints and escorted me to his car. I was charged with home invasion robbery including the use of a firearm. Six days later the District Attorney's Office offered me a plea agreement that would send me to state prison for seven years. I accepted.

It has been explained to me that any crimes I commit on this assignment will be excused, that I will not be held liable so long as my actions were necessary for the fulfillment of my duties. Program directors, however, remained rather vague as to what acts they consider necessary. I begin my investigation with the intention of committing very few crimes indeed.

I never met any of the other RIPs. We are incapable of compromising one another, accidentally or otherwise. Each investigator selected a password, something he would never forget, to be used only in case of deathly peril. I chose "trident." I am instructed to observe, to assimilate, and to document, submitting my research only when I truly believe I have reached the end of this investigative process. The following report summarizes my findings.

4

CHAPTER TWO

I first set foot on B-yard in December, 2005. Imagine a high school football stadium, only in place of bleachers stand long, three-storey buildings crammed with prison cells. The track is still there, but it's asphalt instead of dirt. Inside the track a ring of tables and small bleachers make up what is commonly referred to as the yard.

I showed up at ten o'clock—yard was open. My mind was immediately disoriented. Three other inmates and I were being escorted by a plump, Hispanic woman who looked like she might have purchased the uniform she was wearing from a costume shop. A clever joke for Halloween. More than a thousand men swarmed the yard, each moving with a purpose, somehow aware of where he was going and why. All of them stared at me. Some were dressed in different shades of gray sweats, others wore dark blue pants and light blue shirts emblazoned with yellow letters. None of them was smiling.

We moved counterclockwise around the track, as instructed in the State's Title 15 procedures manual (the reason most inmates choose to walk clockwise). Stopping at the first building, Toro Dorm, we shortened our party by one. Fifty yards and ninety degrees later, we stopped at the door to Whitney Hall. The officer spoke to me. I'm not sure what she said; I must have heard the words, but they didn't communicate anything. I nodded and she turned into the building with the other two inmates. I was alone.

Twenty-four hours before this I had believed myself prepared. I knew how things would go and I was ready. So why was I dizzy? I stood there clutching my paper bag and rolled up wool blanket as members of the swarm zoomed by me. Hopelessly, hopelessly lost.

I noticed one of the men had halted his zooming and was standing five feet away, staring at me. I turned around quickly to see if he was possibly staring at someone behind me. Of course he wasn't. I turned back to him. He was just looking at me. Minutes passed. I felt about twelve years old. Finally, as if sensing my desperation to end this torture, he spoke.

"You just get here youngster?"

"Yeah," I answered stupidly.

"You got everything you need? You got tobacco?"

I looked blankly, first at my bag, then back to him. I'm really not this dumb. He approached me and put a healthy cigarette in my mouth (my hands were full) and stuffed another two in my shirt pocket. As he lit my cigarette with his he asked, "What county you from?"

"Modesto." Modesto isn't a county, but I remembered from the RICAP briefing that this was the correct answer. Things began to slow. I noticed this man stood about five-three and had a face like an old catcher's mitt.

"All right," he said. "You got some good homeboys here. Good motherfuckers. I'll let 'em know you're here." Homeboys. I remembered that too. Your first association in prison is with the men from your own town. The training was coming back. He stepped forward and stuck out his hand. "I'm Mad Dog."

To meet his hand I had to roll my arm so my elbow pinned my wool blanket to my ribs. I shook and smoked in hands-free mode. Puffing, inhaling, I still held the cigarette in my lips as I said, "All right, Mad Dog." Smoke accompanied my words.

He held my clasp and stared at me, clearly unimpressed with my professional smoking talents. Why was he staring? What was he waiting for?

"You got a name, kid?"

Idiot. I must have forgotten introductions include an exchange of names. I replied quickly, "Joseph McCarty."

He tilted his head and smiled at me like he wanted to laugh but had lost the ability to do so. "I'll see you out here youngster." And with that, he left.

The officer returned from the building as he walked away. She spoke with a heavy accent. "Oh, djoo got a smoke! Good for djoo. Let's go." We continued around the track to Shasta Hall. "Djoo can't smoke in the building." I gathered from this that I was going into Shasta. I let the remaining third of the cigarette fall from my mouth and stepped on it.

The hall's front door (its only door, except for the fire exits that have been welded shut) opens in the center of the building to the sally port. It's about the size of a household entry, with barred doors on either side and a wall of bars protecting the cage and sally port officer. My escort and I turned to the left. The B side. The officer told me I lived in "Chasta B, 303." She asked me to sit on a nearby stool while the cage officer processed my movement sheet.

I was immediately approached by a porter, an inmate charged with keeping the building clean and relaying messages to inmates still in their cells. His name was Brent Foreman.

"What's going on, bro? You just rolled up?"

I told him I had. He was closer to my age and easier to talk to.

"I'm Brent. Do you know what cell you're going in?"

"Three-'o-three," I explained.

"Oh, good shit. Blizzard. You got everything you need? You got your paperwork?"

I nodded. Paperwork? What the hell was he talking about?

"That's a good cellie you got," Brent told me. "He'll look out for you."

Evidently I looked as though I needed someone to look out for me. One of the building officers led me up two flights of stairs and down a third tier catwalk to 303. He let me in and locked the door.

The floor and the toilet. Those were the only two things in the cell untouched. Everything else—the beds, the walls, the lockers and the ceiling—was completely covered with pictures from magazines. Naked girls presenting themselves, skateboarding shots, a picture of a waving President Bush that looked like a Nazi salute and a picture of Arnold Schwarzenegger in a triceps pose that definitely was a Nazi salute: there was not a single square inch of anything not coated with images. A television saddled in a yellow mesh bag hung from one of the ceiling-high lockers. The other locker was empty.

I climbed up onto the top bunk and put my pitifully small bag into the vacant locker. Then I stared out the window at the yard. The older convicts from RICAP's briefing had discussed the yard layouts. I tried to adjust my own concepts to match what I saw.

Everything was divided by race. Whites, Blacks, southern Hispanics, northern Hispanics, Paisas (illegal immigrants) and others (Asians, Pacific Islanders, Arabs: they all ran together). White men were my brothers—they each deserved a nod and a handshake. The southerners and

Paisas were our allies. This didn't mean we never fought, and it certainly didn't mean they would help me if I were in trouble. It only meant the three of us share the same showers, the same handball courts and bleachers, and the same workout bars. The other inmates were not necessarily our enemies. They were more like ghosts. Association with them generally led to fighting and bloodshed. We ignored them, and they ignored us.

I located the white area. They were down to the right, three tables and a concrete patio surrounding a light pole. The tables seemed designated. On one, younger men playing cards; the second contained men in their thirties and forties slapping dominos on the table's surface; and to complete the circle, gray-haired men playing chess. I watched them play. I learned chess when I was six years old. I watched them and hoped I would be able to play with them.

At an instant all of their gray heads turned in one direction. I followed their gaze. Two men were fighting at the card table. No. Not fighting. One man was stabbing the other while a third man held the victim in a headlock. I didn't see the knife, just a clenched fist, but he was swinging it in a way that was impossible to mistake for a punch.

The victim's body jolted with each thump. Five, six, seven. The stabber quickly turned and threw the knife like a Frisbee to another inmate, then strolled casually to the domino table. The man who now had the knife walked quickly but breezily toward the bathroom. The headlocker proceeded to beat the piss out of the now fetal-positioned pin cushion.

The intercom clicked on. "Code one, B-yard! Code one, B-yard! All inmates, prone out!" Officers sprinted toward the commotion from all directions. A loud pop sounded and the headlocker dove to the ground. Two officers sprinted right past the man with the knife. He jogged the rest of the way to the bathroom and flushed his cargo, then jogged to the workout bars and dropped to his stomach.

All of it had happened in half a minute. Even as that thought crossed my mind I realized I'd been holding my breath. Everyone was still, everyone lying down. The chess players had managed to carry their boards to a patch of grass and were playing from their bellies. Each guard stood catching his breath while an orange electric cart wound along the track. The victim wasn't dead, but the medical attendant's attitude suggested there was little hope, or at least little reason to fret. Either way, the man's leaking body left the yard on a gurney.

Twenty minutes later the intercom clicked again. "Yard recall for Whitney-A *only*." They were recalling the inmates to their cells by section to minimize the number of men on their feet at one time. I remembered one of the men out there lived with me in this tiny, picture-covered box. I tried to figure out which of them was my new cellmate. Two of the three inmates involved in the stabbing had not been caught. I could see them both. The stabber remained on his stomach next to the domino table. The carrier had ditched his white cap in the workout area and swapped his blue coat for someone else's gray sweatshirt. As long as neither of them lived with me, I'd be okay.

Click. "Yard recall for Whitney-B." The stabber got to his feet, dusted off, grabbed some items from the base of the light pole, and strode toward Whitney Hall. A wave of relief passed through me. Not the stabber. I watched the carrier from sixty yards away and three stories up.

"Yard recall for Shasta-A *only*." Nothing. Many got up, he remained. All the chess players were gone. A few card players and one domino guy were still there. Lots of inmates in the workout area.

Click. "Yard recall for Shasta-B." All but a hundred inmates got up and headed toward me. My dreadful suspense was short-lived, however. With his bulky coat and cap removed I got a good look at the carrier as he passed beneath the window. His shaved head, his neck, his hands: everything was covered in tattoos. His body unmistakably resembled the walls of the cell I occupied.

He arrived outside the narrow cell-door window and gave me a quick glance, then turned around and leaned forward against the catwalk railing. A collage of tattoos covered him and an evil, angry monster stared at me from the back of his head. I climbed down from my bed and stood in the middle of the cell, waiting for the door to open. It did. He walked in and put his hand out. "Blizzard." At first I thought this meant cool or hello in prison slang. I remembered Brent had said it too. Then I realized it was his name. I met his hand.

"Joseph McCarty." I was ready this time.

He released my hand, turned around, and pulled something from his locker. A piece of paper. He handed it to me. I opened it and barely had time to read his name before he interrupted me. "You got your paperwork?"

"Oh." That slipped out. Stupid words slip out when you're confused or surprised. I turned and reached into my locker, all the while wondering if I were about to go the way of the crumpled pin cushion. I dug out my court papers and my classification sheet from the reception center. Steadily, somehow, I handed him both. He gave them a quick glance. "No. Where's you 128G?" I just looked at him. "This!" he insisted, tapping the paper he'd handed me. "I don't care what your charges are. A rape-o can get out and commit a burglary and then his shit says burglar. Your 128 has everything, your whole history. You gotta have it or your through." I stood there trying to look collected. I doubt I pulled it off. "Nobody told you this shit in reception?"

"No. I was only there two weeks," I explained, "and we were on lockdown because of a riot with the Blacks."

"In Tracy?" he asked. I nodded. "Oh yeah. Fuckin' nigs," he reflected. "Look, they'll take you to classification a week from Thursday. You gotta tell 'em to give you your 128G. That's your passport in prison. It says you're not a child molester. Nobody comes back from classification without it."

"Okay." All I could muster.

"How old are you?" Blizzard asked.

"Nineteen." Small words, heart still thumping.

"You look fuckin' twelve." That was true. Even in the Navy I'd heard it. I had shaved my head and face and let it all grow back together to try to look older, but my facial hair didn't grow in everywhere it was supposed to and the patchiness only strengthened the impression. I looked twelve.

Blizzard and I spent the rest of the day talking. He was twenty-five, a skinhead from Marin County. He pointed out all the different areas of the yard from our cell window. He explained the phone line, how canteen worked, what was ours and what was theirs. And somewhere in there he hinted that if I didn't have my 128G a week from Thursday, I would likely be headlocked, stabbed repeatedly, and beaten to death while an apathetic MTA cruised his cart out to my lifeless body. Not surprisingly, I believed him.

That night I stared up at the prostrate whores and skateboarders heel-flipping over crowds of people, thinking about my safety password. I couldn't believe RICAP had neglected something as vital as a 128G. My confidence in the program was shaken. But I calmed myself. I recited my service oath in my head and even laughed at the coincidence of a stabbing occurring on the same day I arrived. That was naïve. I realized later it wasn't much of a coincidence.

CHAPTER THREE

A week from Thursday an escort brought me to the classification committee. I sat at a table across from Captain Tucker, CCI Stoltz, and CCII Erikson. They reviewed my file, they cleared me for yard, and they placed me on the vocational trade waiting list. Erikson had placed me in a GED preparation course but I quickly explained that I had already earned a high school diploma. She agreed to remove me from that list. The meeting went well until I asked for my 128G.

"Ah . . . well . . . ," Erikson rolled her eyes, "we don't give those out." I looked from the captain back to her, waiting for something more in the way of an explanation.

"You see," she continued, "if we give you one, then we have to give one to everybody. The population starts expecting everyone to have one. But there are some inmates who have private information on theirs. We can't give them their 128G because it creates a risk to their security. So by not handing out any, we protect everyone." She said this all to me like I was five years old.

"That's a fine idea, ma'am, but I hope you don't plan to begin this social experiment with me," I argued. "Everyone else here already has one."

"No they don't." She raised her eyebrows and closed her eyes as she said this, like she was explaining to a child how there really was no boogeyman.

I gave up on her and turned to the captain. "If you send me back without my 128G they're going to stab me."

For the first time he seemed concerned with what was being discussed. He leaned forward. "Why do you think someone is going to stab you?" he asked.

"Because I don't have documentation proving I'm not a child molester."

"But your classification score sheet shows that." He was very reassuring. "If you had ever been convicted of a sex offense there would be an E in the box there on the right."

I looked. The box contained a capital F written on top of a blotch of white out. To my left, I saw a bottle of liquid paper sitting in front of Ms. Erikson. I showed the captain. "There's white out."

"That was my fault," Erikson explained. "I made a mistake filling out the form."

"What letter did you originally write?" he asked.

She answered simply. "E."

"Please don't send me out there with only that piece of paper."

"We should probably just give him his G. That looks pretty bad. It looks like he changed it himself." She looked positively offended. "Just give him his G," he continued. She began writing a note as he turned to me and explained, "You'll get it with the mail in a couple days."

That was no good. I was expected to leave this office with that form. "I need it today."

"Well I can't just make it appear," Erikson snapped.

I left the office and stepped out onto the yard. First the workout area, I shook more hands than I could count. I met Blizzard there and explained about my 128G. He nodded. "Right, yeah, they come in the mail." He walked with me to the white tables and directed me straight over to a domino-aged group of men. One had a beard, all of them had tattoos on their necks. He got their attention. "Fellas, this is your homeboy."

"I stuck my hand out to the closest one. "Joseph McCarty."

"Yeah, Mad Dog told us you reported for duty," he remarked without shaking my hand. He stepped to my side and put his hand on my shoulders, turning me to face the group. "Check this out, homeboy. All that Joseph McCarty V-557129 whatever the fuck your number is, that shit's for them." He pointed to the cops. "To them you're that. For us you're Seph now." He sounded like Charlie Manson.

"Why not Joe?" one of the others asked.

"'Cause we already got five fuckin' Joe's on this yard and we got a God damn hard enough time trying to figure out who the fuck we're all talking about. So you're Seph, kid. Like Jo-seph, but no Jo. What do you think, homeboy?" He held his arms half open.

"All right." I was a big talker then.

"That's a good motherfucker!" He practically yelled this as he wrapped me in a suffocating hug. "You're my homeboy, youngster, and I love you to death. I love the fuck out of ya."

I was uncomfortable hugging another man, and I was a little concerned that loving the fuck out of me might entail prison sex. (This was prison.) I learned later how unrealistic those concerns were. There are yards where men have sex with one another—just like there are yards where child molesters and snitches don't get stabbed—but you won't find those yards at Soledad's North Facility.

I met more than fifty men in ten minutes. I tried to block out those names I didn't immediately need so I could remember the important ones. That didn't work. I remembered maybe six names, and half of those I knew already. Brent pulled me out of the mix to spin a lap with him, Glen, and Riotchild. I liked Riotchild: Josh Turner from Butte County, a skinhead. He looked just like my brother, Justin. Not Justin in his twenties, but maybe Justin in his teens. Plus he had on the same sunglasses my brother used to wear. I liked him.

I spent the whole lap listening. Glen had recently been given a job in the lieutenant's office, and his good buddy Brent enjoyed pointing out how Glen's new job was awfully close to being cop-friendly. "Watch out, Seph! Don't walk too close to the building. Fucking Glen here'll give you a one-fifteen."—That's a disciplinary write-up. Only cops issue them.—"He'll put you on C-status and take your yard for thirty days."

"You think you're fuckin' funny," Glen warned. "Keep it up."

"All right fellas, that's enough!" Brent held his arms up to keep a distance between Glen and the rest of us. "We don't want to piss off the captain's son." Glen bore it all in good fun. And Brent continued. "I think these guys have something on 'em. Why don't you put 'em on the wall and strip 'em out."

"I'm about to put you on the fucking ground," Glen threatened.

"Make 'em squat and cough." Brent put his wrist to his mouth. "I've got two ten-fifteens on the B-yard. I'm gonna need some back up." He dodged as Glen reached for him.

"That's right you're scared," Glen taunted. "That's why you roll it up off every yard you've ever been on."

"But I always come back. I admit I was scared and promise not to do it again. So I'm cool."

What did that mean? It was okay to roll up off a yard? The RICAP briefing had clearly explained that was not okay. But RICAP had been wrong once already.

"That shit's only cool with the dudes you run with," Glen continued his attack, "from your rat-ass home town."

This didn't make sense either. They were both from Sacramento. They'd grown up together in the same neighborhood.

"At least I don't suck dick," Brent countered.

"For money! For money!" Glen insisted. "When do you ever make any money? You just live off your rich fuckin' mom."

This was definitely not okay. Why would he admit to giving other men blow jobs? I looked around to see if anyone would attack him for saying this. Riotchild smiled my brother's smile at me and pointed to his crotch as if to say, "Yeah, I got in on that."

"What money?" Brent demanded. "The last dude only gave you two stamps. I'll give you three not to suck dick. I'd give a whole book if it would keep my babygirl's mouth clean." He put his hand on Glen's ass and rubbed his thumb on the base of Glen's spine.

"Stupid motherfucker," Glen laughed and pushed him away. Brent held his hand up a bit as he walked. He was clearly at a loss to explain why Glen would rebuke his perfectly normal advance.

This lap was my introduction to peckerwood humor and my first glimpse at convict games. When it was time to joke around (and even sometimes when it was not) the cons say incredulous things (what they call way out shit) and say them with all the sincerity they can muster. Whoever makes the most outlandish statement, and still manages to pull it off convincingly, wins the game. In this way convicts master the art of lying. They command body language, facial expression, voice tone, and eye contact to lend believability to the unbelievable. I've met cons who can convince anyone of anything. Even reading this I'm sure you're smiling and thinking, "Yeah, but not me."—Don't kid yourself. If you've made it this far into the book, I've already convinced you of at least three things that aren't true.

We finished our lap back at the tables. I broke off from the group and approached the chess table. Mac and Sparky, two of the best players on the yard (though I had no way of knowing that then) were sitting, staring at the board. I asked one of the other men standing there if I could play.

"Sure," he said. "Just tell 'em you want to play the winner."

I turned to the game. "You gentlemen mind if I play winner?" Neither man responded.

"Tell 'em you want tally," my friend encouraged me.

"You gentlemen mind if I have tally?" I don't think I expected a response and I certainly didn't get one.

My sponsor leaned over and rapped his knuckles hard on the table. "Tally!"

The old man on the right wearing the highway patrol sunglasses slowly unrolled his finger and flicked it in my direction. I had tally.

I watched the game. It was flawless. Mac won, Sparky got up, then Mac got up. Both men left toward the bathroom. I heard the man who'd helped me let out a loud tsk of disapproval. He approached the board. "Come on, youngster."

We sat down to play. He introduced himself as Dave, though I later learned everyone referred to him as anger management when he wasn't around. Halfway through our game the intercom clicked on. "All library workers report to your job assignments."

"That's me, kid. I gotta go," Dave explained. He was a point ahead but I had a clear positional advantage. I would probably win. He tapped another of the old guys as he left. "This kid Seph can play."

Frank Owen approached the table. He had a slight lazy eye and bore an unmistakable resemblance to a coyote. I couldn't look at him without thinking of the word *wily*. He outplayed me down to an even endgame, except for his two remaining pawns. Several guys watched as Frank used his king to escort the pawns across the board. I wasn't even playing anymore, just making moves because I had yet to learn when I should simply tip my king over.

I won almost accidentally when Frank trapped his own king between his pawns. My bishop moved over for mate. Voices sprang up and Frank took a little razzing. He stood a moment looking at the board, then raised his head and smiled at me.

I froze. I'm not sure anything has ever affected me like Frank's smile that day. Its bottom half was genuine, like I'd reminded him of some fun we used to have together as kids. But from the nose up it was ice cold. Not angry . . . sorrowful. Probably most of us never realize how much of our smile comes from the eyes. Frank's eyes were pleading. I got the overwhelming impression that Frank had seen, and perhaps caused, unspeakable human suffering. His eyes sat there, atop a typical closed-mouth smile, begging me not to do or say anything that would force him to continue such habits.

I was sitting with my legs tucked under the table (something I don't do anymore). I raised my hand to shake, then thought better of it and brought my hand down on my side of the board. I didn't smile at him—just nodded my head and said, "Good game."

He curled his chin as he nodded, looking back down to the board. Then he walked away.

Smerf stepped into his place. He was as good as Dave. I should have won, but didn't. Frank's smile had shaken me.

CHAPTER FOUR

The racial divide is absolute. It affects everything: chow, showers, sports, where you sit waiting for the dentist. No one questions it. All races seem equally fond of the separation. My own attempts to understand more about how this came to be have earned me nothing but dirty looks from the other inmates.

I've made a point of sneaking the question in only in confidential settings, where a person could answer me without anyone else overhearing. Results are consistently not what I had expected. They look at me as if I were crazy or stupid, as if they feel sorry for me. Some of them thought I was joking around. A few looked like they wanted to hit me.

Only one inmate ever gave me an answer. Mac was known by everyone as simply Mac. He was more than sixty years old. The housing board inside Whitney Hall showed his first initial as T, but nobody knew what it stood for and he refused to tell anyone. I sometimes just guessed. My second week at the chess table he tolerated me long enough to play one game. Toward the end (he won handily), I asked him the same question I had casually put to many inmates who seemed politically moderate. He didn't answer right away, instead looking around the yard without giving any indication he had heard me.

"Walk a lap with me," he said, getting up from the table. I went.

"What we have here is not racism," Mac began. "It's called separatism, and there's a big difference between the two. If you'll notice, even the skinheads don't sit around telling ethnic jokes or spitting racial slurs at people. The worst you can say is they ignore anyone who's not white. But it's not the evil, monstrous racism you learn about in grade school.

"Now as far as separatism goes, I can give you a pretty good reason for why it exists here." We were walking clockwise around the track. "In a second, up here on the left, we're gonna pass by a card table. Don't stare," he told me, "but pay attention to what game they're playing. See if you can tell me who's winning, or even what game it is."

We continued walking. The table Mac mentioned was hosting a card game played by four Asians. I think. More Asians surrounded the four players and seemed just as involved in the game. Cards and dominos moved quickly around the table, sometimes bouncing off into the nearby dirt, and each player's hands flew violently in all directions. They were screaming at one another. One man played two cards at once, then picked one back up. Another player threw his whole hand on the table and shouted angrily at the guy across from him. The person shuffling the cards didn't even turn all of them face down before shuffling. It was straight out of a Lewis Carroll novel—the March Hare's tea party.

"Now I don't speak Asian," Mac said with a straight face, "so I'm a little fuzzy on the details, but apparently one of those guys murdered another player's sister. When we walked by, they were in the process of making death vows and deciding whose family would side with whose."

I smiled, and Mac continued explaining.

"In reality, they were just playing cards. That's how they play. And who am I to say that's wrong? But take a look at this next table."

Just past the yard's toilet facility four southern Hispanics sat playing pinochle. Just four. Everyone else was at least five feet from the table. None of the players spoke.

"See how quietly they're all sitting? If one player even mutters the word bitch at another, they're gonna stab each other. But I'm not trying to put it all on one side or the other. The Blacks interrupt each other, and talk over one another, and yell and scream all the time, but you won't see them touch each other's asses or pretend to want to kiss one another like the white's do."

We had almost finished our lap. Mac continued his lesson. "The point is that each of these groups has a distinct culture with unique habits that seem strange to everyone else. The main divide is loud ones to one side, respectful to the other. But make no mistake, these Mexicans don't like us any more than we like them."

Once the difference had been pointed out to me, I started noticing it everywhere. Words like punk or bitch are go-words for whites, for souththerners, even for Paisas. If someone calls you a punk, you fight instantly, right there on the spot. Black inmates tend to use the terms more freely. I was sitting at our dayroom table, waiting to shower, when some loud voices at the Blacks' shower drew my attention.

"Hey! That's my shower, nigga!" The guy yelling was about medium build and still had his clothes on. He was shouting at a naked heavier guy who had just stepped under a shower head.

"I said that's my shower, nigga!"

"I'm *in* this shower, nigga!" the bigger guy countered. "Nigga this *my* shower!"

24

The fully clothed inmate looked about ten years younger, maybe forty pounds lighter. He paced back and forth for a second, then spoke to the intruder again. "Nigga, I put my soap dish in there!"

"Ain't no soap dish in here!"

"Nigga, I put my soap dish in that shower!"

"Ain't no soap dish in here," the bigger guy said while soaping his chest.

"Nigga, you's a punk!" the youngster fired off.

The bigger guy smiled while lathering his armpit. "Don't call yo' daddy a punk! Yo' mama's a punk!"

"Nigga, I get that shower when you get out!"

"Nigga, I'm in this shower forty-five minute! Take me that long to wash my ass!"

The first guy spat, "Bitch-ass nigga!" He repeated that a few times, then walked away. Maybe he'll shower tomorrow.

The groups are not one-hundred percent racially exclusive. On occasion you'll see Asians who are Nortenños, or even Sureños. And every now and then you'll come across a white kid who thinks he's a Crip.

One week after I arrived at Soledad a young man showed up who called himself Bishop (because he liked to play chess). He was a middle-class white kid from Sacramento, and he told CDC he was a Crip. The youngster's parents worked full-time, so he had relied on music videos for an upbringing. Instead of a suit and tie and six-figure salary, the youngster aspired to one day have the baggiest britches and most platinum teeth in the whole state. All his Crip friends were white kids from Sac. He only knew two Black guys, and they didn't know any other Blacks. But there he sat in the middle of the Black area on Soledad's B-yard.

The Black's didn't accept him. He wasn't from Compton or Watts, he didn't know them, and they didn't like white people anyway. They were disrespectful to each other, but to Bishop they were just nasty. He stood post at the edge of their area (Blacks never stand post) to make sure no one else but Blacks came in. They ridiculed and embarrassed him. He cleaned other Crips' cells and stood in line for them for store or the phone. I watched him spend ninety dollars at canteen and only make it back to his cell with a bar of soap and a tube of toothpaste. His cheeks were always puffy and his eyes were always black.

My cellmate, Blizzard, was the first to address this issue. He hated Bishop, hated the sight of him. The youngster made white people look weak, and Blizzard was the exact opposite of that. Where they abused Bishop, the Blacks feared Blizzard. The youngsters especially. They came from neighborhoods where the only whites they knew looked like Bishop and were always running away. They had never seen a white guy glare at them angrily with a swastika tattooed across his face. When I walked laps with Bliz I saw their eyes widen and watched them move to the other side of the track. On his chest was tattooed the Statue of Liberty holding a gun and a list of ones to kill, atop which could clearly be read the word "niggers."

Bliz planned to remove the white Crip. He hated watching the Blacks turn the youngster into their bitch, and he didn't want them to get comfortable treating whites disrespectfully. He said it was only a matter of time before one of them said something rude to one of our own youngsters, in which case we'd have to rush them.

None of Blizzard's views were revolutionary. All mainline California prisons operate on an all-for-one basis, and none of them allow white Crips to hang out. Most Black convicts grew up in neighborhoods where they outnumbered whites and other races. They're used to grouping up and jumping the outnumbered ones for their shoes and jackets. And in prison, they outnumber the whites. For this reason, most groups hold a hands-off policy. Throw one punch at a white guy and all the white guys will charge you. Sock one southerner and two hundred will attack. Over one punch, entire groups (white, southerners, Paisa, northerners, even Asians) will go to war in a flash.

Blizzard made a plan. Then he decided it was too complicated and he simplified it. "I'm just gonna walk over there and stab the dude. Whoever wants to go with me is welcome. I don't think the Blacks will fight for him, but I'm gonna stab all of them anyway." This was all said in our cell. I helped him make knives that night and the next day he brought all the knives to yard and called a meeting with the other skins.

"This dude's gotta go. I'm going right now." He held one knife in his hand and tossed eight more on the ground amid the circle. "If you'll join me, grab a knife and let's go. If you'll stop me, grab a knife and get your fucking money." Riotchild bent down and grabbed a knife, then nodded to Blizzard.

Some of the older skinheads hesitated. They felt it was too hasty, too immediate. "Hold on, Bliz," one said. "I owe some money. I don't want to skip out. Let me pay what I can and we'll do this tomorrow or Friday." Blizzard agreed and picked up the knives.

That night Bliz came in from night yard worried. (I couldn't go out to night yard because I didn't have a job.). The skinheads had held a meeting without him. No one would talk to him. He speculated for hours on what this might mean, suspecting the others may be plotting against him.

They were.

The next morning at yard release two younger skinheads, Scotty and Eighty-eight, jumped on Blizzard. The official word from the elders was that Blizzard had spoken disrespectfully to his comrades. Scotty and Eighty-eight were sent to check him. That, of course, was bullshit. A check is a one-on-one fist fight to correct poor behavior. A removal is a two-on-one beating. Sending two attackers delivers a clear message to the guards that the victim is no longer allowed on the yard. Blizzard was rolled up.

The three men who made this decision and who fed their lie to Scotty and Eighty-eight were each within a year of going home. They didn't want to risk catching any more time by having any riot with the Blacks. They traded their ideals, their honor, and their comrade for their outdates. I don't want to mention them by name.

Skip from Aryan Front, Con Man from Peni Death Squad, and Jester from South Bay Skins.

These men were the exception, rather than the rule. From my observations, most skinheads are decent and principled, though horribly racist. This episode does, however, demonstrate how convict rules are flexible, subject to change based on who owes money or goes home soon.

Two days later the cops rolled Bishop up—they didn't beat him up; when cops roll you up, they just tell you to pack your property. The Blacks had gotten word the woods might rush them over the white crip. So they tattled. Eight different Blacks sent eleven different notes to six different officers. The kid was removed and life continued.

I got a new cellmate later that week. He was a youngster from Hemet and we got along well. That same week I received a job assignment ducat placing me in a GED preparation course: Adult Basic Education. Evidently my counselor had not removed my name from the list.

My first day I explained to Mrs. Thompson, my teacher, that I had graduated from high school and so couldn't take the GED exam. She had me fill out a form and two weeks later my transcripts arrived, verifying my graduation.

I remained in the class. Mrs. Thompson filled out a drop chrono to remove me from the GED list, but said I would still need to attend until that change was processed. That never happened. My instructor filled out a new drop chrono every month, but my counselor never responded. I was assigned in that class for three and a half years. Most of the other students had no desire to be there, and I was continuously approached on the yard and asked if I could help get someone in to prepare for his GED exam. I never could. Mrs. Thompson let me bring textbooks out for other inmates to keep in their cells, but all work assignments ultimately came from the Counseling Department.

The inmates who wanted to attend school weren't allowed, and those who were forced to attend didn't want to be there. Eventually, I stopped going to class.

CHAPTER FIVE

That summer was pleasant, once you got used to the random eruptions of violence. I played softball all day long. I smoked during every activity except showers, and I spent hours on the yard soaking up the sun. I worked out (mandatory for white boys) and I played chess.

One morning I came out to yard to check out the softball equipment. Riotchild waited with me for the guard to make his way over to the recreation gate.

"I was reading this pamphlet last night," Riot shared, "about how Jews are like flies, how they need disgusting piles of shit to live off of. And that's hella true! Look at Jerry Springer. That dude makes millions off the worst shit in the world, trannies cheating on each other with midgets. Weirdo shit.

"Then I was reading this other article, some ACLU-type shit, about how white nationalists use the actions of one person who happens to be Jewish, and we use that to justify attacking whole buildings full of Jews. But that's bullshit. I mean it's probably true, but look: if one Black takes off on a white dude, we fuck up all the Blacks, right? We don't even care if the one Black who did it is still on the yard. And they do the same shit. There's something to be said for who you run with.

"And then I was reading this other shit . . ." Riot was well read.

He helped me carry the bucket of softball equipment over to the diamond. "I still can't believe that shit with Bliz," he said. "It feels all fucked up. And they smashed on him like that. I know I'm still brand new, but it feels all fucked up." I felt the same sentiments, but I didn't know what to add. We walked a while in silence.

"And then I wonder if me or you are next," Riot picked up suddenly where he'd left off. "Do you get that feeling at all?"

I looked around as I answered him. "There's not really enough dudes on this yard to roll me up." I didn't feel this tough, but it sounded good. I thought it may lend Riot some comfort or something helpful.

"That's fuckin' rad," he smiled. Evidently it worked. "Listen," he said as we picked through the softball mitts. "Bobby from Sac wants to talk to me later about putting in work. We need two guys. Do you wanna go?"

"With you?" I asked. He nodded. "Fuck no," I told him. He smiled my brother's smile at me. "Dude you weigh like a buck-thrity. Who the fuck are we beatin' up? Mini-me?" Still smiling. "I thought you just put in work?" I asked him.

"That was a single," he explained.

"What happened?"

"This dude in Whitney kept sleeping in till like nine o'clock. He'd been told like six times; even did burpies for it. All that missed him. And his cellie's some fuckin' nac. That dude gets up, but he won't tell his cellie shit."

"Where's the sleeper from?" I asked. "Butte?"

"No. Sac."

"Wha'd you do?"

"His cellie brushes his teeth and shits at seven," Riot explained, "but the youngster just lays there with the blanket pulled over his head. Even when the door opens. Straight neglect. So a few days ago I stayed out after breakfast. When his door popped, the cellie stepped out and I stepped in and shut the door. The dude's blankets were over his head, so I sat on the toilet quiet as fuck and let him fall back asleep. I felt like a secret agent, sitting there all stealth."

"What would you have done if he'd have peeked out from under the blanket?"

"Take off on him. I was watching real close.

"So after the gunner's bar had been thrown and the cop was off the tier, I ripped the dude's blanket back and cracked him hella hard, right on his chin. He woke up dazed. And I just fired on him for like two minutes. Then I stopped—he was all balled up—and I said, 'You had enough?' And dude he was like crying. He's all, 'Yes!' And I told him, 'You gonna start waking up?' 'Yes!' And so I got off him and I was like, 'Okay, then we can be friends. My name's Riotchild."

"Then what?" I asked. "You were locked in."

"Then I made coffee."

"You drank his coffee?!"

"I used his cellie's cup," Riot explained. "Then the coffee made me have to shit, so I took a shit in his house. He's all right though. He just needs direction." Some guys had shown up and were trying to pick teams for a game. One of them called my name.

"I hate being picked first," I complained.

"Play like a fag and they'll quit," Riot suggested. We played on separate teams.

That afternoon we met with Bobby. "Your comrades gonna trip on you handling wood business?" he asked Riot.

"No. I checked. Me and Seph are both cool to do whatever."

"Seph, you're a skinhead too?"

"No."

"What's the whole situation?" Riot asked. "Who's the guy?"

"Tommy John."

"Really?" Riot was surprised. Tommy John lived in Whitney. Riot liked him; I didn't know him.

"Here." Bobby unfolded a yellow newspaper article that looked like it was from the gold rush.

> PLAINVIEW, TX—Proceedings continued today in a multiple-defendant drug distribution case. Jury members heard testimony from Thomas Gene Mathews, former co-defendant turned state witness, as Mathews described his role in the drug ring allegedly run by brothers Jacob and Daniel Holden. Before Mathews took the stand Judge Robert Gifford instructed jurors that Mathews was receiving a mitigated sentence in exchange for his testimony, and that the jury should take that into consideration when weighing his statements. Mathews received three years imprisonment following his cooperation.

"Damn," Riot commented.

"We can get you Tommy John's paperwork if you want to be sure it's him," Bobby offered.

"No, I know his last name is Mathews."

"How old is this newspaper?" I asked.

"Don't matter." Bobby looked at me. "What's bad then is bad now."

"I just mean," I explained, "I mean Tommy John's been down like twelve years, right? And he got three years for this. Are we sure it's the same guy? He doesn't look but thirty-five."

"He's over forty. We can show you that too, if you like." Bobby was a patient old convict. "And he had a term between these two. The homeboy who handed me this recognized Tommy first, then had this sent in, not the other way around."

"We got it, Bobby," Riot said.

Bobby smiled. "This is your plug." He handed Riot a tube of paper wrapped in plastic, the size of a broken crayon. "If you get caught—and you'll probably get caught—shout out to the white men when you land in the hole. Shoot 'em your lock-up order, get on roll call, and shoot 'em this kite. You'll want to clean it up and rewrap it first."

"What do you mean?" I asked.

Bobby might have thought I was retarded. "One of you boys is gonna need to hoop this. You'll need to have it up your ass when you jump." Riot looked at it distastefully. "Well don't roll yourself up over it, kid," Bobby scolded. "It ain't no bigger than a mouse's dick. Shit, I keep a full can of bugler up my ass just to save on locker space."

"I don't get why everyone looks so pissed off when they go," Riot said as we walked laps. "I could see if it's your own personal fight and you're mad, but if you're just putting in work, why be pissed?"

"Maybe some guys need to be pissed off before they can fight," I offered.

"Everybody, it seems like. Did you see Hungry jump on Shane over that dope debt? His face was red as fuck and he was holding his breath."

"And you get tunnel vision when you're angry," I added. "Then you lose track of what's going on around you. Your punches don't land."

Riot and I spent the rest of that day planning. Any longer than that and we risk rumor sneaking its way around to Tommy's cellie or the cops. Tommy John played handball most mornings. A gunner's tower stands right over the courts, but that gunner was usually too busy mother-henning the phone line to watch what was happening right under his nose. It was the best place we would get.

I came up beside Tommy and asked who had last tally. As I wrapped my hand in a strip of bedsheet (for handball), Riot walked up from behind and threw his right arm around Tommy's neck in a rear-naked choke. When I heard his feet scuffle, I turned and grabbed Tommy John's right wrist with my left hand. That was it. In two seconds a man who outweighed either of us by sixty pounds was completely immobilized.

I used my grip on his arm to pull my weight into every punch. Slow and steady. One punch per second: one one-thousand, two one-thousand. He went limp on the third, but I continued. Five one-thousand, six one-thousand. Each punch landed with a melon thumping thud.

Finally I released Tommy's wrist and Riot let him sink to the dirt as we started toward the bathroom. Blink and you missed it. We washed up and I flushed my sheet strip, then the two of us headed for the phone line. Still no cops had seen Tommy John's unconscious body. The phones switched and we moved closer toward making a call.

After what seemed like half an hour but was probably closer to ten minutes, the loudspeaker clicked. "Code one, B-yard! Code one, B-yard! All inmates prone out!!"

We proned out.

I suppose I should answer for my actions. Do I feel bad about hurting that guy? No. He wasn't a good person, and I didn't exactly kill him anyway. At the time, I was living in a dangerous place. And when you live amongst wolves, you behave like a wolf, or you are eaten.

CHAPTER SIX

A few months later Riot found me at the softball bleachers. We sat off to one side, where no one could hear us.

"Help me out. I've got this thing I've gotta do," he started. "I gotta hit this guy. It's gotta be in the White area and it has to be at night."

"Okay." I was pretty sure I knew who it was and why they'd have to hit him at night. The guy worked all day and only came out briefly at night yard to shake hands. He stayed in on weekends to watch sports. Riot was talking about hitting the shotcaller for the Whites. I'd heard the smut whispered around all that week.

"But you know how the nightyard cops always hang out by the pisser. And there's nobody out here at night—maybe a hundred guys. They'll see us right away." He glanced over to the toilet, then continued. "If I try to make it to the pisser with the piece, they'll tackle me. So how can I get rid of it?"

The rule is: if you make the knife disappear, the DA won't pick up your case. You'll still get in trouble with CDC, but you won't be stuck with any new sentence.

I had a couple suggestions for Riotchild, but none of them were very good. I felt like I hadn't been much help. The next night he came to find me at the handball court. He wore all State clothing and a pair of gloves as he walked up to give me a hug. I knew then he'd go. I didn't watch, but continued playing handball with Mac and a few other friends. Ten minutes later the code sounded.

Most people, even many convicts, have inaccurate ideas about what a shotcaller does. He's not a king. He's not even a boss. He doesn't get to tell anyone what to do. He's more like a secretary. He organizes things. One guy gets to know all important goings-on. That way we don't stab somebody on the same day four guys are trying to bring a large amount of drugs from one building to another. This particular shotcaller was giving the cops information.

Riot figured out how to manage the trick after all. Once the guy's neck was good and sliced, he tucked the blade into the victim's jeans pocket. Four guys then proceeded to stomp the victim out. It was brilliant, really. The victim gets medi-flighted to the hospital, his clothes get bagged as evidence, then (once the investigation fails to produce any weapon) the case gets dropped and the bloody clothes get thrown out.

I didn't know then where the piece had gone. I stayed proned-out on the damn handball court until midnight, four hours after the hit. When it first happened the cops had rushed over and pepper-sprayed everyone. They took one look at the victim and called for a helicopter. As they gurney-wheeled him out, one of the cops looking for the knife fell to the ground as stiff as a board. He fell from a standing position and smacked his face on the pavement surrounding the light pole. He'd had a stroke. I watched the guards dump the victim (who was bleeding and in critical condition) onto the concrete, turn the gurney around, and go get their coworker. Our shotcaller caught the second helicopter.

Staff took their time searching the area. They were convinced no one had run for the toilet. The knife had to still be there. They turned over tables and trash cans, stripped everyone in the area naked, then stripped everyone else on the yard. They even had each inmate bend over at the waist, spread his cheeks, and cough to make sure nobody had hid the knife up his ass.—Disgusting, right? They wouldn't check if we didn't do it.

The strip-out took hours. We didn't mind, though, and actually had a good time throwing rocks at each other. At least this time they had a reason for taking so long. Hour-long prone-outs are an everyday occurrence at Soledad, but the ones that get to us are the bullshit prone-outs: lying on our faces for sixty minutes for a false alarm or a one-on-one fist fight. I know this doesn't seem like that big a deal, but it is. This is why I'm here. It's what the program is looking for. Bullshit prone-outs are exactly the reason California prisons breed, rather than deter, criminal behavior.

Maybe we need some background.

Imagine a woman robbed at knifepoint while using an ATM. Of all the things she loses there, her two hundred dollars will be the easiest to replace—simply a matter of working a little overtime. And the bruise on her cheek will heal in a couple days. But she loses something more, something much harder to replace. Things made sense before this happened. I work to earn money, so I can do things I want to do and buy the things I want to buy for myself and for my family. But if someone can just take that away, why should I work? And what's worse, she loses her sense of security. She used to pull up to the supermarket and get out of her car thinking about dinner, or an upcoming birthday party, or taking the kids to Disneyland next summer. Good things. Now every time she opens the car door she wonders if someone will assault her, or take something from her, or violate her. [Credit here should be given to psychologists

Frieze and Janoff-Bulman for their "theoretical perspective for understanding reactions to victimization."]

That same list of what the woman loses, those are the reasons why a normal person would feel bad about robbing her. How could we even think of putting her through that? And for two hundred dollars?

But prisoners don't have that. Anyone who has served more than a year in prison is likely incapable of seeing any loss more than the money. We no longer understand the significance of being a victim. California prisons are a whirlwind of victimization. That's just a part of life. And it comes from the other cons, to some degree, but more often it comes from the staff and from the institution. As toddlers, we expect our brother to steal our cookies. And when Mom catches him, we expect her to punish him. Imagine you went to your mom to complain about the cookies, and she slapped you in the mouth and took your ice cream as well. Mom is the prison administration. The prison tells the inmates that inmates are entitled to these ten things. Then it only gives the inmates three of those things.

The prison says yard opens at eight-thirty. At eight-fifteen, the inmates get dressed. At eight-thirty they stand by their doors. But yard doesn't open. Nine o'clock, ten; the unit cop says he's waiting for the call, but he doesn't know why they haven't opened it yet.

It never opens. Not only do we not get yard, but we spent all day waiting by the door so we wouldn't miss the unlock. Staff should tell the inmates when yard is cancelled and why it's cancelled. They don't. Same as with the bullshit prone-outs: they don't care. You're all convicts, lower than snakes, so sit there and shut up.

And I know, I *know*, you're sitting there reading this thinking, "But they *are* convicts. These are bad people who have committed bad crimes and they don't deserve to be catered to or treated like princes." I agree. They are bad people. They should be boxed up and buried deep in the earth. But that's not going to happen. Most of them have out-dates and they will then be released back into society. These men may deserve to be cruelly punished, but your grandchildren shouldn't have to bear the consequences of that punishment.

Compare this with your dog snapping at you. It's unacceptable, and the dog may even deserve a good kick in the teeth. But if you spend three years kicking your dog, you end up with a mean little bastard that bites your kids, bites the mailman, bites your Aunt Sue when she visits. Let reason, not emotion, guide your judgment.

We were some of the last cons to leave the yard. As I passed the White area I waived to Riot. He was sitting there handcuffed amid several comrades: Rooster, Rowdy, somehow Fat Tony had ended up in the middle of everything. That was the last time I saw Riotchild. He went to the hole that night.

CHAPTER SEVEN

I read a lot. Most convicts do. I have my textbooks for school but, recreationally, most of what I read is fiction. I like good stories and characters that really say something about human nature. I mean, if you don't have anything to say, why are you wasting paper?

Still, sometimes I branch out. While I lived in Shasta I read a nonfiction book from the early twentieth century. It was a firsthand account by this guy who'd lived in Europe at a time when the economy wasn't doing so well. He talks about a lot of things—the whole book is just him talking—but one thing he mentioned really stuck with me.

He gets a job at this factory. All the workers there earn below minimum wage, they're all barely scraping by. But you could do it. You could live and feed your family from that small paycheck. Every second week you get your twenty-three dollars. You go down to the store and you buy a two-pound bag of beans and a three-pound bag of rice and you make it last. You buy a little milk and maybe this payday you buy a pair of shoes for your boy who's still wearing last year's shoes. And as a treat, you buy a little chocolate for your family to share. You celebrate payday.

But nobody does this. Maybe a couple do; they all started out this way, stretching their dollars and getting through the weeks. Only it's never enough. What good is rationing to stay alive if, though alive, you and your family are always just better than starving? Life becomes a steady plane of unhappiness with no peaks or valleys, a miserable glide slightly above rock bottom. So the treats get bigger. Last week was a little chocolate, this week you buy a cake. Two months later you've implemented a biweekly payday feast with roast beef and salad.

Of course, to pay for this you have to reduce the amount of food you eat on other days. The feasts get bigger (with beer and applesauce) and the better they get, the less money your family must survive on.

But they're happy. You've given them something to live for, something to look forward to and they will gladly survive on dreams and candle wax during the other thirteen days.

At the extreme, men would spend their entire paychecks in one night. They would even forsake their loved ones and blow everything at the local bar, buying the house a round as each hour struck. Selfishness consumed them. They'd been poor too long and now (against all reason) they give away everything only to experience for one night what it would feel like to be rich.

These kings-for-a-night were the early 1900's predecessors of today's dope fiend.

They don't feed you enough in prison. I should explain that first, or the rest of this won't make much sense. In theory they hit their mark. The prison prepares a two-thousand calorie diet for each inmate, every day. But that's not what we get. First, the inmate cooks and servers take their cut off the top. And if we're eating in our cells because of a lockdown, the building porters take some extra food for themselves. We get less than we're entitled to.

In addition to meager portions, what we eat redefines disgusting. No one cleans the pots. As a result, anything that's cooked in a pot (beans, mixed vegetables, stew) bears the strong and unmistakable taste of greasy dishwater. Our scalloped potatoes can't be eaten (like chewing on poker chips), and we get them every fucking meal. Because of these things, unless you feed yourself you are hungry, always.

Luckily the State allows your family to send you packages with food in them or to send you money for store. So here's the comparison with that factory in Europe. Your package is payday. You could stretch it: you could buy enough cheap food—beans and chips and ramen soups—to put a little food in your stomach every day. And when you start out, that's exactly what you do. Then you get this idea. Why not order a package-day treat? So you get a box of honeybuns and some corn nuts to share with your cellie. Next package it's a bag of pork rinds and some oreos. You stuff yourself that day. Within a year your package contains bags of beef jerky and nacho cheese and packs of grilled chicken. You eat everything in three days.

It gets worse from there. One package day you trade two bags of chips for a joint, or four bags of beef jerky for a twenty-paper of crank. Two days later you double it. Eventually someone else fills out your package list because the whole box is going to him anyway. Getting high is your payday feast, methamphetamine and heroin your beer and applesauce.

Why do convicts turn to drugs? I could sit and think about it for hours and still not come up with a good answer. In searching for release, we trade one prison for another.

At this extreme we find the prison junkie, the dope fiend. These modern-day kings-for-a-night live on narcotics. They don't care where it comes from or how they get it. Most of them have long since been cut off from their families and so have no package coming. They get on the phone and even pretend to speak with someone, but no one listens on the other end and no one will send to the dealer the money they owe. They are alone. They care only for getting high and, somehow, they always find a way to make it happen.

I started getting high as an escape. Prison sucks. It's the worst place in the world—not so much because of the restrictions, but because of the people you're around. And you *have* to be around them. Imagine the most intolerable son of a bitch you know. Multiply that one incredible asshole by two thousand. The lowest, most disgusting people in the world go to prison, and you and six hundred of them live in a building half the size of a football field. You want to eat? You come out and sit at a table with them. A shower? You'll have one on either side of you and a third asking if he can share your showerhead.

Irritation grinds you down, unceasingly, until you hate everything. You stop wanting to listen to music or watch TV. You snap at anyone for anything. You pray for quiet but it never comes. Never. The pressure crowds you from all sides, like being underwater and unable to escape. But waiting for you at the surface, drugs are a breath of fresh air. You don't bother me when I'm high. Shit doesn't get to me. I'm so immersed in what I'm doing and how I feel that no amount of you hanging on my shoulder and talking way too loudly in my ear about how you once stole your grandmother's jewelry to pay for a prostitute can possibly affect me. I'm at peace.

Of course, once I know the air is up there, I'll do anything to get it. Almost. I never traded my television or radio for drugs, but only because of how it would have made me look to the other White boys. I never forsook principle either, but nobody does at Soledad. We run those dudes off.

I used meth more often, but heroin caused me more problems. The worst mess I fell into came when I got a new cellie who used as well. Debt accumulates more quickly when you've someone next to you who's screwing up just as badly as you are. Look, nothing terrible has happened to him yet. Why not a little more? It starts small, too: a twenty on credit, then fifty. In one week we each ran up two-hundred dollars in heroin debt. The skin on my nose was badly peeling from me rubbing my face.

That was my new cellmate's last week in prison. He went home. Everyone else, including myself and all the guys we bought drugs from, believed he still had three months left to serve. We were cellies, we used together, we bought from the same people (I had even picked up dope for him from the connect). According to prison rules I was liable for his debt. Almost overnight I was four hundred dollars down. I didn't know what to do. And I was still high. I'd come down in another twelve hours and that meant two days of vomit and diarrhea. I wouldn't even have time to get my head on straight before my homeboys started asking questions. If I couldn't cover my debt, I'd be gone. About this time the drugs started to lose effect—I knew they were because I actually started to feel some concern about getting stabbed.

I sat on one of the tables in the White area, nodding out, with my feet on the table's bench. I must have sat there all day. Things would be worse if I'd hid in the house; I knew at least that much. Just after two o'clock Teardrop came up and sat next to me. Teardrop had lived in Modesto for his last ten years, but grew up in Inland Empire. In prison he was IE.

"What the fuck's up, youngster?" he greeted me. "You look like shit."

"I feel great," I replied sarcastically. He was looking around to see who could hear us.

"No fucking softball today? I thought you always played ball?" He asked this aloud, then leaned in close like he was kissing me on the neck. He whispered, "You know that Paisa, Conejo, on the A-side?" I nodded and he continued. "You owe that dude any money?"

I hesitated, and considered lying about it. Best not to. "Yeah. I got fifty from him on Monday."

"Okay," he explained. "Don't trip on that. You hear me? Whatever you owe that dude, don't trip."

I didn't really understand what this meant, so I asked.

"They're gonna fucking whack that dude, homeboy." Teardrop had his god damn mouth buried in the crook of my neck as he said this. What a creep. He added, "Ol' Conejo fucked up with these Surennos, homey, and his own people are gonna whack him at breakfast tomorrow. So don't send that dude no fucking money. Them Paisas don't want no piece of those southerners."

He got up, looked around, and left.

They care only for getting high and, somehow, they always find a way to make it happen. Do you remember me saying that? Conejo was leaving. My debt was down to three-fifty and that should have been cause for a relaxing breath as at least some of my debt was lifted. But before Teardrop was out of view I had already formulated my plan.

I was the first one in the building at yard recall, straight to the A-side. I ran up the stairs and down the tier to Conejo's cell. He was home. I knocked on the door and called him to the window.

47

"What's up, my man?" he asked in a heavy accent.

"What do you got right now?" I asked him as I rubbed my face.

He stared down into the soup he was eating out of a bag. These dudes are all the same. Prison dealers want to sell everything quickly. If you're caught with drugs, you lose all your profit, you go to the hole, you catch a new case. Life sucks. But he didn't want to get burned. He raised his head and said, "You owe a lot of money my man."

Shit. My homeboys had put word out not to sell to me. They were trying to stop me from accumulating any more debt. Which meant they'd already begun discussing what to do about my existing debt.

"No," I corrected him. "I owe you fifty, and I owe a guy on my side fifty. That's it. I owed Solo two hundred, but he just called. My money landed today." Conejo played dominos with Solo every morning. He had to know about the money I owed Solo, so I thought I'd use that to reassure him. "Hold on," I told him as I turned around and looked over the edge of the tier at all the prisoners coming in from yard. I pretended to look for Solo, then I gave up and turned back. "My money landed with Solo. I'll send him up to talk with you." I was lucky Solo didn't suddenly appear because my money had definitely not landed.

"Why you no get from him?" he asked. This dude was unbelievable! Didn't he trust anyone?

"Solo's out. He doesn't have any more." I was pulling my own hair out and my strung-out eyes were pleading with him, but he just stared at me.

"When you money land for me you come, I give you more," he offered.

"That shit won't land for three days. I'm coming down, bro, and I don't want to kick right now. Look, I'll send my TV over tomorrow morning and you can hold it till my money lands. Just give me one-fifty. That'll make it two-hundred, like Solo. I'll call my people and have them make it two hundred." I was very reassuring.

He thought it over. "You bring you TV?" he asked.

"The porter, Brent, on my side." I promised, "He'll have it here after breakfast." Five seconds later he slid a hundred and fifty dollars worth of heroin under his door.

I didn't make it to dinner that night. The evening porter, Coco (so-named because he was from Contra Costa County) came to check on me. He peeked in on me through the window and found me sitting cross-legged on the floor listening to Pearl Jam.

"You got more, didn't you?" he demanded. I didn't really answer, just sort of half-assed waved. I wanted to tell him no, to lie, but I was just too high. I could barely sit up. He tapped on my window with an accusatory index finger. "You're fuckin' up, Seph."

I closed my eyes and rocked back and forth to the music. I was still up when breakfast came around, so I went. Coco and my homeboy, Shannon, made a point of sitting with me. As soon as I sat down I pushed my tray forward and closed my eyes. I'm not even sure which of them was talking, but he was trying to jam me up about the debts.

". . . seen too many youngsters go down this road. And you're too good a motherfucker, and too well liked here, for this to be how you go out. So what are you going to do?"

"Why are you sweating this without even having given me a chance to pay the debts?" I asked with my eyes closed. "Half the motherfuckers in this chow hall have owed money that went over a month past due. None of mine's more than a week. My money will land. I pay my debts. So get the fuck off me." They could have been about to jump on me or been pulling knives from their waistbands. I would have had no way of knowing. I was too high.

Once back inside my cell I went straight to the window. From the top bunk (vacant since my last cellie had left) I could see the guys from Shasta-A just starting to head back inside. Now was when they would get him. The other Paisas would have had enough time in the chow hall to work out who would stand in front of him and who behind. I picked Conejo out of the crowd. I saw him, I saw the other Paisas around him, and I watched them all walk into the building. They didn't stab him.

There was a chance they planned to get him once inside the hall. I waited. Nothing. Everyone locked up from breakfast. The doors were shut and the gunner's bar thrown.

Shit.

I looked at my TV, still hanging from the ceiling-high locker. Maybe the Paisas wanted to get him on the yard. Maybe they wanted to do it in front of the southerner he'd wronged or maybe the youngster on deck lived in the other building. Or maybe Teardrop was full of shit. I couldn't allow myself to even consider that a possibility. He couldn't stay. If he stayed, the yard would turn against me. My only choice would be to arm myself and make an absolute massacre out of whichever luckless youngsters were assigned to deal with me. I didn't want that. Maybe they'd get him at yard.

I went out when they opened yard. I had to: as soon as I showed any doubt or fear I'd be through. I said good morning to everyone, the usual handshakes, and walked casually to the phone line. I figured it couldn't hurt if Conejo or the other creditors saw me making a phone call. Everyone likes hope. I considered pretending to talk, making it look like I was making things happen, getting money sent. Then I really did call home. It was Saturday morning and my mom and brother were both there. For twenty minutes I forgot about prison. I entered a world of barbeques and trips to the lake, of funny stories about the neighbors and two little barking dogs. I hated that damn phone.

Conejo met me as I came out of the phone line. I'd seen him waiting in the workout area and I'd spent the last five minutes of my phone call praying he was just there for pull-ups.

"Why you TV no come?" He was pissed.

"I gave it to the porter," I explained, "but we had that new cop in there today. Right now the porter has it in his cell. He's gonna bring it over at nightyard." I couldn't really tell if he believed me or not.

"Your money land with Solo?" he asked.

"Yeah, yesterday," I confirmed. "You talk to him?"

"He's at a visita." Thank God for that. He continued. "So you send it at nighyard, okay?" He walked off toward the Paisa table.

I went back inside at the next inline. As I got up from where I was sitting in the White area, an unusually large number of White boys got up and prepared to go in. This wasn't yard recall, but an optional open door to head back inside. Normally four or five guys per side go. I noticed twelve, all of them quiet and at least half of them stole glances at me. The group moved quickly to put me at its center. Shit.

They more or less escorted me back inside. A few guys broke off and went to their own cells, but more made it up to my sleepy little corner of the third tier than I'd ever seen up there at one time. My homeboy Shannon and his cellie, Whitey, stood next to me by my door. Tripper leaned against the rail to my right, and Brent and Coco stared at me from across the tier. I'd never seen this before, and I had no idea what was going to happen. It didn't make sense. Shannon had taken the keys to the yard since the night Riot left (that meant he was the shotcaller). If I was getting stabbed, he wouldn't be in the immediate vicinity. And if I were getting checked they'd send a youngster, not any of these guys.

When the gunner threw his bar to open the doors, I didn't move. I waited, looking straight forward, calm and patient. No one else moved either. Finally I turned around and with a word of departure, "Gentlemen," I opened my door and stepped inside. All this was slow, steady, but once inside the cell I moved as quickly as I could. I went straight for my pillow and pulled my knife from under it. I turned back to the door, using my body to shield the piece from view.

Shannon had closed my door almost all the way and was staring at me through the window. He just stood there. I, of course, just stood there looking back at him, clutching my knife behind my back. He slowly closed my door until it clicked shut, then walked away. I stood motionless until I heard the gunner's bar go up. When it clacked, I dropped my piece on the ground. What were they trying to do? Scare me?

I had every intention of going to chow that night. I wasn't about to give anyone the satisfaction of thinking I was afraid. Only I nodded off. The sounds of slamming doors woke me as the other inmates closed their cells and headed out. I didn't want to stay in, but I barely had time to get up from my bed before the gunner's bar was thrown. All cells were locked.

I sat in silence for half an hour, thinking. Prison irritates, and most of the men here break records for worthlessness.

Still, a select few were my friends. A handful of these men had proven themselves, time and again, to possess the finest qualities of human character. They were my comrades. Our mutual desire for dependable allies drew us toward one another and, together, we drove the under-qualified from our midst. I loved them, I needed them, and proving that I belonged amongst them made me feel good about myself. Only now these were the men who were coming for me. I hated that. After a year in Soledad I felt as though I could fight the world alone, so long as I never had to lay a hand on any of my comrades.

That's how it goes in prison. If you mess up, it's usually your closest homeboys who come after you. This holds especially true if you're well-liked. I would have difficulty putting into words exactly what produces this result; why the strongest of men would rather stab their own best friend in the heart than let someone else, some stranger, lay a hand on him. Even reading this, I imagine thirty or forty people are nodding their heads, while the rest of us have no idea what I'm talking about. Best just to move on. It is what it is.

Shannon's stare had hit its mark, just not in the manner he intended. It didn't frighten me, it broke my heart. I hated that it was him staring at me, that my friend was trying to intimidate me because I couldn't stop getting loaded. The men who thought so highly of me now had lowered their opinions. It was enough to make me want to throw up. I didn't though. I wanted to save my stomach's strength for the sixteen hour vomitfest that necessarily follows a week-long heroin run.

I got up on the top rack to look down at Shasta-A as they came back from dinner. I wanted to find Conejo. I kept imagining he would look up at me and make some menacing gesture, a hand across the neck or a finger rub for money. Then I heard one of my all time favorite sounds. The loudspeaker clicked.

"Code one, B-yard! Code one, B-yard! All inmates assume a prone position!"

To my right three Paisas were kicking and punching a curled up Conejo. The guards rushed in and sprayed everyone. They hadn't stabbed him, but it didn't matter. Conejo would not be back. In thirty seconds my debt had fallen from five-fifty to three-fifty. I got down from my the top rack and dropped to my knees in the middle of the cell. I thanked God for sending those Paisas to kick the piss out of Conejo. I thanked him for making me sweat and for humbling me with this lesson and I promised, not to be perfect (prison had long ago taken that possibility from me), but to practice more discipline, and to never again break the hearts of those who had faith in me. And since I was already on my knees, I leaned over to the toilet and threw up for forty minutes.

CHAPTER EIGHT

One October morning I sat down to play chess. In the middle of our second game Mac squinted and held his hand in front of his face. "Trade me spots, Seph. The sun's getting me right in the eyes." Mac was old, so giving him my seat was the right thing to do. We swapped, and as I spun the board around Mac got my attention. "Look at me," he said. I did. "Now look directly over my left shoulder." My eyes shifted to the right. "What do you make of that?"

I was looking at the Christian table, the only table on the yard where Blacks, Mexicans, and even some Whites sat together. They used this spot to hold hands in prayer and sing songs. Occupying the table this morning were nine southerners. And not just any southerners. These were some of the big homies, a few younger hitters, and a couple ese's (Sureños, pronounced like "essays") who were well known for carrying big knives. Four Christians—three Blacks and a southerner resident—stood nearby on the track looking lost. One of them held a guitar case.

Prison Christians aren't real Christians. Maybe five percent of them will go to church or live by God's word after release. Inmate Christians run Christian so no one will check their paperwork. They hide in the chapel to avoid violence, terrified that someone will ask them to put in work or that they might have to defend themselves. Conversation with them tends to give you a creepo vibe. These same men will gladly prey upon women and children when they get out, so long as their victims are much smaller than them.

"I'll tell you," Mac said. "I couldn't count how many times I've seen this."

"Someone taking another race's table?" I asked, surprised that he had seen it more than twice in his life.

"No. I'm talking about what caused this bullshit. Last week we got a new captain for this yard. And he's new, and has ideas, and he wants to show everyone he knows what he's doing. So he shakes things up. He decides there's too many tables on the yard. And all the wooden ones, the tables that aren't cemented to the ground, he has them removed. I saw them yesterday. They're all still behind Shasta.

"And this time it was the tables, but it could be anything: how we walk to chow, or unlock procedures. It's always some dumb asshole who thinks he's smarter than the way we've been doing things. Why did he take the tables, Seph?" I was still watching the southerners. "They've never once been used as a weapon or even squabbled over. Until now."

Three guards walked over to the Christian/southerner table. In seconds the noise level on B-yard went from crowded baseball stadium to vacant field on a windless day. It was eerie. I couldn't make out what the first guard was saying, but I heard the southerner's response.

"We're Christians." The yard cop, Alford, said something. The same Sureño replied, "Every Sunday." Another ese stifled a laugh. Alford pointed to the lost Christians standing on the track. "They can come over here," the Mexican insisted. "As long as they're down with God, they can join us."

Neither Alford nor the Christians seemed dumb enough to see this as a sincere invitation. The Christians left, and the cops escorted two of the southerners up to the Programs Office.

"You mark my words, Seph," Mac said. "This bullshit with the tables is going to cause a world of shit. And if Officer Alford thinks he can keep that table for the Christians, he's out of his damn mind. He might as well be trying to dam a river with a single fucking two-by-four."

As I reached down to make my next move, I heard a loud thunk. Someone slammed into my shoulder. My legs weren't tucked under the table, so I was up quickly and swung around the table's corner to let the scuffle pass by. It was Hungry again. Damn this kid put in a lot of work. He landed a series of heavy shots on some guy I didn't know. A slender youngster hopped around the fight, alternating between squaring up and dancing around.

Mac yelled, "Grab the pieces!" as he walked toward the grass balancing the chessboard. Before I could reach for them a rubber block from the rooftop gunner struck our cluster of pieces like a bowling ball. A pawn hit poor Yugo right in the face.

One of the slender dancer's older homeboys yelled, "Get that piece of shit!" The kid hopped in and threw a punch. It was a two-on-one, but with Hungry, it didn't have to be.

As I proned out across from Mac I told him I'd lost a white pawn. He said we could use my ID card.

Staff recalled the yard over the two-on-one. We lost our afternoon yard but walked to chow; no lockdown. My homeboy Greg had moved in with me a week earlier and we had fast become good friends. Greg and his brother Steve were known in Modesto's newspaper as the Comcast bandits. They were portrayed as daring, gunslinger outlaws, but neither of them really belonged in prison. The idea of providing for loved ones at Christmas set the brothers up to be talked into armed robbery. But I think Greg and I got along so well because he was a normal guy—rare in prison.

At dinner we sat with another homeboy, Justin Massengil, and his cellmate Bones (Chris Johnson from Santa Rosa). Our dinner talk was dominated by bullshit and convict games. We all brought our trays to the table, then Greg and Justin headed back to get some water. As soon as they'd left I slid Justin's fork to Bones. I swiped the lid to Greg's cup and hid it up my sleeve, then nodded to Bones who followed suit by stashing the fork. Justin and Greg returned together.

"All right," Greg sighed heavily. "Where's my lid?" He looked from me to Chris.

"Yeah, my fork's gone," Justin noticed.

I returned Greg's stare, then raised my eyebrows and went back to eating. After a second Greg said, "Seph."

I put my fork down, exasperated. "Why do you always look right at me?"

"There's only two of you sitting here," he said defiantly. I tilted my head in Chris's direction.

"I didn't take it," Bones answered.

"I look at you 'cause you do the most sneaky shit."

"Yeah, every now and then," I defended. "Every now and then it's fun to play around. But not every fuckin' night. It's cool if, once in a while, we have a normal fuckin' dinner without the bullshit." I was noticeably irritated, but they weren't buying it. Damn they're good.

"All right, you know what," I continued, "Chris stole your guys' tupperware." I turned to Bones. "Now I'm a fuckin' rat. Are you happy?"

"I didn't steal shit."

"Skin that!" I challenged. As he raised his hand to slap his arm I leaned toward him, "You know what motherfucker," and stuffed my hand into his pocket. I let Greg's lid fall down my sleeve and into my hand. Chris stood up to move out of my reach, but that only raised his pocket above the table and into view. It certainly looked like I'd pulled Greg's lid out of his coat pocket.

I tossed it on the table. "Where's the other one, Bones? Empty your other pocket." I said this because I thought the fork was in his sleeve—a little inaccuracy to sell the idea that I wasn't involved in the theft. Turns out Chris really had moved it to his pocket. He really had no choice but to toss the fork onto the table. His cellmate was waiting to eat. I only meant to let him take credit for about a week, but I think I forgot to ever come clean. Greg and Justin probably still think Chris stole their shit.

The next morning I skipped my regular handshakes to grab a spot in the phone line. Mine was always one of the first cells let out, so I didn't notice anything when I crossed the yard. As the rest of the inmates were released, though, bad feelings surfaced. The atmosphere demanded attention; I don't know how else to explain what was happening. I scanned the yard, trying to figure out what was wrong. Gradually I noticed more and more Crips clustering together in their small area in front of Shasta Hall.

That was it. There weren't any Blacks in the phone line. Maybe eighty percent of the B-yard Blacks stood in the group. Then it moved.

By now two-thirds of the yard had tuned in. The cops still hadn't noticed. Iron Mike, from Sac, was two spots ahead of me in line. He called to a southerner ahead of him. "Hey, homey. Them toads might be fixin' to rush you guys." The southerner took one look, then yelled to another

Sureño to ready himself. That second Sureño knelt down to dig a knife out of his shoe. They left the phone line toward the nearest southerner table. As they jogged past, I noticed both of them were now carrying knives. How do they always have so many knives?

The cops were on their radios. The Blacks had moved along the track. The front end of the group reached the pisser. Every toilet had a crip with his hand down his pants, supposedly hiding his piece. Each of them had another crip posted-up behind him. The force they had mustered was impressive, and the southerners at the ex-Christian table were basically surrounded.

This was a role reversal. Most prison riots are caused by Blacks fucking up. They'd get too comfortable, disrespect another race, and that race would attack them. To see them pushing an issue and rushing anyone was surprising. To see them preparing to rush the southerners was unbelievable.

I stared intently at the crotches of the men at the urinals. I didn't care if they thought I was gay or what-the-fuck-ever. I wanted to catch a glimpse of metal. If the Blacks brought knives, they were here to fight. If not, it was only a bluff, a muscle flex.

Riots are dangerous places: not just for the groups involved, but for men on the sidelines as well. Let's not forget most of the men on any three yard are violent felons in their own right. They're not here for using violence on behalf of their groups, but for using it on their own behalf. They're angry men who like to hold grudges. I once watched someone walk up to a guy he hadn't seen in years and sink a metal spike into the guy's chest. We keep anger. And a riot is the perfect chaotic atmosphere to get away with clearing old personal debts. An aggressive block during a football game, cutting in line at store; maybe an Asian guy overheard me joking in an exaggerated accent; maybe my downstairs neighbor was trying to go to sleep early when I yelled out my window last Thursday evening. Convicts remember insults. If the Blacks and southerners got off, they'd be the only people not on my radar as I tried to find a safe place to sit.

The intercom clicked on and asked all inmates to take a seated position. Sure. No problem. That announcement might as well have been a starting pistol as just about everyone took off running in one direction or another. The ese's swelled into groups, the Blacks moved their army to the basketball court, and the cops spun circles in a mild panic.

I noticed Iron Mike was still standing in line. I walked over and joined him. "Can you believe this shit, youngster?" he asked. "This shit's fuckin' crazy." I liked Mike.

Nobody fought. Somehow everyone ended up proned out. The cops strip-searched everybody, found no knives, and escorted everyone back inside.

Once back in the cell, Greg and I prepared a spread (one big bowl of food with lots of things mixed together) and shared versions of what happened. Just as we'd finished eating a code sounded. "Code one, Toro Dorm! Code one, Toro Dorm!" And then seconds later, "Code three, Toro Dorm! Code three, Toro Dorm!" The southerners in the dorm had rushed the Blacks. So much for flexing muscle.

Cops ran for Toro from all directions. After the initial cheers and yelling died off, the yard was quiet again. Everyone waited to see who was brought out, and what condition they were in.

"Tie yo' shoes tight, nigga." At first I thought this came from one of the cells below mine. But all my downstairs neighbors were Whites or southerners.

"Why?" came a younger voice.

"Nigga, do what I say!" I slid my mirror out the window to see. "And pull yo' pants up. Fix yo' belt so they stay up."

"That look stupid!"

"You can sag 'em back down when we get to the hole."

"Why we goin' to the hole?"

Two Blacks sat on the curb below my cell. They had been up at Medical when everything happened, and were being escorted back to Shasta when the dorm cracked. Their escort had left them to run toward Toro.

"Now you listen to me, nigga. When I take off runnin', you run too. Run as fast as you can. And when we get where we goin', you show the world you can fight."

I turned in to face my own cell so my voice wouldn't carry out the window. I asked Greg, "You hear this?"

"Rec gate," he answered.

I looked. Education had been releasing inmates when the code sounded. Seven cons sat outside the gate: two Whites, two southerners, a Paisa, an Asian, and one Black guy. No cops anywhere around them.

Staff had dragged eight Blacks out of the dorm so far, no one else. All of them were sprayed and handcuffed. As the first southerner came out of the dorm, the two Sureños at the rec gate attacked the Black. Those two Blacks in front of my cell really did haul ass, too. They beat the cops there by six seconds. They didn't save the other Black guy from his ass whoopin', but they did get some shots in before the cops got control of the situation.

CHAPTER NINE

Monday, February 6. The southerners and Blacks had been slammed for three months following the dorm riot. The two groups were on sight with one another for the first thirty days of the lockdown. Two Blacks got beaten up, another was stabbed. I don't even know what agreement had been reached to end the lockdown, other than the Surennos kept the table.

This was an ordinary Monday, except that it followed an unusual Saturday. Saturday morning we'd gone to breakfast. Everyone was happy, everything normal. We came back to our cells and prepared for yard, thinking we'd go out and enjoy a game of football. Yard never came. Not only were we locked down, but the entire prison was slammed. Nobody knew what had happened, and staff made sure we had no way to find out.

We shrugged it off. Greg and I worked out in the cell and tended our two gallons of homemade apple wine. On Sunday we got drunk and watched the Superbowl. Lockdowns aren't so bad if you know ahead of time you'll be locked down.

On Monday, the porters came out to serve breakfast. As they were finishing, the Asian porter walked down the tiers calling out, "Normal program," at every other cell. We got our things together, gloves and coats, and prepared to head out. Within minutes, though, Coco showed up at our door. He looked at me, then whispered into the door jam,

"Mandatory yard." Pulling his face back into view through the cell window he asked aloud, "Did you hear me?" I nodded.

These are some of the most ominous words in prison. Mandatory yard. It means something happened. Something's up. And we're involved, so bring your ass outside 'cause we're probably fighting someone.

My cellie and I talked it over, trying to decide if we should bring our knives to yard. Greg hadn't been at Soledad for out last mandatory yard. I had. We'd grouped up against the Blacks. We looked tough, the Blacks looked tough, then the cops called a code and everyone proned out. It really was a poo-butt affair. And all the White boys were left trying to hide their knives before the guards stripped them out.

Greg was generally opposed to hiding anything in his ass. He understood, though, that if anything did happen, a knife could save his life. It's not even about stabbing anyone else. Just having a piece in your hand lets you choose who to fight, rather than have six guys charge you at once. If you're armed, other cons will only engage you if you come at them. If you ignore them and give them a choice, they'd much rather rush a guy who's not armed.

We decided against bringing the knives. It was just too likely this was some dramatic, soap-opera bullshit. Plus we figured if anything did happen, we'd be all right so long as we stayed near one another. We broke our knives apart and flushed them, then made a solemn homeboy vow that if anything did happen, we'd stay together.

We met Shannon on our way down the tier. "Come with me," he asked. "We've gotta go talk. Pretty much I just need some homeboys there, in case the group needs to be disagreed with." That our homeboy had keys for the yard was the only reason Greg or I were involved in the yard discussions. This was fine, though. At least we wouldn't have to wonder what was going on.

"Some shit happened in Whitney," Shannon said, once we were on the yard and could stand by ourselves. "Woodpile's coming out to run it all down." Woodpile was from Stockton, essentially a homeboy. He lived in Whitney but worked on yard crew. The prison had split the two halls apart on a rotating schedule, so Shasta Hall inmates had limited access to Whitney's guys. Woodpile was by default a common go-between.

Men began to join our circle. Woodpile was the last to arrive. We said our good mornings, then everyone was quiet while Woodpile spoke.

"All right, Saturday morning when Whitney's first group was going in for chow," he began, "some fucking shit happened. All of Shasta was done feeding and back inside. Most of Whitney's first group was in and sitting down there in the chow hall. And our tables for that group are in the back right there, next to the entrance line for feeding.

"So the very last guys are coming in, and all of our guys are already sitting down. Well this fuckin' Crip, he's like eighteen, he just got here. He sees these dudes at the very back of the line he knows. And he's all smiles and shit, and he yells hello. Then he gets up from his table and walks over to them. He walks right through our tables.

"So Mad Dog, he gets up and tells this kid what-the-fuck, ya' know? He explains to him, look, these are our tables. We don't walk through yours, and you don't walk through ours. And this kid's acting like, 'Who the fuck is this dude?'

"Well his people wait, they don't move forward in line. So that gets the cops' attention, and they come over. Then all the cops outside the chow hall come in. And this kid, I don't know, maybe he thinks like he's running out of time to figure out what he's gonna do. The cops close in, and this kid cracks Mad Dog.

"And the cops are all over it. Mad don't even get a shot off and he's hemmed up, and the cops are radioing for squad. They take Mad Dog and the niglet up to the patio,"

"Why didn't the motherfuckers in the chow hall jump?" Jay interrupted. "Who the fuck was in there?" Jay was from Fresno, the only guy there besides me under thirty.

"They said the cops were already on it. Anyway that's not really the issue." I couldn't believe Woodpile had even acknowledged him.

"The fuck it's not! Every motherfucker in that chow hall should've got off," Jay insisted. "They're all pieces of shit."

That'll be addressed in turn, Bubba," Shannon told Jay. "What Woodpile's saying is there's a more pressing issue right now. Did you come here to argue, or to listen to Woodpile explain what-the-fuck?"

Jay shut up.

"So Mad explains to the lieutenant, he says he can fix it so we don't have a full-out riot. He tells 'em they've got to bring both of them back to Whitney.

"So they do it. And on his way back Mad gets at their people in Whitney and runs it all down. And dude already knows what time it is. He says the Crips already talked it over. He says they'll have the kid checked on the track, right in front of the White area.

"Mad's cool with it. The Black shotcaller, he says it won't be two-on-one, but the Crips promise to send a big guy. He gives assurance it'll be decent, and Mad tips his hat and goes along on his way.

"Only they don't open yard all day. That kid gets rolled up and the cops move him over to A-yard. Mad gets his door open and goes back to dude's door. And the black shotcaller says 'don't trip.' He says he's already sent a kite over through the kitchen. He says they'll do it over there on Monday, and the Woods over there can verify it was cool and done in front of our area and shit.

"Well the Black dude shows up yesterday at Mad's door. He says the kid is so-and-so's fuckin' nephew over there, and they like him, and they'll explain to him how he was wrong, but they don't want to smash him over some shit that happened on another yard. Basically they're not gonna do it.

"And Mad told him it might be okay. And he wants to come out and talk before we do anything."

Everyone but Jay waited to make sure Woodpile was done. "It ain't Mad Dog's fuckin' call," Jay said.

"He ain't sayin' it's his call," Woodpile returned. "He'd just like to put in his piece before we act. It was his face was struck."

"Mad Dog's face don't just belong to him in this situation," another man put in. "We were all punched in the face here, and all of us have cause to feel offended."

"I agree." Stoner, from IE. "It's not Mad Dog's call."

"The point is," Whitey said, "if we don't answer this, the fuckin' nigs are gonna get way-the-fuck casual in how they come at us. If we don't bite their ass every now and then, they forget we have teeth."

"Yeah," came another voice, "but it's not really their fault the dude got taken off the yard. They offered to check him."

"Bullshit," Shannon explained. "The cops brought dude back here on Saturday. Why would they take him off the yard the very next day unless one of them dropped a kite to avoid seeing the kid beat up. Probably twenty kites were dropped." This looked to be a short discussion. "So, what?" Shannon asked. "Go in and piece up during lunch? Rush 'em this afternoon?"

Jay didn't give anyone else a chance to put in. "No," he said. "We called mando yard this morning. We're ready. Why give rumor a chance to work its way over to their side?" That was actually a good point. The Blacks had evidently been told everything was cool. Twenty of them had started a game of football.

Shannon looked around for any more questions. "All right," he said. "Get every White man over to our tables." The group dissolved.

I sat with Shannon and Greg in the White area. Frank and Mac sat nearby, playing chess with their running gear on. I thought about going over and telling them not to go running, but they'd likely already gotten word. That's probably why they weren't running. Dave said something to me. So did Travis, then someone else. I ignored everyone.

I was trying to remember everything I'd heard from older cons about surviving riots. Stay on your feet, and move around as much as you can. Don't lock in on one guy. Try to break your time up evenly between finding motherfuckers to land shots on and finding other Whites who need your help. Don't panic, and don't get excited. If you knock someone down, resist the urge to follow them to the ground. If you're on top of him, then you're under his homeboys. Don't look at faces—they're all the same. Watch hands. Look for knives. If a guy's hand is open, he's on the defensive; if it's clenched, he's about to strike.

"Hey Seph!" A freckled youngster named Buddy called for my attention. "You wanna play chess?"

"What?" I looked at the empty chessboard he was pointing to. "No."

"Why not?" he asked. "You and Mac always play, but you never play with me. Am I not good enough?"

I remembered then that Mac and Frank had just been playing. They were gone. Scanning quickly, I found them jogging toward the pisser, about to start their run. Nobody'd told them. I wanted to run after them, but couldn't. Already one of the three yard cops was staring at us, and our numbers continued to swell as more White boys showed up.

"Or I'm not cool enough?" Buddy continued.

"Buddy!" I snapped at him. "Do you see how everyone's grouped up? Shit's happening. Pay attention."

"Okay." He stomped off, pouting. Where the fuck am I?

Shannon got up and clapped me on the arm. "Ready?" I was. Greg and Coco followed. The whole group shifted in one direction. The gunner atop Shasta was staring now. If the Blacks had been grouped up as well, instead of playing football, the guards would have called in a code.

The southerners had a small three-on-three game going on right in front of us, between our area and the Black game. They looked surprised to see us.

"What do you think?" Shannon asked. "Start at the football game?"

Greg answered. "We're not going to make it long standing here like this."

Sporty, one of the Sureños playing football, called to us from their game. "Did you guys want to play?"

"Let me see that ball!" Coco yelled. The southerner threw it to him. Coco wound up and spiraled the football high and deep, straight for the Blacks' game.

It was just like a kickoff. As the ball left us everyone broke into a dead sprint. Mine and Greg's sprints are a few steps faster than anyone else's. We were quickly out in front and could see only each other and the Blacks in front of us. The charge was surreal. We were wolves, two brothers rushing full speed into a herd of caribou. The herd scattered, leaving two isolated targets: a middle-aged Crip too surprised to run right away, and a youngster, just stupid enough to stand his ground. I went for the older, Greg the younger.

My guy took off running as I closed in. I dove and swatted for his feet, knocking one leg behind the other. He stumbled, somersaulted forward, and was up and running again before I'd even realized he'd fallen. As I hopped to my feet I heard the loud speaker calling code three.

The entire yard was in an uproar. The first thing I did was lose track of Greg. Shannon had the younger Black in a headlock. The kid was taking more fists to the face and knees to the ribs than anyone deserves. His legs gave out, and the White boys around him began stomping on his head. The entire Woodpile surrounded him. He was our prize—our payment for having been punched in the face—and if the Blacks wanted him back, they'd have to come get him.

The basketball courts cleared as Blacks rushed for the middle of the yard. The forty Sureños playing handball, though, couldn't see the main fight. Their view was blocked by the front end of Toro Dorm. They saw three dozen Blacks charging through their area and decided the Blacks must be getting their runbacks for the Toro riot. The southerners nearest the Blacks attacked, while those in the back dug knives out of the sand. Now we had Whites and Sureños fighting the Blacks. We would have won on our own; with the southerners in the mix, it was a blowout.

A scrimmage line formed between the two groups. For the first thirty seconds we had cops yelling orders and spraying random bursts of pepper spray. When their cans ran out, the sergeant did a quick head count and they all marched, single-file, to the patio. They just left the yard. An officer explained to me months later that's actually in their training manual. The gunners save their ammo, the yard cops leave, and they wait for more officers (or until we're more tired).

I have no idea how many punches I threw: somewhere between three and a hundred. I kept repeating the older cons' advice in my head. Stay on your feet. Move around. Find a target. Help somebody.

At one point Chris ran past me, calling for his cellie. Justin was alone out by second base, squared up with four Blacks. As we approached, all but one of them hopped backward. I got there a split second before Chris, and as I set my feet he came flying over my shoulder in a superman punch that knocked the Black guy out cold. I was shocked, and even one of the Blacks behind this fellow snickered. Chris weighs like one-fifty and this guy was easily two-forty.

I turned back toward the center. I was at the end of the scrimmage line, looking down a long tunnel of fighting convicts. I made my way down it—fighting, moving, fighting, moving. The tunnel pinched shut in front of me as Rambo reached out to grab hold of one of the Blacks, pulling him to our side. As he struggled to get loose, Brawler sank a metal spike into the guy's stomach. Dumplin stumbled and swayed at my side and I pushed him back into our group.

I found Greg in mid-swing as he knocked some guy's tooth out. I was so happy to see him I was in the process of yelling "Hi Greg!" when somebody caught me in the face, knocking my sunglasses into three pieces. Foolishly, I stopped to pick them up.

I put the pieces in my back pocket, but when I came up to continue fighting the tiniest little female officer was pointing her spray at me and ordering me to prone out. I put my hands up and even started to bend my knees, but I was really looking around to see if anymore fighting needed to be done. As I turned my head back toward her she let loose, hitting me in the face with her blast. I didn't prone out right away, but stumbled back. She sprayed again, yelling "Prone out!" and I yelled back "Please stop spraying me, ma'am!" She yelled "Prone out!" again, so I did.

The officers moved down the line, putting inmates on the ground. But since they didn't leave anyone behind to keep us down, we got right back up. I cleaned my face with my torn slingshot undershirt. Blocks flew in every direction. I got hit twice, and I'm pretty sure everyone else did too.

Tear gas canisters landed with a thud then expelled a cloudy ring of gas. The rooftop gunners only stopped firing long enough to dig out more boxes of blocks. Some Mexican had taken one cop's blockgun and all the other Mexicans were cheering him on. I felt like I was in a war movie.

When I finally proned out for the last time I was lying at the front of the cluster, between Greg and Hot Rod from Bakersfield. Hot Rod's neck had been sliced open and he was bleeding badly. He asked me how bad it was and I lied. Someone threw him a T-shirt and I helped him put pressure on the cut. Another guy flagged a sergeant down to tell him we had a man in critical condition.

"We've got lots of guys in critical condition," the sergeant replied.

"No, this is a White guy," our Comrade explained. The sergeant just shook his head.

Fifteen minutes passed before they got Hot Rod onto a stretcher. I figured if he'd made it that long, he was probably going to be okay. As I watched his stretcher leave through the patio gate, I heard the intercom click again.

"Code three, Whitney Hall! Code three, Whitney Hall!" The voice was much less frantic now. Some well-armed prison guards ran for Whiney as still more jogged onto B-yard in tight formation. The inmates in Whiney's dayroom had figured out who was fighting whom out at Shasta's yard session. They followed suit.

Minutes later the speaker clicked again. "Code three, Toro Dorm! Code three, Toro Dorm!" Through the building's barred windows we could see men throwing objects and swinging at each other. Everywhere on B-yard the southerners and Whites were attacking the Blacks. I sort of wished they would stop. The pepper spray in my eyes and nose hurt much more as the adrenaline left my body.

Once staff had suppressed each pocket of violence, they combed through the groups looking for serious injuries. Fresno Jay was the third guy escorted up to Medical. As he walked by the front group Coco yelled to him. "D'you get stabbed, Homer?"

"No," Jay shook his head.

"What happened?" Coco asked.

"I got sprayed, dog."

Coco yelled back, "We all got sprayed you fuckin' puss!" Everyone laughed.

Having taken care of the seriously injured, the guards began to strip out the remaining prisoners. Anyone with marks on his hands or cuts on his face was taken to the chow hall to await transfer to Ad Seg. I looked at my hands. They bore matching cuts, one on each ring finger. I rubbed both with dirt. My gum was cut too, just above my front teeth, but that likely wouldn't be seen in the search.

Greg had asthma. The pepper spray had given him a rough time, but he was beginning to settle down. "Am I cut anywhere?" he asked me, still a little out of breath.

"Yeah, I answered. "Your nose is bleeding." He wiped it with his hand, spreading the blood around and not stopping the flow. I took off my badly ripped slingshot and tossed it to him. "Use this."

Greg held the cloth to his face for less than a second, then he jerked and threw my shirt back at me. It was so saturated with pepper spray you could have wrung it out and had enough to spray down a whole new guy. I hadn't realized it was like that when I'd offered it to him. Greg broke into a coughing fit that drew attention from several officers. They demanded to know what was wrong.

"He has asthma," I told them. "If you could just walk him over to the bathroom so he can get some water, he'll be all right." Greg's face was blue.

As they escorted him toward the pisser someone called to me in a loud whisper. "Seph!" I ignored the voice. They got closer to the bathroom area, but didn't seem to be veering toward it. "Seph!" came the whisper again.

"Hold on," I answered. They turned Greg left, toward Medical. "Mother fucker," I said out loud.

"Seph!"

"What?!" I turned. It was Buddy, the freckle-faced chess player. He had crawled toward me when the cops weren't paying attention. He stretched in my direction and spoke in the same loud whisper, "I shit my pants."

"What?" I tried not to laugh, but I'm sure I at least cracked a smile.

"I shit my pants," he repeated.

"Well that's okay," I told him. "It's not like, the end of the world or anything." Then I smelled what he was talking about. It was terrible.

"I was on the ground and they were kicking me," Buddy explained. Maybe. He might also have shit them when he

74

saw everyone around him take off running into battle. "What do I do?" he asked.

"Nothing," I told him. "You know, shit happens. But, tell 'em. When they go to strip you out, just tell the guy, 'Hey, I shit my pants.' Don't just drop your pants and surprise him." Buddy seemed okay with this plan. I moved a little further away from him.

Most of the Whites made it back into their cells, but very few from the front group. I felt like I had lost all of my friends. When Greg didn't come back that night, I packed up all of his things.

The following day the local news reported the riot. More than four hundred men were involved in the fighting. Some guards had been injured. One Indian was assaulted during the chaos. Cops had rushed over from thirty miles away. Of the twenty-six men flown or driven to nearby hospitals, twenty-three were Black. And all of this occurred because one nineteen year old threw one punch.

CHAPTER TEN

From the moment we were back inside our cells, the blacks and Whites were on sight with each other. That means exactly what it sounds like. When we see each other, when we have any sort of access to one another, we fight. It doesn't matter if that guy just got here and has no idea what's going on. It doesn't matter if two cops are escorting me and four are escorting him. I will attack him. I'll get to him, I'll bring him to the ground, and I will hurt him. Hurting blacks takes precedence over school, over store, over visits. It's the only thing that matters.

Why does this happen? It sends a message. We are unwilling to accept the conduct that led us all to this situation. We cannot abide by any other race laying hands on a White man for any reason. If a White stole from you, burned you, tell us. We'll take care of it. But you will respect our boundaries.

And, of course, words like these are only effective when they're backed up with force. The riot was force. It delivered our point handily, better than any messenger could have done. But it's not enough. Did you really think one day of fighting would even the score? You crossed the line. We have an unlimited supply of kill you, and this is not over until we decide you've understood us.

The blacks, understandably, respond in kind. They'd rather not let us think they're afraid of us, and if we want to fight, they have every intention of bringing it to us directly.

They're sure as fuck not going to sit around waiting for us to attack them.

The cops picked up Greg's property Tuesday evening. I didn't think they would leave me in a cell by myself for long. We had guys going to the hole, guys coming out of the hole to make room for the new guys; consolidation and cell moves would be quick.

Chris lived below me. Justin had gone to the hole with a big egg on his head and a broken pinky, so Bones was now single-celled. I called down to him, yelling out my window loudly enough for him to hear. "Chris!"

He yelled back. "Yeah!"

"Did they pick up Justin's shit?"

"Yeah," he answered.

"Do you want to come up?" Moving someone you like in is always better than letting CDC pick your cellmate, or taking your chances with someone off the bus.

"Yeah," Bones agreed. "But do you want that cell, or this one?"

"Up here's better." Some cells have four plugs instead of two, some have faucets that stay on instead of push-button timers. 303 was one of the first cells unlocked for any release: good for phone line, good for store, good for a lot of things. "I'll try to get at the cops. You try to."

"All right," Chris answered.

The evening regular, Atkins, showed up at my door two hours later with a movement sheet and some large plastic bags. Bones must have talked to him.

"McCarty," he said after keying the door.

"Yeah."

He tore three bags off his roll. "I need you to pack up all your property, get ready to move."

"Where'm I goin'?" I double checked.

"Cell one twenty-three."

"No I'm not," I told him. He looked down at his movement sheet. "I already talked to my homeboy out the window," I explained. "I'll go to two 'o-four, or two 'o-four can come up here."

"Well, for right now you're going to one twenty-three." He was irritated, probably stressed out.

"I bet I'm not."

He showed me the movement sheet. "McCarty, I've got to get all these moves done before my shift ends."

"Well your best option seems to be moving Johnson, from two 'o-four, into this cell. Your other option is to go get the goon squad, and we'll see if you boys can get me out of this cell and carry me down to one twenty-three. I don't see it happening."

"McCarty, it's the same captain on tonight who had to deal with this fucking riot last night," Atkins said. "Do you really want to piss him off?"

That was a good point. Going to the hole for refusing a cellmate was bad enough; dong it while we were on sight would be inexcusable. "All right," I told the cop. "Please let Stoner know I'm coming down." I'm such a bitch-ass.

I showed up at Stoner's door holding a box. Stoner had no idea I was coming down, so I arrived unexpected with my move-in shit like it's already my fucking cell. That was rude, if unintentional.

Long lockdowns create a unique program. Every day, the same thing. We have no weekends, no Friday, no upcoming holidays to look forward to. Nothing changes. Stoner and I got up every day at the same time. We worked out at the same time. This monotonous repetition plays tricks on the mind. Sometimes days flew by; sometimes it felt like time was at a dead standstill.

Any stored food we had was gone after the first two weeks. Hunger set in. Our stomachs were empty, and the daily drive made our bodies even greedier. We needed more food than came on the small trays twice a day.

By the third week some of the cubans and indians were up and moving around. We traded hygiene products for sugar, and collected apples from the fellas. Eight apples makes a bitter batch of wine, but Stoner had a trick. "That same batch can be boiled off into two sixteen-ounce tumblers of White lightning. Sometimes we didn't even use apples. We'd use prunes, tomato paste, even potato flakes from the kitchen; as long as we had sugar, we had lightning.

The key was to make a good stinger. Canteen sells little piss-ass stingers—metal coils you can drop into a cup and plug into the wall outlet to boil yourself some coffee. Those don't work. Stoner had taken two of the washers that secured his table off their bolts. He spaced them out with a toothbrush handle and then attached each one to the broken cord from an old hotpot.

We'd throw the wine into one bag, then connect that with another, empty bag using an empty creamer canister. Once everything was tightly sealed, we'd rip a hole in the wine bag and drop the stinger in, retying the bag around the stinger's cord. We flipped sugar into whiskey, twenty dollars a tumbler, all day long. Two alcoholic indians kept us alive during that lockdown. Tuna, beans, soup: we even had enough to send food around to the other Whites.

By the end of February, staff began letting one race at a time out to shower. The catch was, we could only come out of our cells wearing boxer shorts and shower thongs.

This has been an issue for the Whites for the last ten years. Southerners never come out without their shoes on, blacks never care. On most four yards we hold the same policy as the ese's. Many three yards are the same, but some aren't. I've seen different buildings operate on different policies on the same yard, and I've even seen the same building go one way one year, then switch up the next.

The refusal started as a protest. We should be able to shower, and we shouldn't have to put ourselves in a vulnerable position to do it. So we refused to come out. We did this to send a message, but staff never cared. Actually, they're quite happy only having to shower one-third of the inmates on lockdown. Now the only message we send is that we're scared to come out of our cells without our shoes on. Personally, I fight better barefoot.

Still, almost always: if we're on sight, we don't come out.

When the cop came by to ask if we wanted showers, we said yes. He opened the door and said, "Boxers and shower shoes only." We both yelled fuck-you's in response. To avoid this awkwardness, veteran guards don't even ask if we want showers. They just come by and say, "Boxers and shower shoes" with a question mark on the end of it.

A cell near ours housed a youngster and a not-so-with-it older guy. They came out in their shower shoes. Stoner called them over when they tried to walk past. "Hey motherfucker," he told them through the door jam, "we don't come out in flip-flops here, and we sure as fuck don't do it when there's tension."

The guy looked around. "What do I do? Lock back up?" He didn't want an argument.

"Yeah, bro," Stoner explained. "It's no big deal right now. Go in and do some burpies. A hundred and twenty-three for you, a hundred and twenty-three for the youngster. Sound off when you're done. But if you go shower, it becomes a big deal."

They locked up.

So how can I say they should be reprimanded for coming out when just six paragraphs ago I said I disagree with the policy? Easy. I adhere to the strictest standard suggested. I don't nap during the day, I don't share food with other races, I don't even talk to the other races. This practice leaves little room for some coward-ass fuck to smut me up behind my back.

This same thing happens in yard politics. We could have three guys saying someone should be two-on-oned and one guy saying he should be stabbed. Regardless of who's right, the most extreme position wins out every time. No one wants to be the guy who defends the bitch side of any discussion. That's why the older homeboys should talk these things over: guys who have plenty under their belts, who stab people just to pass the time, the way other guys play dominos. No one can accuse them of being scared of the knife.

Anyway, coming out or not isn't that important, but unity is. Forget the message our refusal sends to staff. All of us doing the same thing sends a message to these other races. It tells them we're a unit, a well-oiled machine, and we've got our shit together so they better watch the fuck out.

Once finished documenting all the White and southerner refusals, the cops let the blacks out to shower. This illustrated for us the bad shape cell one twenty-three was in. We had crips on both sides of us. And not just crips, big ass crips. Four more cells across the way, the corner cell on our side: all black.

"You not coming back?" I asked

"No, bro," he told me. "Lieutenant wants to see you means you're going to the hole. Remember that for future reference." He was strapping his Velcro back brace around his torso.

"You don't want me to pack that in your shit, Stone?"

"No. Medical gave this to me, but they never sent me a chrono for it. If it's in my property, they'll just take it out." The cops were having trouble getting the door open. "I need it for my back. If they want it, they'll have to fight me for it."

Stoner ripped the spoon from the door and tossed it to me as the lock clicked open. The cops examined the lock for a second, then handcuffed Stoner and escorted him out of the building. They walked him across the front of Shasta and, sure enough, forgot the lieutenant's office and turned Stoner down the path to Ad Seg.

I yelled to my old cellie as he left. "Stoner!"

"Yeah!" he called back.

"I'm keeping your hygiene you asshole!" I didn't though.

We got a kite from Stoner from the hole. He said the cops had received a tip that he was instigating racial tensions. That made sense. Stoner was a big guy: six-five, two-sixty. The blacks wouldn't want him in the building.

CHAPTER ELEVEN

The lockdown was long. We never came out of our cells, not for anything, and I felt like I was forgetting what prison was like. By May a porter came around and said the Whites would be escorted in groups to the canteen window. I was one of the first guys on the list.

Our ranks had changed since February. Of the five Woods I went to store alongside, I only recognized two of them. We'd lost guys during the riot. New guys had shown up to replace them. We'd lost a few in isolated attacks as well. But we weren't on sight anymore. The green light had been called off in April, so things should settle down.

A similar group from Whitney was finishing up at the canteen window. Mac was the last guy. I got in front of our group as we lined up so I could talk to him.

"I didn't know you had any money."

"It's only about six dollars," Mac chuckled, "but I'm spending it."

"It's good to see you, Thadius. I was worried you might have died," I told him. "Not from the riot. Just, you know, in general." Mac was old.

He ignored my joke. "I have been hearing some good things about you, mister."

"Like what?" Like what?

"From the riot," Mac explained. "Everybody I meet has got a god damn Seph McCarty story. One guy says you knocked some guy out over by second base." That was

85

Bones. "Another guys says you kicked somebody in the face over by Toro." Maybe. "If you put everything together, you stabbed six blacks and two cops, then socked up some of your own guys for not fighting hard enough."

I tried to explain to Mac. "I didn't even have a knife."

"Then Tony's got this story he's told about six fucking times," Mac continued right along, "about you and Greg charging into a pile of crips to save Irish from being stomped to death." That didn't even sound vaguely familiar.

"Wait," I stopped him. "Tony lives in my building. When'd you see him?"

"At Medical," Mac explained. "Everyone's been putting in medical slips. That's the only place the fellas can meet. Put a slip in, Seph, and you'll see what I'm talking about."

"When should I put in?"

"It doesn't matter. We're only allowed up there two days a week. You're bound to see somebody you know."

"I didn't even know," I complained. "Nobody told me about Medical."

"You didn't notice so many guys being escorted up there all the time?"

"No," I told him. "I'm on the fence side now."

"Well that's why," Mac said. "You're way the fuck up there in bum-fuck nowhere. Probably nobody's had a chance to talk to you. I'm serious, though, Seph. You should be proud. You did good."

"No, Mac," I corrected him, "most that shit you just said isn't even true."

"Listen to me, kid," he said, lowering his voice. "At the very least you did as good as anyone else. Why don't you go to Medical, and you'll see what I'm talking about. You're not the only guy being talked about, but you *are* being talked about." He raised his wispy grey eyebrows at me and lowered his head. "There's simply no reason for you not to enjoy it."

I went to Medical that Tuesday. Mac was right. Nobody told me any stories, but there was a definite change. Guys I'd never met came up and said hello—big guys with lots of tattoos, guys who looked like they'd been doing this for a while. Plenty of friends clapped me on the back and told me they'd seen me from out their windows in Whitney.

Some new guys asked about the riot: what caused it, how it went. Fat Tony told a story with me in it, but not the saving-Irish thriller I'd expected. I hadn't heard this one before, and it was almost halfway true.

A youngster named Red went next, telling his own story. He gave an exciting account of how he'd chased two bloods around the horseshoe pits, and cut one of them from shoulder blade to love handle. What interested me, during this powerful narration, was the response he got from his listeners. Nobody cared. The general opinion of this kid actually dropped as he described his amazing feat. And his story was probably more true than mine. The difference was, he told his own story. One of the best lessons I've learned in prison: nobody wants to hear you talk about how bad-ass you are. If you're really that rad, people will already know. They'll know because someone else will tell them. And if nobody talks about you being bad-ass, maybe you should take another look at your reasons for thinking you are.

Bottom line, don't talk about yourself. No good can come of it.

By June staff began a progressive release. All inmates who were fifty years or older could come out on regular program. That meant Mac and two other guys, one southerner, and about fifty blacks. Luckily the blacks didn't want any further trouble, though I think Mac would've made them work for it.

Two weeks later the bar lowered to forty and up. Another two weeks, thirty-five. I had just turned twenty-one. My wait would be long.

Convicts generally agree that lockdowns breed lockdowns. When things are going smoothly, we can stay up for six months or more. Trouble comes in bunches. First we're locked down for a week, then back up; next we're slammed again for five days, back up. Then it's a month.

A steady flow of trash hits any prison yard at a constant rate, people who have tattled or touched kids. Six months of lockdown means we're six months backed up on no good. Lots of guys need to be cleaned up, and the longer we wait, the longer our list will get. We tried to get the work done without causing too many waves. The key holders for each race got together and worked out a schedule—southerners one day, Whites the next. The blacks even got a couple clean-up days in.

Sadly, we were the ones who wrecked the train. We were supposed to smash a guy from Whitney on Tuesday, but he didn't come out. On Wednesday, we let the southerners do their thing, then we got our make-up move in. I guess the ese's figured that meant to hell with the schedule. They got another guy twenty minutes later. Three two-on-one's in sixty minutes. The prison locked us all back down.

When I finally did hit the yard, I was only out there ten minutes. I sat down to play chess with Mac, he told me staff was moving him and the other lifers to A-yard, and I told him that sucked. Before I could even think of anything else to say, I watched two southerners walk right in front of the cops and start swinging away on each other. That's crazy. A one-on-one fist fight, right in front of the cops? These two had to be in the hat for this.

Staff responded. About the time the last few cops sprinted over the loud speaker clicked. "Code one, B-yard! Code one, B-yard!" The cops all smiled at the late announcement. Alford even put his hand up, as if to say, "Yeah. We got it."

The intercom clicked again. The woman in Control was screaming frantically, "Handball court! Handball court! Code one, handball court!"

We looked. Sure enough, eighty yards from where the cops stood, five southerners were stabbing the shit out of one of their own. The cops were all out of breath and their cans were half empty. The best they could do was jog over and try to stop the attack.

I'll tip my hat to this one. You have a dark gift, surennos. That was devious.

CHAPTER TWELVE

Things changed once yard opened up. I had felt regret over my performance in the riot, even a little ashamed. But the treatment I received now showed me that the small amount I did do was enough to earn me top honors. I felt like Henry Fleming from *The Red Badge of Courage*. "He had slept and, awakening, found himself a knight."

I remembered walking up to the chess table for the first time, almost three years earlier—how the men had ignored me. That couldn't happen anymore. Now I just walked by a table and guys said hello. And not just our race. The southerners said good morning. A northerner named Doc, from my hometown, stopped me on the track to tell me how he and a friend had shared a bag of chips while they watched the riot. Said he was proud I'd held it down for Modesto.

Respect from the other convicts felt good, and it was quickly the only thing I cared about. It was better than heroin. I was young, but that would eventually change, and I felt as though I alone possessed the secret knowledge of how easy standing was to come by. I wanted more.

I found myself with friends, listening to Bones recount his version of the riot. I interrupted him at a given point, so he wouldn't have to tell his own knockout story. "Yeah, 'cause Justin's way the fuck out over there." I pointed. "The fighting's over here, and Justin's, like, over here in the black area, all "Oi! Come on! You wanna fight, ya neegras?"

Everyone laughed. "And he's fightin' like four dudes. And me and Chris ran up, and three of the blacks hop back. But this one dude, he stays.

"Well I get there first, 'cause Bones is a slow-ass," more chuckles, "and this dude squares up. He's hoppin' his fists up and down like, 'You want summa dis, cracka?' And Bones comes flyin' over my shoulder—it wasn't even a punch. It was like someone molded Bones into a superman punch position, and then swung him onstage with a rope. Like he was in some old school production of Peter Pan and shit. *We can fly! We can fly!* wha-THACK! motherfucker!" Laughing. It was a funny story.

"And this was a big dude. That's what made it so fucked up. Look at Bones. He's like one-twenty"

"I'm one-seventy," Bones corrected.

"You're a damn liar," I told him.

He argued, "Look at my legs."

"I don't care about your legs," I said. "Look at your arms, you skinny bastard."

"Let's go to Medical and weigh me right now."

"Who's telling this story?" Actually he was, at first. "In my version of how this went, you're a hundred and twenty pounds."

"What happened next?" someone asked.

"I don't know," I answered. "I stopped fighting, right there. I was so fucked up by what I'd seen that I just sat down and pondered shit for the rest of the riot."

We'd been off lockdown for a couple months when Scotty came to find me at the chess table. "Seph," he asked, "you play handball?"

"Yeah, I'm all right."

"I need a good partner," he explained. "Come play a game with me."

I went. Scotty had the keys to the yard. Even if I were the best handball player on the planet, there's no way this dude I barely know comes all the way across the yard to recruit a partner. Something was up.

We went over to the dirt behind the handball courts. Soon Boxcar and this youngster, both from Sac, joined us. I'd met the kid before, but I couldn't remember his name. "Everybody know everybody?" Scotty asked. We all nodded. "Okay," Scotty says to the kid. "Go ahead."

The kid looked at me with his eyebrows raised, as if to say, "*This* is the guy we were waiting on?" Still, he spoke, albeit to Scotty and not to me. "Well," he began, "I came back from Medical yesterday late, and it was already count time. I came in and they told me to stand by my door while they finished count. Boxcar too. He was at Medical with me.

"Anyway, I'm runnin' around, checking to see if any of the fellas need shit ran. I run by Wingnut's house." Wingnut's from Modesto. "And I'm just crusin' by, ya know, giving a thumbs up to make sure they're cool. And I look in and Wingnut is suckin' his cellie's dick." What the fuck?! "And I pop out of view," the kid continued, "and peek over and look again, just to make sure. Wingnut is just yackin' away on this dude. The guy's got his head back and his eyes closed and he's just enjoying the fuck out of it.

"So I leave. I go flag Boxcar down, and he comes runnin' upstairs. And I tell him to go look in Wingnut's cell."

Scotty turned to Boxcar. "You see the same thing?"

Boxcar nodded. "Yeah I kicked the door for ten minutes and yelled 'What the fuck?' about a dozen times."

"So they know it's coming," Scotty continued. "Which explains why neither guy is at yard."

"You did well to go tell somebody," Scotty told the youngster. "If you'd have said anything right off, it would have been both their words against yours. Things wouldn't have been so clean cut."

"I've been through it before," the kid said. "I caught somebody shootin' dope from a black's door. It was his word against mine, and he said I was makin' it up 'cause I owed him two jars of coffee. I really did owe him coffee, too. Shit got all fucked up."

"The thing is," Boxcar was talking to me, "this is someone we hang out with. We share coffee cups with him, share cigarettes"

"I know the score, thank you." I was shorter with Boxcar than I meant to be.

"His cellie's gonna get hurt, but Wingnut's gotta go first," Scotty explained.

"I'll take care of it." I walked off while those three took turns shaking hands and congratulating each other on what a fine conversation they'd just had. I was a little too irritated to shake hands.

What the fuck is wrong with people? I mean, what the fuck is wrong with people? You know? . . . I mean . . . just . . . what the *fuck* is *wrong* with people.

Three months ago Bakersfield had two-on-oned a rapist. Since then they had been ridiculed and laughed at. Sex offenders were to be stabbed. So, too, would Wingnut be. Modesto would not join Bakersfield in the poo-butt parade. The problem, though, was that I had never stabbed anyone. Which meant I couldn't ask anyone else to stab someone, and there weren't very many Modesto guys left after the riot anyway. But that was fine. It was hard to see this as anything but another opportunity to gain standing.

That afternoon I asked my homeboy, Donny, to sit with me at the bleachers before yard recall. "I need you to go up to Wingnut's cell when you go in," I told him. "I want you to read this shit to him through the door."

He looked over the paper I'd just handed him. "Don't give it to him?" he asked.

"No. He can't have it. No matter what, don't give it to him. Just read it off. Tell him these are the rules he has to live by if he wants to stay on this yard."

"Say it's from you?" he asked.

"No," I told him. "Don't put anyone's name on it. Say it's from the fellas on A-yard. Say it came down from our homeboys over there."

"I can't read him this, bro."

"Why not?"

"Look." He pointed to one of the entries on the list. "The others ain't gonna let him shower in their shower."

"He's not going to shower there," I explained. "Wingnut's a punk. He got caught sucking dick."

"What the fuck?!"

"Yeah," I continued. "He's gonna get dealt with when he comes to yard. But first we need him to come out of his house."

"Who made the call?" he asked.

"Are you raising your hand to do it?"

"No."

"Then don't worry about who made the call," I answered. "Read him the fuckin' list."

Donny squinted at the paper. "He's not gonna believe this shit, Seph. He's gonna know something's up."

"Trust me, he'll believe it. The dude's a fuckin' lame."

I came out to night yard and walked laps by myself. I walked slowly by the pisser. Wingnut drinks twelve cups of coffee a day. That means, between six a.m. and noon, he uses the bathroom every twenty minutes. I knew I could count on this. He's not going to stop drinking coffee, for fear of the blinding caffeine headache, and he can't just hold it. No matter what he did or where he went when he came to yard, he'd have to use the toilet.

I didn't need to be out here. I knew this layout by heart. But night yard is a quiet environment when you're left by yourself: fresh air, clear thoughts.

Did Wingnut deserve this?

Hell yes. Official reasons aside, Wingnut's dick sucking was like a stiff slap in the face. It woke me up. I remembered things he had said about missing his son: his body language, tone, the little grunts and grins that accompanied his words. He was a born child molester. That he had now proven to be sexually immoral made me grateful this man was in prison and nowhere near his four-year-old boy. I remembered him joking that he couldn't wait to get another girl pregnant, because what he really wanted was a daughter. He wasn't joking. God help the poor girl who gives Wingnut a daughter. She'd be begging for heartache.

I walked over to take a piss, staring in front of me at the horseshoe pits. Anyway, this was my job. Earn stripes to move myself into the inner decision-making circles. Was I then to pick and choose how I earned them? Even if I should, I'd choose Wingnut.

The gravel under my feet caught my attention as I left the toilet. I noticed that gravel surrounded the area on all sides by at least ten feet. Probably the prison had done this intentionally, to hinder inmates from sneaking up on one another at the pisser. We'd deal with it.

I spent my morning at the back of the phone line, letting everyone pass me by each time the line moved. Wingnut was at the softball bleachers, one of the places the A-yard homeboys told him he could sit. He'd bought it. Of course he'd bought it. He was in trouble. Guys who are in trouble will always latch on to any excuse to believe they're not in trouble anymore. I'd asked some of the youngsters to play a rowdy game of horseshoes at the second pit, right in front of the bathroom.

Later than expected, Wingnut got up from the bleachers and headed for the pisser. I left the phone line and walked up to three blacks who were standing on the track by the rec gate. "Excuse me, fellas." They looked at me. "I know it's kind of unusual, me coming up to you like this, but I'm hoping you can help me with something important."

They were confused. The two closest to the phone line were over thirty, the one on my right looked about twenty. I kept my back to the yard. I had my jacket collar flipped up, the way the blacks wear theirs, and I'd put my beanie on without folding it so it was loose and floppy at the top, just like the blacks. If Wingnut looked over, he'd just see fo' bruthas, choppin' it up.

"A friend of mine is walking toward the pisser," I told them. "Don't look." The younger guy looked. "I have a surprise for him. But I need to make sure he doesn't see me coming." They must have thought I was out of my mind. Just walking up to them dressed like a black dude was crazy. Maybe I should crump, just to fuck with them.

"Don't look yet," I continued, "but when he gets close, can you peek over and tell me if he's facing me, or the horseshoe pits."

"What?!" the youngster blurted.

"Nah, I gotchu, Wood," one of the older two answered. "Don't trip."

"What he say?!" the youngster spat.

"Just don't make eye contact," I said. "If he looks over here, I'm hoping he just sees four of you guys."

The older guy laughed. "I ka' see dat," he smiled. "Yeah, nah, I ka' see dat. You pull it off."

"When he gets close, please look," I asked. "Not you," I told the kid. "I need you to look at the store line."

"The sto'?" He looked for two seconds, then shot back. "Who at the sto'?!"

"Please keep looking," I requested.

He turned back to stare down there, this time for four seconds, then he turned back and almost yelled, "I'o'neeven *see* nobody!"

The older guy spoke. "He got his back to you."

"Thank you." I spun away from them and walked quickly across the track.

As I approached the gravel the horseshoe players began to argue, loudly. Good lads.

"What the fuck good is keeping score? Every time you're over here you drop rocks on your side of the boards!"

"Bullshit!"

"You do not have fifteen fuckin' points!"

Wingnut watched them, and I made my way quickly across the gravel.

I didn't feel exhilarated. I didn't feel butterflies or any adrenaline rush. I felt like it wasn't me doing it, like I was playing a part in a movie, and one I had seen a dozen times. I knew already how this scene unfolded. I don't think this feeling came because of the program. I believe most convicts feel this sense of dissociation during a hit. For a few seconds, it's something else entirely.

I pulled the blade from my waistband as Wingnut watched the horseshoe guys through his expensive sunglasses. Hopefully he'd drop those and one of the fellas could have them. My plan was to grab hold of him, but when I was two feet away his head turned slightly to the right. Then he bolted, dick out and all.

I swung frantically, over the top, and hit him on the back of the head. I didn't even think I'd cut him. I thought I'd missed, just sort of punched him. Before he was passed the gravel, though, blood was gushing from a four-inch gash.

For a quick second, I felt like everyone on the yard was staring at me. Then that second was gone. The horseshoe players were playing horseshoes, the blacks from the rec gate were lost in a discussion amongst themselves; everyone was back to doing whatever it was they did. The only unusual activity on the yard was Wingnut sprinting toward Medical with his expensive sunglasses still on his face. I flushed the piece and made it back to the White tables before any code was called.

By the time I made it back into Shasta Hall, everybody knew. The blacks knew, the northerners knew, even the asians knew. I got nods from everyone, handshakes from all kinds of people. One southerner gave me a cigarette, which were harder to come by since some asshole had taken tobacco out of the prisons. Several of the White boys had cigarettes for me.

Some brilliant and far-sighted official somewhere had taken tobacco out of the prisons, supposedly to cut down on the cost of lifer inmates developing emphysema and other lung disease. That was just stupid.

Making tobacco illegal doesn't remove it from prison. It just makes it cost more. Heroin is illegal, but I can still go to any yard in the state and buy enough to kill myself. And, because tobacco is worth smuggling in, but rolling papers aren't, we smoke out of inky Bible paper and dye filled mill text, which are a thousand times more carcinogenic than tobacco.

You cut away the revenue prisons pulled from their huge mark-up on tobacco, and added to their operating costs. Each prison now needs an extra SHO to process all these tobacco write-ups and write-ups for bullshit caused by tobacco. So now you're handing out classification points like Halloween candy. Some inmates who are trying to turn their lives around are sent from two yards to three yards, or three yards to four. And for what? Smoking? That's not a good reason to level somebody up. So good call on the tobacco thing you stupid fuck.

I smoked six cigarettes that afternoon while I waited for staff to come get me. I figured Wingnut would tell. I had my plug with me when I went, and I saw no reason to get rid of it now. But night came and passed. I flushed the kite in the morning and went about my routine. I couldn't believe Wingnut didn't tattle. A punk with a gangster's heart? More likely he was too busy running to get a good look at who was behind him.

On the third day of lockdown, early in the morning, five cops showed up outside the door. "McCarty," they called. "Lieutenant wants to see you." That figures.

My property was already boxed up. The last thing I said to my cellie was, "Tell Scotty I lost my plug. Ask him to send a new one as soon as he can."

CHAPTER THIRTEEN

The porters were still cleaning up from breakfast. The clack and clamor that filled the dayroom died off as the cops brought me out of my cell and down the stairs. The porters stopped working, a lot of convicts stood in their windows. They were all looking at me. Look, they got him. That's him. That's the dude who whacked that motherfucker. I was surrounded in green, handcuffed, with a cop holding each arm. I felt like the toughest guy in the world.

We came out of Shasta and headed east along the track. For the five-hundredth time I got to see one of the most impressive sights I've ever encountered.

The sunrises at Soledad take your breath away. Enormous billows of fluffy cotton glide effortlessly over humble mountains, lighting up like jack-o'-lanterns as the sun's first rays bring life to the valley. My thanks to whatever brilliant asshole came through this beautiful corner of the Salinas Valley and said, "This looks like a good place for a prison . . . . Fuck it, let's build two."

The single-storey roof above the laundry room and canteen window forms the bottom of a U-shaped bowl, with two-storey buildings on either side: the gym and chow hall on the right, the education buildings on the left. The whole section wears a shawl of coiled razor wire. An old, run-down gun tower leans out over this bowl from the right, and a mysterious strip of state blue and a handful of

100

plastic bags snagged on the coils lend just the right touch of realism to the scene.

Every morning the sun splits these uprights. It always made me feel like an artist, that I could see how powerful this scene was, and if I had even an ounce of ability I'd have painted this picture a hundred times. Such heavy contrast rendered me insignificant, and *happy* about it. It was nature versus civilization, God's creation against man-made. It was unbridled, uncontainable freedom cut harshly with captivity's depressing gloom.

We turned right just before the chow hall. Apparently the lieutenant would meet me in Ad Seg.

The cops escorted me into X-wing, the more serious of the two Ad Seg units. They stripped me out, threw everything I was wearing in the trash, issued me a hole jumpsuit three sizes too big. While they were busy trying to find me a roll of toilet paper two shaved heads appeared in a cell window above the cops' office. They didn't say anything, but showed me a piece of paper with writing on it and gave me a come-here wave. Shoot your paperwork. I looked up at their cell number, took note of it, and nodded.

They put me in cell three thirty-five. It's very important to look up at your cell number when you enter a cell in Seg. Otherwise, when someone calls down and asks what cell you're in, you have to say "I don't know" and sound like a complete fucking idiot. Three thirty-five. I was thankful for the advice the older guys had given me.

The first thing I did was clean the cell. I was just about finished when a mexican accent spoke to me from the small air vent above my sink. "Hey neighbor."

I climbed up on my sink and spoke in an equally mexican accent. "¿Samos vecinos, no?"

He spoke back, something long and in Spanish. It sounded like thirty words, but he was probably just saying hi.

I interrupted him. "Nah, I'm just fuckin' with you. I don't speak spanish." He chuckled, so I continued. "What's going on, homie?"

"Good morning, friend. Are you a Wood?"

"Yeah, I'm a Wood," I told him. "My name's Seph."

"Good morning, Seth. My name es Feo. I'm a Sureño."

"Feo?" I asked.

"Si mon."

"Well you sound like a handsome young man."

"He chuckled. "I am. I don't know why they call me that." We both laughed. "Hey, what are you here for, Seth?"

"Nothing." I was adamant. "I'm completely innocent."

"But what do they think you did?"

"Fuckin' cut somebody," I told him.

"¿Serio?" he asked. "But you're innocent? ¿Palabra?"

"Innocent until proven, buddy."

"Oh, yeah," he said. "No, me too." He paused here, maybe waiting for me to say something. When I didn't, he wrapped up. "Well it was nice to meet you, Zeth. I'ma letchu do your thing."

"All right, Feo. Hasta." As I stepped down off the sink a cop slid a piece of paper into my door. I pulled it in and read it. CDC-114: lock-up order. Inmate McCarty, blah, blah, blah . . . assault with a deadly, blah, blah, blah . . . against inmate Steele. Yep. That sounds about right. I planned on pleading not guilty. Maybe I could get Feo to represent me as legal counsel.

I laid down on my stomach on the freshly cleaned concrete and yelled out the bottom of my door. "Excuse me on the tier! This is three thirty-five. Can I get a White man on the tier?"

The answer was prompt. "Yes, sir!"

"This is Seph McCarty, Modesto," I yelled. "I've got my shit headed up the tier."

"Okay, hold on," came the response. "Thank you on the tier!"

"Thank you on the tier!" I repeated. 'Up the tier' meant to a higher cell number—two forty-eight in this case. The first numbers don't matter. Forty-eight is higher than thirty-five."

"Excuse me on the tier, Seph!" A new voice this time.

"Yes, sir!" I yelled.

"Street sweeper!"

". . . Okay," I answered. What the hell did that mean? "Hey Feo," I called up toward my vent. I heard him climb up on his sink and answer "Yes sir," through the small grate. I was about to ask him what street sweeper meant when I heard something skid past the front of my cell. I looked. It was half of a toothpaste tube with a long, slender string attached to it. "Okay," I yelled. "Okay, hold on."

"Yes sir," Feo repeated as if he hadn't said it once already.

"Sorry, Feo. I was gonna ask what street sweeper meant, but I think I figured it out."

"You forgot to say 'Thank you on the tier,' Seth."

I was already up ripping my sheet off my bed. I slid back to the bottom of my door and shouted, "Thank you on the tier!"

"You're supposed to say that every time, Seth."

I had no razor to cut strips from my sheet, so I was biting the fabric. "Shit!"

"Seth, are you okay?" Feo asked.

"Yeah. I think I cracked my front tooth." I switched to my canines. The strips I tore were not slender. I packed wet toilet paper into the strip's folded hem to use as a weight, and slung the sheet-strip under my door. Not long enough. I tied another strip to it. Almost a third of my bed sheet was out on the tier.

"Excuse me on the tier, Seph!"

"Hold on. I almost got it," I shouted. ". . . Over."

Feo laughed. "Seth, it's not a walkie-talkie."

"You're having fun with this, aren't you?"

More laughing. "Seth your line looks like a tugboat rope." I kept slinging my weighted end out there. It went far enough, but I couldn't get my strip to hook under the front end of the toothpaste container.

"Seth, I would help you, but that's your people's shit. I'm not allowed to pull it into my house, you know?"

"Thank you, Feo. You're being very helpful."

"Excuse me on the tier, Seph!"

"Hold on! I almost got it!" I really did. I had slid my line under his and was slowly pulling it in. I watched under my door to make sure I didn't pull my weight right under his line. Too hard. "MOTHER FUCKER!" I shouted. I heard laughter from several cells. Good. I'm glad everyone's having a good time with this.

"Excuse me on the tier, Seph!"

"Yeah . . ."

"Bro, do you need me to recast?"

"No. I don't think that will help," I explained. "Hold on." It was closer now. Another couple throws and I had my weight wedged under his toothpaste-car. I pulled steadily, watching under the door. It was perfect. I wasn't even under his line; I had the car. It was about three inches away when the line and car both went zooming off up the tier. "No!" I groaned loudly under the door. "I almost had it!"

"Excuse me on the tier, Seph!"

"Yes sir!" I answered casually, like it was the first time anyone was calling me. We'd been fishing for more than twenty minutes.

"Shoot your line out all the way," the voice yelled.

"Okay!" I did. The car came zooming back down, crossing right by my door. The line was so close I could almost reach out and grab it. Fifteen minutes later I had it in my cell.

"I've got it!" I shouted. I waited, but no response. "Now what?!"

"Excuse me on the tier, Seph!"

"Yeah!"

"Whatever you've got coming down," my friend said, "please tie it on." He sounded a bit exasperated.

I twisted and wrinkled my 114 into a tube, then tied about six knots around it with this guy's line. As I pushed it under the door I yelled, "Okay, go!"

The line disappeared. Six seconds later I heard my partner yell, "That's a touchdown! Thank you on the tier!"

"Thank you on the tier!" I repeated. I got up and put my bed back together.

"Excuse me, Seth." The vent was calling me.

I climbed up onto my sink. "Yes sir."

"Hey, Seth," Feo said. "I got a little care package for you. I got a little piece of line you can use, a lure, and the waistband from a brand new pair of boxer shorts. Do you know how to spin line?"

"No," I confessed. "But thank you."

"If you want," he offered, "you could stand here on the sink, and I could explain how to pull the band apart and spin it up."

"I suppose you want me to fish your line in to get this stuff?"

"No, don't trip," he said. "Look . . ."

I heard Feo climb down off the sink. Three seconds later there was a clack outside and a red disk slid under my door. It was a Folger's lid, cut down to fit through the narrow gap, and tied neatly inside were the items he had mentioned. This bastard had bounced this thing of the curb and under my door like he was playing a game of air hockey. "That's fuckin' out of line," I yelled as I untied the gift basket. Then I climbed back on the sink. "Thank you, Feo."

He told me how to pull the elastic and binding strands out of the waistband, and as I followed his instructions I asked him about why he was in the hole.

"The homies rushed the cops."

"Oh, I remember that," I said. "On A-yard, at night."

"Si mon."

"I was at the end of Shasta Hall, in cell one twenty-three, when they escorted you guys to the hole."

Yes sir," Feo said. "It was right after your guys' riot with the blacks."

"What happened?"

"The homies were handling a two-on-one," he told me. "The two homies were beating the homey's ass, and the cops came and broke it up. And this punk-ass yard cop is hitting the homies while they're laying on the ground. The homey is covering his head, and the cop yells for him to put his hands out on the grass. But every time the homey puts his hands out, the cop cracks him again.

So the big homey gets up and runs over there, and the cops all back up and spray him and shit. And he's the first one they escort off the yard. The two cops walking with him are gavas, you know? So the homey looks at the homey in the phone line and says, 'Guerra en la placas, ahora.' Do you know what that means?"

"Yeah," I answered.

"So I'm over in the workout area, and the homey in the phone line signs to me, and tells me to get the homies ready." This guy calls everyone the homey. That gets really confusing. "So when the cops tried to escort the homies who were fighting off the yard, they walked right between the two groups: the phone line and the workout bars. It was like a gauntlet of homies. Do you know what a gauntlet is, Seth?"

"Yeah."

"There was two cops on each homey, plus a sergeant. So it was seven juras against like thirty-five homies. We all jumped at once, and the juras didn't know what to do. We took their batons, their pepper spray. I seen the homies who were already handcuffed run to the bathroom to wash the pepper spray out of their eyes. And the cops who were still in the middle of the yard came to help the juras, but right behind them were thirty more homies from the bleachers. It was crazy, Seth."

"It sounds crazy," I agreed. "Okay, I've got this band apart. Now what?"

"Okay, hang a paper clip in the far end of your cell," I did, "and set two bars of soap by the door. You wanna tie the threads to one soap, go around the paper clip, then tie them to the other soap. Do it a couple times, back and forth, back and forth. Two times is cool, but three is better."

I just did it twice. "Okay, now what?"

"Okay, hold both strings in your left arm—one in your hand, one in the crook of your elbow—so that the soaps hang up off the ground."

"All right . . ."

"Now spin the soap. Make sure you spin them both in the same direction. Then when it's too tight to spin, just tie the soaps together and let it all unspin itself." He got down off his sink and left me to it. The process worked. I made string, though it was sort of kinked and scraggly and didn't look much like the line that came from Feo. I was halfway through my second piece when the guys up the tier called again. "Excuse me on the tier, Seph!"

"Yes sir!"

"Street sweeper!" the voice yelled.

Thanks to the line Feo shot over I was much faster this time. I pulled long sections of string into my cell until I found little packets tied on, one after another. They were all tightly folded and wrapped in cellophane. I untied them from the line and called back, "That's a touchdown! Thank you on the tier!"

"Exxcuse me on the tier, Seph!"

"Yeah!"

"How many times?" he asked.

"I counted the packets. "Four times!"

He yelled in response, "Thank you on the tier."

I wasn't sure if I should yell 'Thank you on the tier' again. I'd already said it once. I just let it go, and set about unwrapping the packets. The first was my 114. They had smoothed it out and folded it up neatly. The second was two more 114's, I was guessing from the guys who lived in that cell. The third package was a baggy containing all sorts of little things: a pen, an elastic band, a razor blade. The last was a kite.

Seph—Greetings and White Respect, White Man. My Cellie and I send Ours, FULL
BLAST. I'm Brodie, from Ventura, and I run the program here in the back. Roll call
is 7am and shutdown is 9pm. We are awake all the day long, with mats rolled and
senses alert. At roll call, my cellie will call your name. Please respond, "Yes, Sir!"
When he says "Good morning to you, White Man," please respond as follows: "Good
morning to you, to your cellie, and to all the Active White Men on the tier. Thank
you!" We Drive 5 days a week, to each his own on non-yard days. Sound off upon
completion. We maintain a respectful tier. No profanity, no casual conversation.
Please fish quickly and quietly. Now to more specific issues: Your 114 shows you to
be here for stabbing another White Man. You should have been given a plug from the
Man with Responsibility for your yard. The kite therein will explain the reasons for
this as a called shot. Please shoot that kite. And please do not tie any more knots in
my line. That shit is not appreciated. All one-ways are to be wrapped in plastic, and
a single slipknot on the line will suffice. We are in cell 346 if you have any questions.
Shred and flush this kite. That said, I leave you as I came. Full, Heartfelt, White Love
and Respect—Brodie, Ventura & Clown, Paramount.

This entire letter was written on a slender, eight-inch
strip, like cracking open a fortune cookie and finding a
short story. Three rows of text for every line on the paper.
Prisons are generally run from the back, meaning most calls
sent from the hole override those that might be made on
the yard. If Brodie had keys for the hole, he was basically
the shotcaller for the prison.

I wrote back, explaining everything—the reasons for
the hit, why I didn't have the kite. I told them the next plug
coming from B-yard would, I'm sure, verify everything.
Then I called to Brodie and asked him to send his line
down. I sent my note alongside the two 114's I had barely
glanced at.

"Excuse me in the vent, Feo," I called my neighbor.

"Yes, sir."

"What's a one-way?" I asked.

"A kite," he explained. "It's a hot kite that you flush when you're done reading it. Sometimes it's called a one-time. A note that, you know, it's not like you're asking for coffee or something. It's got sensitive information in it."

"No, I get that. A hot kite," I said. "I just hadn't heard the term before."

"You were on B-yard, so you probably don't know the homey Pecas. from A-yard. Do you know what Pecas means, Seth?"

"Yeah," I smiled. "Is he tough?"

"Si mon. His other name is One-ways. He's here with us. When he goes to shower you can see he has 'One-ways' tattooed on his chest. He's not our shotcaller, but a few years ago on the four yard, he was the big homey. His name was One-ways 'cause his kites only went one way. Like, 'Here's what you need to know; here's what you need to do; don't bother writing back, 'cause your opinion doesn't matter.' Words went one way."

"All right. Thanks," I told him. "I was just wondering."

"Your people got at you?" he asked.

"Yeah. They sent me a gift basket with a waistband and a pen, and a razor blade, which will make things easier."

"I know," Feo explained. "I wanted to send you one, but I couldn't."

"Why not?"

"It's just one of those things," he said. "What if something happens, and the homies and the Woods go on sight? And you use that razor blade to make a knife, and cut a homey with it? Then I gave a Wood a knife that he used to cut a homey."

"That seems a little unreasonable," I argued.

"The easy answer is to not give weapon stock to anyone but homies."

"Excuse me on the tier, Seph!" How did they have an answer already? It had only been like five minutes. I fished in another kite. A one-way.

Seph—Ours to you White Man. wingnut is on the first tier in O-wing: single-cell, walk-alone. He locked it up. That corresponds well with your version. Of course we will wait patiently for the kite from B-yard. You have friends here who vouch for you as a Solid Comrade. Your Homeboy Greg recently left. He ran the program back here the last few months he was with us. Shannon before him. With that said, I leave you as I came. Enjoy the rest of your day. White Love & Respect—Brodie, Ventura

They had sent me a green scrub pad in the baggy earlier, and I spent the rest of the day cleaning. I scrubbed the sink, toilet, window sill, everything. Prison cells are filthy until you make them your own.

CHAPTER FOURTEEN

"Do you see where the seams come close together?" Tim Pitassi was looking down at me. "They bend in near each other, here in the middle.

"Now every time you throw, first I want you to take a second and look down at the ball. Make sure your first two fingers are across both seams. I know it feels like you're wasting time, but a good throw will make up for that extra second. You understand?" I nodded. "Okay, we're going to take turns throwing the ball over to coach Mike, over at first. I want you to look at him. Don't look at the ground; don't cock your arm way back and stare up into the sky. Look straight at Coach Mike. If you look at him when you throw it, the ball will get there."

I stood at second base with my green OBA jersey on. There was chatter all around me. "Hey, batta batta batta batta batta. Hey batta batta batta."

I looked down into my glove, then turned the ball so I could get my fingers across both seams. He was right. A good throw always made up for that extra second.

"Choke up on the bat, son!"

"Eye on the ball, Mathew! Eye on the ball, buddy!"

"Excuse me on the tier! Seph!"

I sat up, confused, trying to make sense of what was going on.

"Excuse me on the tier! Seph!"

I jumped out of bed, clumsily, slid to the bottom of my door and, still groggy, shouted something that sounded like "Feelum der!"

"Good morning to you, White Man!"

"Good morning to your cellie, and to all the Active Whites, and you and everybody, who's on the tier, and Active and White! Thank you!"

". . . Thank you." He didn't sound very enthusiastic. For my part, I was just happy he continued down the tier. I wasn't off to a very good start.

A few days later staff released Feo back to general population. I got a good look at him when they escorted him out. That really was the ugliest mexican I had ever seen.

Feo's cell had only been empty ten minutes when the cops brought someone up. He was a tall White guy, about forty-five, with long, hippie hair. I figured he would make a good neighbor, but the cops escorted him right past Feo's cell and opened my door.

"You guy's all right together?" the guard asked.

"Yeah." You always answer yes. Unless it's clearly not a White guy, you always answer yes. They moved him in and closed the door.

"Hey, bro. My name's Tennessee."

"Seph."

"I got my paperwork in here." He reached into a brown bag. My own 114 was within arms reach, but I waited. I watched his hands digging in the bag, waiting for them to re-emerge. I had this vision of him pulling a metal spike from the bag and shoving it into my chest, uppercut-style. When he did pull paperwork from his bag, I grabbed mine and we traded. His 114 was for battery. He handed me his 128, too, but it smelled awful.

This is not the most difficult thing in the world. Get yourself a Bic pen and knock the back end out of it. Then get another Bic pen, a Round Stic, and cut it in half. Put your tightly rolled paperwork into the back half and stuff the stopper from the first pen into the freshly cut opening. Now you have a canister to hold your documents. And if you can't hide this small tube comfortably up your ass, you just don't belong in prison. Ideally, your paperwork would be rolled in another piece of paper and wrapped in cellophane before you put it into the tube. There's just no reason you should ever hand someone a piece of paper that smells like ass.

"Shit, bro," Tennessee said. "They got you for a stabbing?"

"I'm innocent. What was your battery? A two-on-one?" I had developed a talent for keeping conversation focused on the other guy.

"Yeah. That dude's still good though. It was just a checking. He's here with us. We've been back here for almost a month."

"How'd that all unfold?" I prodded.

"Man." He reached into his bag. "It started when we were on lockdown from the incident with the northerners." He began making a cup of coffee and asked me if I wanted one. Good. Story time.

Most guys you live with will tell you stories. If you end up in a lockdown environment with him, he'll tell you every story he has four times. In ten days you'll know everything about him. With little plastic surgery, I could pass for any one of a dozen guys in front of his own family. Of course

I remember what I named the dog you bought me when I was in second grade.

"Me and my cellie, James, lived in Lassen Hall." Tennessee moved his hands when he spoke. He motioned in whatever direction he thought Lassen might lie in. "So did Shameless. He's the reason we're back here. We had an incident with the northerners last June. Not a riot, nobody fought, but we grouped up. The cops locked us all down.

"So we're not on sight, but we are locked down, so most of us are coming out for showers in just our shower shoes. Both buildings on A-yard do that, you know?" I didn't know, but I nodded. "But some guys aren't. This dude Shameless has been down for a while, like twelve years, and on various four yards. He's on his way back from Medical. And my neighbor, next door to me, he's a northerner. But Shameless knows him from the four yard. Shameless is talking to him, and I'm on my bunk and I can hear every word he's saying, so I know my cellie can hear it 'cause he's on the door listening.

"Basically, Shameless tells the northerner that all the Whites in Lassen Hall are lames, poo-butts for coming out of their cells in their shower shoes. Shameless tells him we're lucky the northerners aren't going to rush us over the group up, 'cause if you discount all the lames the Whites are heavily outnumbered."

"Fuck," I commented.

"Yeah," he continued. "Then he went on to tell the dude all about how he was basically the shotcaller, how him and his cellie were the only White boys in the building who were about shit. When the northerner joked that he'd be in trouble for talking to northerners when we had tension, Shameless shrugged and said he'd have to send a kite to himself to have himself whack himself, 'cause he was the only motherfucker in the hall with a man-sized pair of nuts."

"Damn," I said. "Well did he lean over and spit on your window while he was saying this?"

"No. He stopped short of that. But James said as he was walking by he looked in and made eye contact with him. I've never seen anybody so mad. James wanted to kill him."

"I bet."

"But there was really nothing he could do. Shameless never came out for showers, and even when we did come off we couldn't really fight right away. We had to kick back and see if that shit with the northerners would turn into anything. Bad idea to take White boys off the yard when we're about to go to war."

"Yeah, I get it," I told him.

"Well neither me or James is letting anything go. The dude basically called out the whole building, but we're not gonna go run and tell everybody, 'cause he'll just say he never said it. But I heard what he said, and my cellie heard what he said. So we both decide we're gonna call Shameless under the stairs for a one-on-one. You know, first I'll do it one day, then James'll do it the next day, or something like that. But it needs to be answered, and we're the ones who heard it, so we're the ones who should answer it.

"We're locked down for a week or so longer. But then the second day after we come off, Shameless gets taken to the hole. The cops say they received a kite saying Shameless was about to be the victim of a stabbing."

"Oh, you don't say?" Ninety-nine percent of the kites that say someone is going to get stabbed are bullshit. Notes like those are written by someone who has a reason to want that person off the yard. Often the person mentioned is the author. GET ME OUT OF HERE!

"And the way he left had everybody fucked up. He went up to Medical, but he didn't have a ducat. First the cops said they found the kite on him. Then they said, 'Oh, no, we found it in the mailbox on the patio while he was on the patio.' Nobody knew what the fuck was up.

"And the same norteño Shameless made his comment to—my neighbor—said he was on the patio at Medical, and he seen the whole thing. He says Shameless was at Medical, he walked up to the patio cop and said something, and the cop made him go sit in the lieutenant's office."

"He rolled himself up," I concluded.

"It seems that way, yeah, but there's really nothing solid to go by. The cops don't know what the fuck happened; or they're not telling. The northerner's version sounds bad, but you can't take his word for it. The norteños will lie just to see us stab a White guy.

"Anyway, James and I don't even tell anybody about the shit dude said on the tier. We told a couple guys, but it was just talk amongst close friends. Nobody officially put word out to the fellas. Nobody smutted him up.

"Well two months later he shows up in Whitney Hall. The cops decided there was nothing to the information they received, and they bring Shameless back and put him on B-yard. And the first week he's back there's all this drama, questions being asked, and somehow he says what he says and he's all good. Somehow, he's all good.

"So, now, there's this insult waiting to be answered. I'm willing to just deal with it when I see him, but my cellie's kind of hard-headed. He doesn't want to let it go. He sends a kite to Whitney telling Shameless he wants to get something off his chest, so meet him in Education on Monday. But

Shameless doesn't go. And one of our homeboys sees him at
Medical and tells his 'What the fuck?' And he says he never
got any kite.

"So James writes a new kite, to the homeboys in
Whitney, telling them to make sure Shameless gets the
message. He tells 'em Shameless called us both lames, so
he needs to be told to go to Education on Friday for two
one-on-ones: first with James, and then if he can still fight,
then with me.

"And I say 'Yeah, I'm cool with it,' you know? The
youngster's running this one, pretty much. So we both go
to education."

"You didn't think they'd get caught on the first one?" I
interrupted.

"No. The kids got this corner in there he says you can
fight and nine times out of ten get away with it."

"Well, not *nine* times out of ten," I laughed. "You are
in the hole."

"We didn't even get to use it!" He swung his arm up
when he said this, spilling coffee on the floor. "Shameless
didn't show up. Some other dude named Trigger shows up.
I've never met him before, but he's evidently got the keys
for Whitney. And he won't even talk to James, 'cause he's
twenty-two. He talks to me, like I know what the fuck's
going on. So I ask him where's Shameless. And he starts
defending him. He says he seen the lockup order and he's
confident that Shameless didn't roll himself up, and he says
what me and James are doing is wrong, 'cause Shameless
told him how we're trying to smut the dude up 'cause we
owe him money."

I laughed out loud, then apologized for laughing.

"It's okay," Tennessee continued. "I dealt with it real
calm. When it was my turn to talk, I just told the dude,

'Look. If somebody told you they wanted to get something off their chest, would you stay at home and send someone else in to plead your case? If you're worried it's gonna be a two-on-one, or five-on-one, or what-the-fuck-ever, then bring a knife, or a couple homeboys and make sure it's a one-on-one. But what fuckin' prison yard have you ever been on where it's okay to just not go? Why is that dude not here? How can you defend a motherfucker who won't show up to defend himself?"

"Wha'd he say?" I asked.

"Nothing. Not a motherfucking word." I smiled, and nodded at him. Score one for Tennessee. "See? When daddy speaks, motherfuckers wise up."

I laughed for a while at this one. No way was this burnt out hippie daddy. "So did he show up?"

"Fuck. You would think that would be enough to make shit unfold properly from then on out, but no, it wasn't. That weekend the IE fellas came to our door and wanted to know why we were so determined to fight Shameless. So we explained the situation, and they said they wanted to think it over. Then they came back the next day and said, since we both wanted to fight him, would we mind making it a two-on-one?

"The one homeboy, Scott, said he had no problem believing Shameless had said that stuff. He said Shameless had told *him* he thought everyone here was a lame. Of course he said it. But they said what makes it bad is when he says it to another race who we're having an issue with. Like he's undermining all the effort we put into making ourselves look respectable. They said he definitely needed to be checked, and checked well.

"After we both agreed to do it, they told us they'd already personally gone over to Whitney and told Shameless to come to Education to catch a heads-up."

Throughout the telling of this saga, Tennessee had made his bed, unpacked his belongings, and pissed twice. It's a wonderful way to pass the time.

"So we're in our cell, talking about how things should go, and James starts throwing these punches at the air. He's kind of holding his breath, and with each punch he's saying, 'W'SUP?! W'SUP?! HUH?! W'SUP-U-FUCKER?! W'SUP-U-FUCKER?! W'SUP?! W'SUP?!'

"And I'm thinking to myself, man I'm glad it's not a one-on-one. I mean, these punches look like they'd hurt, but he's holding his fists way down by his waist and his head is just wide open. I was worried somebody's lucky shot would knock him out. So I stop him from this 'w'sup-u-fucker' thing and I ask him, you know, 'James, do you want me to grab the guy so he can't run or, I mean, how do you want to do this?' And he says no, let's just both unload on him. He says four fists are better than two.

"Well we get into Education first—me, James, and another homeboy named Ice—and James and I go into the hallway there. Then Shameless comes in from B-yard with another homeboy with him, Spinner. And Ice goes up to them and tells Shameless, 'Go in the hallway and catch your heads-up.' Then when Shameless starts to go, Spinner goes with him. So Ice grabs him and tells him, 'Shit's goin' down a certain way. Stay out of it.'

"Shameless comes in and I'm in the middle of the hallway. James is hiding behind the door, so you can't see him. And Shameless walks in with his hands open and says, 'What?' But then he turns, because he sees James, and James is grinnin' this evil grin at him. Shameless gets this deer-in-the-headlights look. See Shameless still thought he could talk his way out of it. But when he seen James he realized James wasn't there to talk about anything.

"Even then, though, Shameless starts to talk. I think the first word he said was 'Do,' but there's no way to be sure. He didn't get it all the way out. The first shot caught him hard, and Shameless backed up into the wall, bent at the waist, and put his arms up for protection. And then the sup-u-fucker machine went to town. I couldn't believe it. W'sup-u-fucker is the most devastating fighting style in the world of martial arts. Every punch landed with knockout power, and every thud was accompanied by a loud 'W'SUP?!'

"I ran over to help, but I couldn't really land any punches except to the top of his head. He was already curled up. So I grabbed him in a full nelson,"—He was dancing excitedly around our small cell, demonstrating the sup-u-fucker, the nelson, and everything in between.—trying to hold him so he couldn't cover up, but he wrenched free.

"Then he grabs James' shirt sleeves and ties him up, you know, like a boxer would. And I just get tired of this whole game, so I reach down and yank both of his legs right our from under him." He was proud of this; you could tell.

"So he's on the ground, and now me and James are both on him, and Spinner comes flyin' in throwin' punches at James. And I get up to help with Spinner and I'm just pepper-sprayed to shit. It was like six cops showed up all at once, all with cans a'blazin'. You couldn't see in the hallway, the spray was so thick. Poor James, he got the worst of it. His whole face was orange."

"Orange?!"

"Yeah."

"Not the new O-C spray?"

"Yeah bro. It's horrible."

"Isn't it?" I agreed. "It's the most disgusting thing in the world. It's like the devil is having sex with your face."

"You're telling me."

"Did you ever figure out why it makes your balls hurt so bad?" I asked.

"No, bro, I don't know. But they sure did hurt."

"So what the fuck?" I asked. "They brought you all here?"

"First they broke us all up." Good. Continue the story. "One cop was saying he seen pretty much the whole thing, but he waited for backup to arrive before diving into that mess. He says it was a three-on-one. Then this other cop says no, one guy came running in afterwards to fight the two who were on top. So they figure it was a two-on-one, and the last guy came in to help his buddy. Then they tried to figure out who was who. They argued amongst themselves for like five minutes, then one cop actually turned and asked us which one of us was the victim. I woulda laughed, but I was in such bad shape from the spray that I didn't think anything would be funny again.

"Finally they just said fuck it. They wrote it up as a melee, brought us all to the hole, and put each guy in a cell by himself. I thought melee was when you cut somebody's eye out or cut their arm off. Dismemberment."

"That's mayhem."

"Oh. Well they changed them all to battery that same day. When they figured out me and James were cellies in Lassen, and Spinner and Shameless were cellies in Whitney, they figured that must be how the lines were drawn. Then they just took a guess. Even though Shameless was all beat up, they wrote him and Spinner up for battery as the assailants. They changed mine to a D-2 fighting and they let James off Scot-free as the victim. He's already back on A-yard."

I had to laugh. "Was that the end of the drama?"

"Of course not," he said. "Remember, Shameless had just left the hole. He'd been back here for two months with these guys, working out and yes sir-ing to you sir on the tier with everybody. He was everyone's best friend. The first thing he did was shoot a kite to Greg—It was before Brodie got here—telling him how it was supposed to be a one-on-one, but I asked James to jump in 'cause I was too scared to fight him myself.

"Spinner was right next door to me the first day, so I slung a line over and asked him for an explanation. He had this whole other version of things. Shameless had told him that, when he'd got rolled up, me and James talked his cellie into not sending all of his property. And then we got dibs on that property since we were his homeboys. And now we were trying to smut him up so we didn't have to shoot back his CD player. It was the biggest bullshit cluster fuck I'd ever been involved in."

"But it worked out?" I asked.

"Yeah. Greg, he was real cool about it. Did you meet him? He was on B-yard before that big riot."

"Yeah, we met."

"He was real patient. He wrote kites to everybody, getting everyone's side of things. Plus we had the plug. That made our story gold and everything else irrelevant.

"I guess A-yard wrote back here, saying all four of us should still be on roll call, and that Spinner should be checked for running in. For some reason, Greg wrote down and asked me how I felt about it. I told him as far as anyone being good or no good, I didn't care. And as far as Spinner being checked, I didn't care. I felt disrespected over something that was said and I wanted to fight about it, and I did that. So now I feel better about myself and we could all be friends. But I said I wasn't mad at Spinner, if that's what he was asking. Friends are gonna do what friends do. That's just the way that is.

"Greg wrote back and told me he sent a note back to A-yard. He said he told them Shameless and Spinner were cellies. He said he wasn't going to ask Shameless to check Spinner over Spinner rushing in to save Shameless from getting smashed. It was just too much. He said Spinner would be back on the yard in four months and if they still felt he needed it, they could check him then."

"Tennessee . . ."

"Yeah, bro?"

"That's the craziest fucking story I've ever heard." It really wasn't though. Stories like his were actually common.

"I got plenty more stories," he said.

"Good. We're gonna need 'em."

"Oh, yeah," he said. "A stabbing? You're gonna be back here more than a year. And that's if they don't send you to Corcoran, and if the DA doesn't pick up the case. Did they find the knife?"

"What knife?" I told him. "I honestly didn't have anything to do with the stabbing."

"Damn," he said. "What evidence do they have to say you did do it?"

"That's what we're waiting to find out, buddy."

CHAPTER FIFTEEN

Feo's old cell filled up the next day. The blacks had handled a two-on-one on A-yard, but all three inmates had done more jumping around and woofing than actual fighting. As a result, none of them was very beat up, and the cops had a difficult time sorting out who was who. One of the assailants was sent to O-wing as the victim, and the real victim and the other assailant had been put in a cell together next door to me and Tennessee.

Apparently the victim was up on his rack as the assailant paced the small cell. We could hear the one yelling at the other.

"Don'tchu fuckin' look at me, nigga! Readjo' fuckin' book, nigga! . . . Yo' ass is lucky I don't do something to yo' ass." Still pacing. "I can't be*lieve* these motherfuckers put me in here like that. Yo' ass is lucky I don't do somethin' to yo' ass." He went on like this for more than twenty minutes, warning his cellmate to stay on his bunk, asking him to read his book, and reminding him of how lucky he was. Tennessee and I tried not to laugh.

When a cop walked by, the loud one got his attention. "Man, get me outta this cell before I do somethin' to this nigga!"

"What's the problem?" the guard asked.

"Man, I'ma *do* somethin' to this nigga! I swear to *God* I am!"

The cop radioed for help while the assailant continued to yell. "God damn you's a lucky nigga! Lucky I don't do somethin' to yo' ass!"

Once the sergeant arrived they handcuffed the loud one and backed him out of the cell. When the door closed, the victim got off his rack and stood looking through the cell window. The cops were waiting to hear back over the radio what cell they should move this guy to, and as he stared through the glass the loud one got extra tough.

"Yeah. Yeah, you's a lucky-ass nigga. Lucky, punk, nigga."

The sergeant interrupted him. "We can put you back in there with him." He slid his key into the door.

"Nah, it ain't even like that, Sarge! It ain't even like that!" His voice had quickly become high and submissive, pleading. When it became apparent the cops were not going to put him back in the cell, he got tough again. "You's a lucky-ass nigga. You lucky. I shoulda done somethin' to yo' ass." He continued to rattle this bullshit off as the cops escorted his down the stairs. He even turned to tell one of his escorts how lucky that nigga was.

Anyway, Tennessee and I had long since been unable to withhold our laughter. In case you're a White boy or a sureño reading this, and you're wondering what you should do in that situation, tugging on the cop's sleeve is not the right answer. That's a PC move, and it will just about end your career.

If the cops put you into a cell with someone who's no good, wait till the cops leave and take off on him. Beat his ass until he screams for help. And if he's too proud to shout out, choke him out and hog-tie him with his own bed sheet, then slide him under the bunk. (LEGAL DISCLAIMER: DON'T REALLY DO THIS.) When the cops come by for count, then you can tell on yourself. You've already proven you're fairly bad-ass. When they ask where your cellie is, tell them he's under the bed. If they ask why, just shrug and say, "Maybe he feels safer under there." But don't ask the guards to protect you. Tattling is only okay when the blacks do it.

Just hours later the cops moved the victim over to O-Wing. Then they brought up a new guy to live in Feo's old cell. He was almost as ugly as Feo, but he was White and older. We let him settle in, then called to him through the vent. His name was Danny Boy, from Sac.

"I've been back here four fuckin' months already," he said, "down on the first tier. Them fucking cops kept promising to move me to the third tier, but it's been a pain in the ass trying to keep them to their word."

"I landed up here right off," I told him.

"Yeah, you're lucky. Wha'd you say your name was again?"

"Seph, from Modesto."

"Oh, yeah. We're almost homeboys."

"Almost," I agreed. "My cellie's name is Tennessee. He's from Tennessee."

"I'm not from Tennessee," my cellmate corrected me.

". . . What do you mean you're not from Tennessee?"

"I'm not from Tennessee. I've never even been there."

"Then why do they call you Tennessee, Tennessee?" I couldn't believe this.

"I don't know, bro. They've just always called me that."

I turned toward Danny through the vent. "My cellie's out of his fuckin' mind."

"Well we all are a little bit," Danny answered. "Elsewise we wouldn't be here." That seemed like a good point. "Hey I'm gonna birdbath, kid. I'll get at you in a bit."

"All right." I hopped down.

Five minutes later Danny was back in the vent. "Hey, kid."

I climbed up onto my sink. "Yeah."

"Who lived in this cell before me?"

"Blacks."

"Really? That's surprising."

"Why?" I asked.

"'Cause it's clean," he said.

"Oh. No. They were only in there for a few hours," I explained. "Before that was a mexican, single-celled."

"Yeah," he said, "that makes more sense."

"You done birdbathing?" I asked.

"Yeah," he said. "We can talk."

"That was quick."

"Yeah, I try not to get too clean. I got a reputation to keep up. What happened to the blacks? They were just on time-out?"

"No," I told him. "It was a two-on-one. Only I think they put the one in there with one of the two. Dude told the cop he couldn't live in there 'cause his cellie was no good."

"Shit, that ain't surprising," Danny said. "What's surprising is the blacks actually did a two-on-one. That dude musta done some fucked-up shit if the other bugs actually decided to jump on him. What rack was he on, do you know?"

"Sounded like the top."

"All right. I'll scrub that one extra good."

I laughed. "What do they got you in the hole for, Danny?"

"Shit." He took a deep breath. "It's a mess, kid."

"Why?"

"Just this whole new technology way of doing things. The internet has yet to fully reconcile itself with our way of doing shit. It used to be you had paperwork in the hand, else you didn't open your mouth to speak on shit. Now they've got this Megan's this-and-that online shit, a motherfucker can be found out for what he is, you know?

"Well I'm not gonna put dude's name out there, 'cause it don't need to be out there just yet, but dude comes up to us in Rainier and tells us his old lady found some shit on the internet about this youngster that's in our building. Says the youngster statutorily raped a fourteen-year-old girl.

"So the fellas tell him, you know, internet's all fine and good, but you need that shit on paper, in here where we can read it. And dude says, 'Yeah, yeah. It's already being sent.' Well fucking two months goes by and this shit never shows up. Dude says he sent it but it got sent back, he'll send it again, fucking, jackoff, whatever.

"Then it comes out dude's cellie owes the youngster almost a hundred fucking dollars for tattoo work. And the cellie says he only got the ink work 'cause he knew he wouldn't have to pay the kid. Well that excuse makes its way to the fellas, and they jam the cellie up, saying why the fuck are you getting tattooed on by a piece of shit? And he says, 'Oh, no, what I meant was, I already got the ink, and I had the money ready to pay, but I don't want to pay the kid 'cause he's a rapist.' Meanwhile this paperwork still has not shown up.

"Then three more guys come forward, saying their mom, their girl, their fucking Aunt Mildred seen that shit online and it's true. They say it's even got the kid's picture there. How they could verify it's his picture over the phone, I don't know. But not two days later it comes out all three of these dudes just recently got tattooed on by this kid." If you're still following this, you're a better listener than I am.

"Apparently it was some fucking free-for-all. This kid can tattoo, so all these motherfuckers caught wind of him being on the shitlist and ran in to get free work done. Why a motherfucker would want ink from a fuckin' sex-offender is beyond me. Bunch of youngsters running around showing off their chomo decals."

"What are their names?" I asked. He told me. "Maybe we'll take care of it if we make it back that way."

"They've already been checked," Danny said. "Checked, but they got to keep their ink. Those motherfuckers are fortunate I'm back at level four points for this shit."

"What would you rather be done?"

"I'd make 'em cover that shit up!" He just about yelled this at me. "I'd hold 'em down and tattoo over it myself if I had to, and I can't draw for shit. Anyway, one of them already paroled, another went to fire camp. Even the dude who originally brought it up left. He came back here for a sec, then went to B-yard."

"What was his name?" Tennessee called from his rack.

"Tell him Shameless, from IE," Danny answered.

"No fuckin' way," I said.

"Why?"

"Nothing," I told Danny. "I'll tell you later. What happened to the youngster?"

"Pfff, drama," he went on. "More bullshit and drama. We finally approached the kid and just told him what questions had been raised. The kid's 128 was clean, but the fellas told him about this printout he could get at some website. They told him he had three weeks to get his, and the kid said he'd get it. He told us that shit online was his dad. He's a junior, and his dad's got the same name. He says if we'd actually read it we'd see it says a man in his thirties had sex with a fourteen year old."

"Did he get the printout?"

"He didn't get a chance," Danny said. "I had my old lady go to that website. She said it was all there. In 2005, nineteen-year-old kid statutorily rapes fourteen-year-old girl.

"I told her these cops are trippin' on paperwork in the mail, but I told her just send the dude's fucking picture. Sure enough, six days later I got a love letter from my old lady and a picture of her nephew. We got at his homeboys that night.

"His one homeboy, Tug—this is all Shasta County—he was already up on what's going on. He says it's *his* homeboy, so he'll handle it. Only he wants whoever's making the call to go with him, since there's no paperwork. That way whoever he gets to the hole with can say, 'Yeah, I seen he's a rapist.'

"And we tell him that would be cool, but we got this skinhead youngster who's been waiting to put in work, and we already told him he could go. So Tug says okay, that's cool, and they come up with this idea to get him at dinner. We're cell feeding 'cause the ese's are still locked down for smashing the cops, and Tug says he'll get the skinhead pulled out to help, says he'll poke the kid and the skinhead can just stay on him while he ditches the knife.

"Well me and David run some bullshit about sick call and get the fuck out of our house, just so these three aren't the only White boys out when this is going down. We're on the second tier watching, and the two go up to the youngster, and the youngster is ready. He fires on the skinhead, and fucking Tug's piece-of-shit ass grabs the skinhead in a choke. It's some old jank-ass PC move. So we run the fuck down there and beat Tug's ass. He balls up like some little pussy. The skinhead's already fuckin' the rape-o up, but I go to help just for good measure and David stays on Tug.

"Anyway, we all get back here, and Tug writes this high-power proclamation to Shannon, telling him 'There's no black-and-white paperwork' and 'This ain't how shit's done' bullshit."

"How'd that go over?" I asked.

"Fuck. Shannon's a solid motherfucker. That's your homeboy. You ever met that dude?"

"Yeah, we met."

"First time those two hit the yard he had about six knives swingin' at 'em. I never seen any motherfuckers so fucked off."

"Damn."

"Yeah," Danny said. "Shannon's good shit. Fuck the bullshit. All right, fellas, I'm off the sink. My feet are startin' to hurt." We said goodbye.

That evening, as Tennessee and I were preparing for bed, Danny called to us again. "Hey, you guys shit in the morning?"

I got up on the sink. "Shit?"

"Yeah, you know, drop a fuckin' load? You do that in the mornings?"

"Yeah," I told him. "Usually alongside the morning cup of coffee. Why? What's up?"

"Just try and hold off, if you can," he said. "I'll get at you in the morning."

The next day I called Danny. "Excuse me in the vent. Danny."

"Yeah, you guys ready?"

"Yeah, I'd like to use the restroom. What's the deal?"

"Hold on," he said. I heard him flush his toilet three or four times. Still standing on his floor he called up, "Okay. Go ahead and shit. I'll shit too."

I didn't really know what to make of Danny Boy. I had used the toilet and Tennessee was halfway through when I heard someone yelling loudly from down on the first tier. "Please stop flushing your toilets!" the voice screamed frantically. Meanwhile Danny began flushing continuously. He stopped only to call over to us.

"Hey fellas, keep flushing."

"Danny, I think somebody's toilet is broken down on the first tier."

"Help me out, kid. Flush that motherfucker till your finger breaks." That was it. The homeboy asked for help. No more questions. I flushed maybe forty times, until the guards turned our water off.

"Hey, Danny . . ." I got up on the sink. "What was all that about?"

He climbed up on his sink and spoke quietly. "Yeah, I'll run it down to you," he started. "You live in three thirty-five, right?"

"Yeah."

"And I'm in three thirty-six."

"Okay."

"See we share this pipe chase: us, the two cells below us, and the two on the bottom tier. All six toilets are connected.

"Well down there in one thirty-five are two caucasian pieces of shit. And next door to them are two northerners who are no good. And this whole fucking tower of six toilets works kind of like a bird feeder. The pipes narrow there at the bottom, just below the first tier, and that creates sort of a bottleneck.

"Well one of them fucking toads left his filthy fucking bed sheet in here, bunch of watch springs and shit in it. So this morning when you said you had to shit, I flushed that whole fucking sheet down the toilet. Then we all shit. See once that sheet catches in that bottleneck, the pipes back up and flood. All that shitty water comes shootin' out of the bottom two toilets at about sixty miles an hour."

"That's fucking gross."

"Yeah, it's nasty," Danny continued. "I heard that motherfucker yell out the bottom of his door, too. It takes some sand to put your head at the bottom of your door when there's shitty water runnin' all over the ground. Either that or he's just nasty. His face must've been right in it."

"How the fuck did you even think to do that?"

"How old are you, kid? Twenty-three?"

"Somewhere around there," I confessed.

"An older convict showed me that, back before you were even born. You got to be quiet about the whole thing, though. We're supposed to leave them dudes be. If you can't get at a motherfucker to lay metal to him, then you've got no business talking to him, or kicking his door, or anything. We don't ever lower our high White Power standards to their level. You know what I mean? As far as I'm concerned, flushing that sheet was an accident. I was just trying to wash it in the toilet and down it went."

"All right."

"Maybe we'll wait a week and then accidentally do it again." That made me laugh.

"What's up with this dude on the other side of me?" I asked.

"A White guy?"

"Yeah," I told him. "His last name's Mitchell."

". . . No . . . I don't know . . . . What's he look like?" Danny asked.

"Skinny, short brown hair. He's got a beard he's just starting to grow."

"Oh, that dude? No, fuck that dude."

"Yeah?"

"Yeah," he said. "Yeah, fuck that dude." That was all. No explanation. My neighbor was no good. If our doors opened at the same time, I had to rush him, and hurt him to a degree that would demonstrate exactly what I'm about.

CHAPTER SIXTEEN

"Excuse me in the vent. Seph."

"Yes sir."

""Hey, fish over here, kid," Danny said. "I got something going down the way."

I fished him in. I had learned to operate the string and car better in the past two weeks. The kite I pulled in had the number two sixteen written on it—straight across from me, but on the second tier. "Two sixteen?" I asked.

"Yeah, look," he said. "Normally we slide this shit across the top catwalk. But they got these fucking carts up here, so that way's all blocked off. Just send it down all the way, and they can cross over down there and go through the back stairs."

"'Kay." I was already sliding an opened-up paperback book under my door to use as a ramp. I shot my car off the third tier and let it dangle, then pulled and slacked the line to start it swinging. As the pendulum swung under our tier I yanked hard, slingshotting my car across the building and onto the second tier. Another foot to the right and I would have knocked on 216's door.

"Hey kid," Danny called me to the vent when I was done fishing the kite over.

I climbed up. "Yeah."

"You're here for a stabbing, right?"

"Yeah," I answered, "but I really didn't have shit to do with it."

"Yeah, you can save that shit," he said. "My birds don't lie to me." I smiled, but he couldn't see me. "They're probably gonna do your hearing today," he went on. "They always do 'em on Thursdays, and you been here two weeks already."

"Okay."

"Listen," he said. "This shit ain't hard. Whatever they got, they got. And they're gonna do what they're gonna do. If they think you're guilty, they're gonna find you guilty. And just so you know, you wouldn't be here if they didn't think you were guilty. But we got a policy. We don't talk to the cops. Not for shit. All you ever say at a write-up hearing is 'no comment.' You understand?"

"Yeah, that makes sense."

"Don't go in there trying to talk your way out of shit. I'm saying this to you 'cause it seems like you got this idea you can do that. Elsewise you wouldn't be telling me and everybody else you really didn't cut nobody. We already know you did, and we already know why. But these dudes don't care what you got to say. You're a liar to them. All you're gonna do by opening your mouth is get yourself a rat jacket and end up on the no-good list."

I was quiet a moment. "Thank you, Danny. I'm glad we talked."

"Yeah, well, you just remember what I said. 'No comment' is all you got."

I had my jumpsuit ready to put on as I laid on my bed thinking about what Danny had said. Tennessee leapt down from his rack and looked over his shoulder at me as he walked to the door. "I'm gonna sound off, kid. You cool?"

"Yeah, that's fine."

He went to the bottom of the door and yelled, "Excuse me on the tier! This is Tennessee, and Seph, sounding off today's mandatory in-house routine! White Men, thank you!"

Twenty voices yelled thank you back in unison. As he got up I asked him, "Hey, Tennessee?"

"Yeah, bro?"

"Do you think we should ever actually work out?"

"Yeah, we can if you want to, bro. I don't mind." The escorts came to get me twenty minutes later.

"Okay. We have inmate McCarty, Joseph, victor one four five one eight, appearing today in front of the Senior Hearing Officer, charged with assault with a deadly weapon . . ." I listened to this asshole rattle off five minutes worth of dates, times, and formalities. "Inmate McCarty, do you have anything to say in your own defense?"

"You mean besides that I didn't do it?" He looked at me, waiting for more. "Look, I said. "I know I'm not exactly entitled to the whole innocent-until-proven-guilty thing, but if you'll clue me in on why you think I did do this, it shouldn't be too difficult for me to prove myself innocent."

He shuffled a couple papers while the other two staff members looked bored. "McCarty, you are charged with assaulting inmate Steele, Daniel, with a knife, whereby you inflicted a three inch long laceration to the back of his head. This occurred on B-yard at approximately nine forty-five on the aforementioned morning. Where were you at that time?"

"I was on the yard," I admitted. "Over by our tables."

"'Our' meaning . . . ?"

"The Whites. I was at the White tables."

"Staff received two separate confidential notices identifying inmate McCarty as the assailant who stabbed inmate Steele."

"Can I see them?"

"We don't have them here today, but they both said, basically, 'inmate McCarty in Shasta is the one who stabbed Wingnut.' We take that to be Steele."

"They both say 'stabbed'?"

"I'm sorry?"

"Stabbed," I said. "Do they both say I 'stabbed' him?"

"What's the relevance there?" he asked.

"Because he wasn't stabbed. Your report says he was lacerated. That means sliced, cut."

"It's a small distinction," the SHO said.

"But it is a distinction. It shows the guy who dropped the kite didn't exactly know what he was talking about. Do both kites use the same language?"

"There are some spelling differences," he said.

"Right, 'cause he wanted to make it look like a black guy wrote one of them. But I'm guessing they both refer to me as 'inmate McCarty in Shasta,'—which is a weird way to identify someone—they both say stabbed, instead of cut, and they both refer to Danny as Wingnut instead of Danny. More people know him as Danny. Wingnut's not even his handle. It's just some stupid name these dudes use when they're making fun of him."

He opened a resealable baggy from his file folder and pulled out two folded strips of paper. What a lying piece of shit.

"I realize you probably recovered those from two very different locations, but that doesn't amount to much either. If I lived in Whitney, I could easily drop one kite at Medical and another in Shasta Hall. But if the language matches, I think it's a safe bet one guy wrote both kites." He sat looking at both notes, a colleague leaning over each shoulder.

"Lieutenant, look at me," I continued. "I'll take my jumpsuit off if you want a better look. I'm probably the only inmate in your entire prison with no tattoos. And I've been here a couple years now: plenty of time to get some. But I don't do that. I don't get tattoos, I don't use drugs, I don't politic, and I sure as hell don't stab other inmates. I do the college courses you guys offer through the mail. That's what I do. I've earned sixty units in the last two years, and I'll dig my transcripts out of my property if you want proof of that.

"And so, what? You guys are gonna give me a fifteen month SHU because some asshole wants me off B-yard?"

"Why would someone want you off B-yard?" the woman on the right asked.

"I don't know." I liked the direction this conversation had taken. "A handful of guys owe me money, but it's not much. They just borrowed a jar of coffee, or a toothpaste and deodorant. And I don't hassle anyone. I know they're broke when I give it to them."

Two of the officials leaned together to speak quietly. I spoke over them. "I realize you probably already asked Danny who did it, and he probably said he doesn't know, and you probably think he's just scared or whatever. But you can make this real simple if you'll just go ask him if McCarty did it. Give him a chance to tell you it wasn't me. Danny and I are friends. Still. I don't care if he's no good or whatever. That's the messed up thing. It's not so much that I don't cut people. I wouldn't cut Danny."

The lieutenant said something quietly to the woman on the right. She shrugged back and said out-loud, "I'm a believer."

"Okay," he said. "It does appear that these two notes are indeed one note, written twice, with words intentionally misspelled, which tends to show some deception on the part of our anonymous informant." This guy was incredibly pleased with his own use of language. You could tell. "These notes then become unreliable and, in their absence, there isn't much of a case. So, we are going to dismiss this write-up due to insufficient evidence. You can go back to your cell, and you'll likely be transferred back to B-yard either today or tomorrow."

I'd like to thank the Academy. I'd like to thank all the little people who really make these things happen but never quite get the credit they deserve. Most of all, I thank Greg, Bones, and Homeboy Justin and all the bullshit dinner parties we shared. Every time you caught me with your lid was a lesson in believability. Make eye contact, but don't stare at the guy's pupil like you're trying to see if he's high. Go ahead and smile, since you probably would smile anyway if you were falsely accused. And don't be afraid to argue some off-topic, meaningless point, like this argument isn't the most important thing to you. Take a second to think about how you would react if what you were saying were really true. I didn't even know Wingnut's name was Danny until that cop read it from his paper.

When the door opened I smiled at Tennessee. "Not guilty, buddy!"

"Oh, that's great, bro," he said. "I'm happy for you. What happened?"

"They didn't ask me shit," I told him. I was fairly certain Danny Boy was listening in the vent. "They just talked shit about the sergeant who originally filed the incident report."

I heard two loud feet climb up onto the sink next door. Loud, for my benefit. "Excuse me in the vent, Seph."

"Danny, what's up?" I climbed onto my own sink.

"Wha'd they tell ya', kid?"

"Not guilty."

"No shit?"

"They asked me what-the-fuck, and I said no comment. But they didn't even look up. You were right; they didn't care what I had to say. But they pretty much said they don't like Sergeant Herrera."

"Yeah, I don't like him either," Danny said. "He's a punk."

"So the dude said they had two kites with the exact same wording, same handwriting, but one had words spelled wrong. They said it was clearly one dude writing both, but trying to make it look like two dudes. Then they said that looks deceitful, so fuck the kites.

"They talked this way and that way, and finally the dude just turned to me and said, 'Did you cut this inmate?' I told him no. I know I'm just supposed to say 'no comment,' but the dude asked me straight out. Am I in the hat for that?"

Danny was quiet a moment. "No . . . . You still shoulda said no comment. But that's all right. We'll give you a pass."

Tennessee and I celebrated with a cup of coffee.

CHAPTER SEVENTEEN

The lieutenant had said one or two days before I would be back on B-yard, and that really did sound good at the time. In practice it was closer to two weeks. When they finally did send me back, it was to A-yard, not to B. Lassen-A, 305.

My escort took me as far as the culinary gate, then handed me my movement sheet and told me to find my own way. The entire yard was empty, a result of the worst fog I had ever seen settling down over the prison. I couldn't see more than six feet.

I stopped my cart in front of Lassen Hall and yelled up to my new cell. "Three 'o-five!"

No answer.

"A-side! Three 'o-five!"

"Yeah," someone shouted from the window.

"You got a new cellmate," I called back.

"No, I don't want any new cellmate." . . . That was Greg's voice.

"Who the fuck is that?" I asked.

"It's Greg."

"Greg Dunn!" I shouted, truly happy to see my friend. "Hi, Greg Dunn!"

"Come on up!"

"Are you my new cellie?" I asked.

"Yeah."

I yelled violently, "Well then where's your fuckin' paperwork?!" Some of the other windows laughed.

"How the fuck did you make this happen?" I asked Greg as I unpacked my property.

"Mac did it," he explained. "He's the Unit Five clerk now. He's been following you on paper. He brought us the incident report, and he knew when you were found not guilty. Then he saw your name on the list of who's coming back, so we moved my cellie to the second tier, and here you are."

We shared stories and caught up. I was glad to be back. Coming out of the hole is a good feeling, almost like you just paroled.

"But we need your help."

"Why?"

"'Cause," Greg said, "our football team is 'o and four."

I shook my head and sighed heavily. "Damn we suck."

"Yeah, well, we're better now. We'll have you at wide out, plus another homeboy is coming over from Rainier. He's a former Downey guy too. Ricky Deathriage." Downey was the high school I had attended.

"I don't know him."

"No," Greg said. "He's older than you. Like twenty-seven. But there's another Downey alum just landed on B-yard right after you left. Bones." My heart thumped, but just once. I knew Bones. I knew everything about him. His name was Timothy Brigham and he'd been a senior when I was a sophomore. We'd met at a few parties, gone skateboarding once. But he definitely did not remember me as a drug-abusing armed robber. If anyone had questions about my arrest, it would be him.

To make things worse, Bones had a habit of sniffing asses. He wanted to know why you didn't get taken to the hole in this riot, what you were arrested for, whether you had any relatives who were rapists. He wanted to know. He was here on a murder case and had spent the last two years at Solano, toeing the convict line and smashing anyone who didn't. I made my mind up not to run into him.

The fog count blended into staff training, so we were slammed until dinner. When I left my cell for chow, the first man I met was my neighbor, Eddie. He was rough-skinned, with long hair and a few teeth not quite in the right place. I always half 'spected him to spit t'backer at my feet.

"This the one you was waitin' on?" he asked Greg.

"Yeah. Seph, this is our homeboy, Eddie. He lives next door." I shook.

"All that shit we hear about you true?" Eddie asked.

"Half," I told him. "There were two Sephs on B-yard. Sometimes the stories got mixed up. The other Seph was a big guy, from Fresno." I held my hands up over my shoulders. "Big guy."

"Is that right?"

"Honestly? I don't know," I told him. "Anything's possible."

"Yeah, okay." Eddie reached out to grab me and I dodged backward. "We'll be watchin' you, big dog."

Our walk to chow reminded me of my first day on B-yard. There were more new names and hands thrust in my direction than I could possibly remember. I did my best. Greg's last cellie, Steve, left his usual seat in the chow hall empty, opting instead to sit with his new cellmate a few tables over. Greg wasn't offended, but still gave the kid a hard time.

"Greg!" Steve got his attention. "Can I use some?" He held his hand over his tray like he was sprinkling pepper over his food.

"Oh no," Greg laughed, holding up his shaker of chicken adobo seasoning. "This is for this table. You give up the table, you give up the seasoning."

"C'mon!" Steve pleaded.

Eddie sat at the table between these two. He interrupted, "May I please get some of that, big dog?"

Greg handed it to him and continued speaking to Steve. "I can't just share with anybody, Steve. It'll run out by tomorrow." Meanwhile Eddie shared the seasoning with everyone at his table and the next. Poor Steve.

I lagged behind as we headed back to the building. There were hands to shake and names to exchange. I tried to catch up with Greg, but ran into Steve and his new cellie first.

"Hey," I tapped Steve's elbow. "Help me play a joke on Greg."

"Okay."

"Just walk like ten feet behind him," I said. "I'll toss you something, you hide it, and then we'll go from there."

I reached around Greg's right side and tapped him on the chest while I picked his left pocket. "Hey," I asked. "What's this guy's name?" I pointed in front of us, and Greg's seasoning shaker was sailing through the air before I had finished my question.

"Crabtree," Greg answered.

"Not his last name," I clarified. "What's his handle?"

"Oh. Grimlin. You just met him at the chowhall."

"Yeah, but I got like forty fuckin' names I'm trying to remember."

"He's short and has tattoos all over his face. Should be easy," Greg argued. "Grimlin. From Yuba Hardcore, I believe."

"Is it Gremlin, or Grimlin?" I asked.

"Grim, with an 'i.' He lives on the second tier with Slash."

"'Kay."

Greg didn't miss his shaker until the next morning when we woke up to go for breakfast. "Seph, did you see where I put my seasoning?"

"Where do you usually set it?"

"Right there on the shelf."

"I don't know," I offered. "We were moving shit around all day yesterday."

"No, I had it at dinner," he insisted. "Remember?" I leaned my head down off my bunk to look at the windowsill and anywhere else I thought he might have set it. My helping him look ended the conversation.

We sat down in the chow hall for breakfast. After giving his potatoes and eggs a healthy coating of chicken adobo, Steve asked Greg if he'd like some seasoning.

"Oh, you motherfucker!" Greg shouted. Everyone involved in the prank enjoyed a good laugh as Greg retrieved his shaker. "Yeah, I'll be watchin' you, motherfucker," Greg warned the youngster.

As we came back into the building Greg asked me to talk to the cop with him. That's standard. We always speak to the cops in pairs so no one ever wonders if somebody else is giving up secrets. As soon as Greg began speaking, though, I picked his pocket and took off for the second tier.

As I passed Steve I handed him the shaker. "Hold this please." Then I came down the back stairs and hurried back through the crowded hall to Greg. I was behind him again when he turned around, so he assumed I had been there the whole time. "What do you think?" he asked.

"Probably that dude won't do shit for us."

"I asked as nicely as I could," he said.

"That's true," I agreed. "You were polite."

We climbed the first flight of stairs, but Greg stopped there. "Hold on," he said. "I want to talk to Steve." We turned down the second tier.

"Yeah, I'm watchin' you," Greg said as we approached Steve and Jimmy. "I didn't know you fucked around. But that's fine. I'm real good at the sneak games, and you don't even want to fuck with this guy." He tapped me on the chest and I smiled at Steve. I don't know how these guys kept a straight face. I sure as hell couldn't.

"I'll tell you this, though," Greg told Steve. "Now that I know you're one of them, it'll be a cold day before you get anything out of my pocket." Greg grinned and nodded. "Yeah. I'm watchin' you." I found it a little ironic that Greg would say this at a time when Steve was once again in possession of his shaker, and Greg was once again unaware of its absence. Before heading back to our cell I pointed to both my eyes, then at Steve. An ominous parting gesture.

Back in our cell, Greg checked his pocket before taking his jacket off. "Mother Fucker!!" he shouted. Then he turned on me angrily. "Are you helping him?!"

I burst out laughing and nodded my head, then Greg gave me a hug that turned into an all-out UFC grudge match.

The prone-outs were different now, because of the southerners attacking the cops. No more just sitting down, no more taking your time to find a nice spot. Everyone had to lie on his stomach promptly.

But the yard was still the yard. I made new friends and ran into old ones—Brawler gave me a big bear hug—and of course we worked our way around to telling stories about the riot we'd fought in together.

Brawler held five listeners captivated. "So these two big-ass lines have formed: all the blacks on that side, all the Whites over here. I'm gettin' em up with this crab right here." A crab is a crip. They don't like us calling them crabs, so we do.

"And Greg's over here," Brawler pointed. "He cracks one of 'em right in the mouth. And I'm getting' 'em up, and I look to my left, and here's Seph on my left, getting' em up with some crab. And I'm like, 'All right. Right on. Fuck yeah. Fuck yeah.'" He had this big loping nod that accompanied his words, and he threw air punches throughout the telling of this story.

"And I'm gettin' em up, and I look over to my right, and there's Seph, getting' em up with that crab over there. And I look back to my left real quick, and he's still there! He's still getting' em up with this dude! There's like six Sephs, runnin' all over the yard, kickin' everybody's ass!" Some laughter from the fellas.

Obviously, Brawler put something extra on this story because he liked me, and because he was happy to be reunited with his Comrade. But friends will do that. Being someone's friend can make you a hero in his story, just like one exciting day can earn you a reputation for something you really don't do very often.

CHAPTER EIGHTEEN

I wasn't back on the yard a week before Mac got me reassigned to Education. According to my counselor, I was still trying to earn my GED, but unofficially the Education staff made me a clerk. The job gave me access to glue and other supplies, access to the copy machine, and I could usually talk the guard into letting me out to yard with the other building. I met the Rainier guys—the older homeboys, the close custody inmates.

I sat at the White tables one morning with Jimmy Jet. I'd met him once before. He talked like Charlie Manson.

"I lived over in Airport, last time I was out. But that was damn twelve years ago. I been doing time, all through, what seems like forever. And I met everybody. I done time with every motherfucker anybody's ever met or heard of twice over."

As I sat listening to Jimmy I watched one of the skinheads walk over to Rainier. He shouted up to a window, made a sign to show he needed a wick, then stood there waiting. The youngsters back at the table this man had come from had a joint they wanted to smoke together. Moments later a tightly rolled rope of toilet paper sailed out from a window and landed on the track, lit on one end like a cigarette. The skinhead picked it up.

The gunner was on it from the start. By the time the runner returned to the table, radios on the yard were rattling with cops' voices.

". . . but I really do like this prison, the weather is especially nice . . ." Jimmy was still talking.

The youngsters noticed the cops' attention, and the skinhead grabbed the now extinguished wick and took off down the track. Haywire left the table too, but toward the cops.

"Look at me, youngster," Jimmy made sure he had my attention. "I want to tell you something. I want to explain to you, why I like Haywire. Look at what he's doing right now."

I watched. The second Haywire stepped onto the track he made eye contact with the approaching officers. He stutter-stepped and looked around, like he might be trying to decide which direction to take off running in. Then he surrendered. His shoulders sagged and he raised his hands and turned around so the cops could pat him down, shaking his head as he turned.

"These fucking kids over here," Jimmy motioned toward the table of youngsters, "ain't worth god damn two cents apiece. I wouldn't give a nickel for the whole lot of 'em. They're all just gonna sit there, and shrug their shoulders, and act like the weed that's sittin' on that table ain't theirs, and they don't know how it got there. They're lucky Jason's got some sense, and grabbed something he can't get in trouble for and ran outta here like he stole something. And they're even more lucky for Haywire. Even with all this goin' on, Haywire has the presence of mind to notice he's wearing the exact same clothes that Jason has on: gray beanie, gray shorts, blue state jacket."

He was right. As I was looking down at Jason, now fifty yards down the track, so were the two yard cops who had begun to search Haywire. The Rainier gunner was on the radio trying to tell these officers they were searching the wrong inmate. One officer thrust Haywire's jacket back at him, and as they jogged off toward the skinhead, Haywire walked calmly back to the table.

The guys at the table still didn't get it. They laughed and gave Haywire shit. "Ahhh! Haywire thought he was busted!"

"You shoulda seen your face."

"You were fuckin' scared."

"Why don't you stupid motherfuckers shut the hell up?"

". . . Who the fuck are you tellin' to shut up, Jimmy?"

"I'm telling you, Topper," Jimmy clarified. "I'm looking right at you, and I'm telling you to shut up."

Topper looked around for a second. "I guess I better shut up then." Everyone laughed, but the moment had been tense.

"You kids ought to pay attention and learn something from Haywire. Of course he'll let the cops search him. He knows he ain't got nothing. Hell, I'd squat and cough thirty fuckin' times if it'd help another man get away from these cops."

Jimmy turned back to me, letting his lecture end. "What are you doing out with Rainier yard, anyway?"

"I got a Medical ducat for ten," I told him. "The Education cop let me out."

"Me too. I'm going to Dental at ten. We'll go up there together." Someone called Jimmy's attention. "Excuse me, youngster," he said. "Let me talk with this man real quick."

He stepped away from the table we'd been sharing, leaving me sitting there with just my thoughts. The morning's incident had raised an interesting question. What made someone a part of the decision-making process? What made a guy's voice count or his opinion matter? There were men on A-yard who had been down twenty years, who had put in work, and no one consulted them on shit. They weren't even expected to make decisions for themselves.

And what did Haywire do? He did the best thing anyone can do: he showed quick, sound judgment. It's not about stabbing someone or putting in work. He got in the cops' way. And not in a stupid, oafish manner that would get him taken to the hole—Haywire did it with finesse and subtlety. He made them stop him.

Jimmy was done talking with the other older guy and was horsing around with Topper and the youngster Topper had been sitting next to. They were shadow boxing, with Jimmy muttering something about 'learn ya somethin, teach ya somethin,' the whole time.

"Years ago, Jimmy had been a boxer in prison. Now he was feeling all of his fifty-nine years. He cut the horseplay short, but the youngsters wouldn't quit. They darted in, tapping punches on Jimmy's arm—first one guy, then the other, then both at the same time—subconsciously taking revenge for being told to shut up. Jimmy's voice became angrier and the situation became more strained. I was unsure how it would end. One thing I did know: I wasn't going to let my sixty-year-old homeboy fight two young men all by himself.

I got up from the table and walked off toward the phone line. Once I was past the youngsters' vision, I circled around and came quietly in behind them, almost close enough to touch either guy. They were both bigger than me. If this turned into a real fight, though, I was certain I could at least leave Jimmy with a fair match.

"See that's the problem with you damn kids." Jimmy held his hand up to stop the younger guys. "You're all so damn worried about how to stand and how to hold your hands. But it ain't no damn use teaching you how to fight when you don't god damn pay attention to what's going on around you. This whole time you're fart-assin' around, my homeboy just snuck right up behind your ass. He's got you dead to rights."

"So I say this to 'em, and they turn around and see the kid standing there with his foot all cocked back." We were up at Medical and Jimmy was relaying the story to another older convict, one I had never met. "And they look at him, and he looks back at them, and they look at each other, and then they go sit their asses back down at the table. And I walk forward and ruffle up his hair, you know, he's a good kid. Ane he tells me, 'I had 'em,' all slick and shit with his little sunglasses on."

Jimmy's listener had some serious ink: warbird on his neck, bolts behind his ear. I knew enough to just sit there quietly and accept the compliment. Grace and humility go a long way.

"And I like that this happened because, he's my homeboy, and, to look at him, you know, you gotta ask yourself, 'Will he? Or won't he?' Well I found out today he will. Like a motherfucker he will.

"We already knew some bits about him," Jimmy continued. His listener never said a word, just stared at me and occasionally nodded. "When he come out of the hole, Iron Mike sent word over saying what he did there and a bit more about him. Mike says the kid caught him slippin' one day. He says this youngster set half a can of bugler up his shirt sleeve, and carried it through a sally port crowded with nine fuckin' cops. 'Oh, excuse me, officer. Pardon me, lieutenant. If you could just step aside there. How's your day goin', sarge? Okay Mike, here's your god damn contraband.

Now let's get the fuck outta here before these bastards get to arrestin' somebody.'" Jimmy chuckled as he relayed his idea of how this must have gone down.

"He just strikes me as kind of a throwback. His first week on the yard he went to store. And we're all in our house, you know, he lives over in Lassen Hall. But he stops by with the yard crew worker out there, and asks him if he knows the older Modesto guys in Rainier. And the guy tells him, 'Yeah, I know all of 'em.'

"Well the kid makes up three bags, with coffee and soups and all kinds of shit, and sends 'em in with Scott. He sends one to my cell, one to EZ's, and one to Robert Bree. Then he leaves Scott with a cold soda and tells him thanks for helping.

"And I know that don't seem like much. If you'll remember back, when we were his age, that was simply what you did. You know, the older guys don't get many packages, don't have money to go to store, so those of us who *can* look out for a motherfucker where and when we're able. That's just how we were brought up.

"But now you've got this new Pepsi generation of youngsters. They're all over the god damn yard, listening to rap music, got their damn pants around their thighs. I got to track a motherfucker down just to get in a good morning. And it makes me feel like maybe I didn't do as good a job as did the fellas who brought me up, like I'm letting these kids down. Well this morning this kid made me feel like maybe shit's not going downhill as fast as it seems.

"I don't know," Jimmy finished up. "That's the way I see it." They called my name for Medical and I excused myself. I never did hear that other guy speak.

CHAPTER NINETEEN

Weeks later I stood in the workout area across from the phone line, the same spot where the southerners had rushed the cops at night yard the year before. I wondered how much blood had been spilled, over the years, in the exact spot I was standing. With all the violence and chaos this prison had seen in the last fifty years, I felt almost like I was living on the site of a Civil War battlefield.

"Hey Seph." Greyhound had come up beside me. He lived down the tier from me in Lassen, but had made it to yard with the Rainier group. I liked him.

"Help me out," he said.

"What's up?"

"They called me to get a package, but I got my knife on me." He held an empty laundry bag in one hand; his other hand was stuffed into his pocket.

Inmates get patted down as soon as they step onto the patio. There's no guarantee the cop will find the knife, but why give him a chance? "I have a pocket," I answered, deliberately looking away from Greyhound and toward the phone line. He slipped the piece quickly into my coat pocket and walked away.

I shouted after him, "I'll be expecting a candy bar from your package."

"I don't buy sweets," he lied.

So few Haywires, so many Greyhounds. Another youngster who carried a shank around without any specific plans to use it. He actually relished these occasions when he was obliged to ask someone else to hold it. I was just one more guy who knew for sure he carried one, and this was one more time he got to feel cool, and gangster, and dangerous. I used to do the same thing on B-yard. As often as I had a piece on me, though, I never once used one that I just happened to have when the need arose. We carry them for nothing.

I planned to put Greyhound's knife down into my shoe at the first opportunity. I stood where I was for maybe ten minutes. Just in case Greyhound walking up to me had piqued the gunner's interest, I gave plenty of time for him to lose it. Next I sauntered over to the pull-up bars, shook a few hands, did a set. The pull-ups gave me time to look around. When I came down from the bar I knelt, stuffed the knife deep into my shoe, then untied and retied my laces. No hurry. Nice and easy. No awkward, jerky movement and no reason to freak out. If you panic, the other cons will notice. They'll look at you. And ten convicts looking in your direction is a good way to get the cops' attention. So relax. Pretend like what you're doing is not against the rules.

This shouldn't be that big a deal. Stuff something hot into your shoe—I've done it a thousand times. But it really does take fifteen minutes. The first time you half-ass it, bad things happen. Getting caught with weapons or drugs in prison carries heavy consequences, so if you're going to do this a thousand times, you had better make sure you do it carefully every time.

One set of pull-ups was enough. I stood around bullshitting with the other guys. Jimmy Jet approached the group and I said good morning. He was distracted.

"Everything all right?" I asked him.

"Com'on, kid. We got to help my cellie." We started walking.

I had only ever seen Tex from out my window. He was the grandpa version of Yosemite Sam: white hair, long white mustache, not quite five feet tall. As we came onto the track I could see him walking toward us.

"Keep goin', kid," Jimmy said. "Don't look at Tex when you go by, but let him know he's hot. Say, 'Tex is hot!' nice and loud." Jimmy stopped in his tracks and stared at the horseshoe pits. I continued on. Tex was coming toward me, slow-trailed by two yard cops about thirty meters behind him and closing.

I turned and shouted to the guys at the pisser. "Kahuna!" Kahuna looked. "Tex is hot!"

"He is?" Kahuna answered.

"Man, Tex is hot as fuck!"

"That's news to me." Tex hadn't looked at me, but said this aloud as his old-man's shuffle intercepted the conversation. Kahuna went about his business.

I remembered the knife in my shoe, then approached the cops as they came by. "Hey Hughes . . . ." I pointed at the rec gate. "We've been trying to get the softball shit out all morning. Can you help us out?"

"Hold on." He almost had to push me aside to get by as I really was right out in front of him. They continued on. Once they were by me I walked over to the sink and washed my hands, watching the pursuit. Tex entered the group in the workout area and the men closed behind him. Almost immediately he emerged from the other side wearing a completely different set of clothes. I've seen magicians on stage, quick change artists, who were less impressive. His grey beanie and sunglasses were gone, replaced with a bulky blue jacket. He had even managed to tuck his hair into somebody's blue ball cap.

Tex went straight to the dip bars and began doing pull-ups. Hughes and the other officer were on the track. Both touched their earpieces. I looked up at the tower. The gunner was running the show.

Both cops went straight for the pull-up bars. They went right past Tex. As soon as they were by, Tex hit the track and made straight for the pisser. The fellas in the workout area spoke loudly and asked the cops any question they could think of. Finally Hughes stepped away from the commotion with a finger to his ear. He looked down at the toilets.

Hughes braced his belt and leaned in a little. For a second I thought he might sprint after the old man, try to catch him before he got there, but it was too late. Tex was already just feet away. He reached down and set something into the bowl, then flushed a few times. By the time the cops made it down there he was already washing his hands.

"Hawkins!" Hughes called him over.

"What can I he'p you with, off'cer?"

"What did you flush?"

Tex hesitated a second. "I didn't flush anything, off'cer." He looked genuinely surprised at the accusation.

"Bullshit," Hughes said. "What are you doing at the bathroom?"

Now Tex seemed a little peeved. "I am an old man, and I have a bladder problem."

"You are an old man, and you have a drug problem," Hughes retorted.

"That is a hell of a thing for you to say to me, off'cer. I wish," Tex squinted at him, "I wish, somebody, had taught you to respect your elders." Yosemite Sam. He shuffled off and Hughes let him go.

Of course, Tex never really flushed anything. Likely one of the guys at workout bars was holding whatever the old man had been carrying. I read in a book once how you could trap raccoons simply by tying a coin to a log. Raccoons like shiny things. Once one of them gets his hand around that piece of metal, he'll never let go. He'll sit there pulling on it until someone comes to collect him, or until he starves. Tex may swallow it, but he would never flush his dope.

The whole time I watched this ordeal, I felt like I was seeing something important. Prison is sometimes referred to as crime school. It's where lawbreakers go to learn the more technical aspects of their trade, and where they develop the attitude and conviction they'll need to ply that trade. It turns hoodlums and vandals into calculating criminals. Four years will earn you a degree. But what happens to the man who attends college for thirty years?

Tex is a master convict. He has two Ph.D's, a handful of honors, and an associate professorship at a prestigious university. He can swindle the bottlecap off a twenty-ounce soda without touching it, and I'm not exaggerating. What chance does the world have against him? Society's only consolation is that these men are so old by the time they reach this level of deception that they will die before doing much more harm.

Of course, not all lifers are like Tex. Just a few cells down the same tier lived Mike Grady. Mike had been a driver for an armored truck service, and so carried a firearm on his belt. One day he stopped at home for lunch. Halfway through making a sandwich, Mike heard a noise in the back of the house. He and his wife lived alone, they didn't have any children, but someone was in his home. Mike drew his gun and headed back toward where the noise had come from.

When he reached the back room, Mike found a stranger plowing his wife. He started yelling, the stranger got up from the wife and came toward Mike, and Mike shot him.

Mike will tell you that he didn't mean to shoot the guy, but that point is irrelevant here. The court examined Mike's case in detail. He was tried, convicted, and sentenced to fifteen-years-to-life. That means fifteen years, and the parole board may choose to extend Mike's sentence based on his conduct while in prison.

Mike Grady has been in prison for twenty-four years. He has never received a single disciplinary write-up. I feel like I should repeat that, just to emphasize how amazing it is. Most guys can't go three months without a write-up. In two-and-a-half decades, Mike has never once talked back to staff, never been late for a lock-up, never missed work. His C-file contains nothing but college credits and vocational learning certificates, along with his completion chronos for anger management, alcoholics anonymous, and narcotics anonymous. Still, every few years the board denies Mike his parole.

The parole board bases its decision on Mike's commitment offense. You killed someone. Letting you out of prison would be unfair to the victim's family. But the parole board is overstepping its bounds. If the court felt Mike's crime warranted twenty-five years in prison, it could have sentenced him to twenty-five-years-to-life. It could have sentenced him to life-without-the-possibility-for-parole. It did not. After twenty-four years behind bars, the parole board should be required to show some justification, other than his initial crime, for denying him his chance at a new life.

There are thousands of men like Mike Grady—men held in prison past their release dates, men who have served thirty years with only an occasional minor write-up. These men are so unlikely to reoffend that I find myself wondering how they ended up in prison in the first place. They are not criminals. If you let them out today, they would go fishing, they would get jobs, and you would never hear from them again.

California's prisons are overcrowded. Complaints come in from all directions: there's not enough staff, not enough medical, housing conditions are unsanitary. We have too many inmates. But these non-criminal lifers amount to roughly three thousand beds occupied unnecessarily. Release efforts, however, concentrate on low-term, nonviolent offenders. We would rather release a guy who's been arrested for auto theft four times in the last five years than release a guy who, twenty years ago, shot someone in the heat of inflamed emotions. Stupid. The car thief will be right back.

And these lifers are not the only inmates who could safely be set free in the interest of justice. Robert Boyd was a normal guy. He had served in the Navy, he belonged to the Local 104 Sheetrock Union. He never stole anything, never used drugs. Never once had a criminal thought passed through his head. But he liked to drink. Robbie enjoyed being the guy everyone at the bar cheered on to chug, chug, chug. He got into his truck one night, tried to drive home, and wrecked into another car. He killed two people.

The court sentenced Boyd to twenty-two years. The length of this sentence was not necessarily meted out to punish Boyd (men have maliciously murdered, raped women, hurt children and received far lighter terms). Instead, the court heaped so many years upon him in the hope that other alcoholics, reading about this in the paper, would take notice and understand that drinking and driving is no minor offense.

For his part, Boyd was changed after just one year. He never drinks. I sat with him as he asked his cellmate to move out because the cellmate liked to drink pruno—Boyd can't stand alcohol—and I have seen Boyd write countless letters to his victims' families, apologizing for their loss, wishing he could take it back, and wishing he could be forgiven. He never even sent any of these letters out; he just ripped them up and flushed them down the toilet. For the last twelve years Boyd has felt nothing but remorse, and disgust with himself.

Robert Boyd should be released from prison. The newspaper's message to those other alcoholics was delivered loud and clear, and his release today would receive far less attention. His release would in no way undermine the initial point's impact. With one stroke we can gain a valuable member of society and free up a bed in our crowded prison system.

I've met a number of younger inmates, especially, who did not belong in prison. They aren't really out to hustle or get over on anyone, they try to avoid violence. But prison has a way of stealing innocence away from the younger guys, and it does so because of a very fixable flaw in CDC's classification structure.

I remember one nineteen year old who didn't belong in prison. His name was Adam. I can't recall his last name, but it doesn't really matter because now he definitely does belong in prison. Over some trouble with his girlfriend, and him trying to run another guy over with his truck, he was sentenced to fourteen years in prison, which put him straight onto a three yard.

The yard level you go to depends on your point score. Adam got two points for each year of his sentence. Then they tack on points for all sorts of ridiculous shit. If you're under the age of twenty-five, you get six points. I don't know why they do this. Let's see . . . the guy is young . . . he's impressionable . . . I've got it! Let's put him in with the most dangerous convicts we have. They'll put a knife in his hand the first week he's there. It'll be great.

Unmarried? Four points. No children? Another four points. Family history of heart disease: eleven fucking points. And then the factors that might actually indicate some hope for a normal life barely carry any weight at all. Adam dropped two points for having graduated high school, another two for this being his first arrest. The career criminal with a four-year term and a fondness for stabbing people goes to fire camp, and the drunk driver who's riddled with remorse gets sent straight to a level four kill zone.

You drop points for good behavior, whether you want to or not. Soledad's level-three housing is cell living. Dropping to level two gets you sent to the dorm. But the dorm is terrible. The bunks are packed tightly together, there's no privacy, the noise is unbearable. And to make it even worse, since Soledad had such moderate weather, CDC had spent the last year filling more than half the bunks in each dorm with triple-C, psych med inmates—the lunatics who shit themselves and walk in circles.

Behave yourself, attend work, and you will drop points. Drop points, and you will be moved to the dorm. It was interesting to see the antics some of the inmates pulled to avoid being labeled well-behaved.

CHAPTER TWENTY

It was nine-thirty: after lock-up from night yard. Greg and I were lying in our respective beds, watching some nature documentary.

"ALL INMATES, GET ON YOUR BUNKS!" We turned the volume down on the television.

"GET ON YOUR FUCKIN' BUNKS YOU PIECES OF SHIT!" We looked out our window. The door to Fremont Dorm was wide open, spilling light onto the darkened prison yard. Two cops stood in the doorway, and thirty feet in front of them stood an inmate, holding the cops' bullhorn in his hand.

"BOTH OF YOU COULD STAND TO LOSE A FEW POUNDS."

Officers came onto the yard from all directions. The cop from Lassen was first to him and the inmate took off running. They played ring-around-the-rosy around the softball backstop, in the middle of which the convict put the bullhorn against the chain link, right by the guard's head.

"NO YOU CANNOT HAVE THE BULLHORN BACK."

As more officers closed in, the inmate cut through the on-deck opening and sprinted for left field.

"SUCK MY DICK."

By now the cheering from the cell windows was drowning out most of the inmate's witty comments. The cops tackled him. They sprayed him, thoroughly beat his ass, recovered the bullhorn, and escorted him off the yard. We settled down and went to sleep.

"The fuck was that all about?" Greg asked Eddie as we walked to breakfast.

"He didn't want to live in that dorm," Eddie explained. "Last night they cuffed him up and walked him over there. So, he give 'em hell."

"Who?"

"Gleason."

"That was Gleason?!" Greg asked, incredulous.

"Not bad for an old man," Eddie chuckled. "They dropped him to level two last month. Dropped him and Polish Joe the same day. Surprised you ain't got yourself back up to level three by now, Joe." Polish Joe was right in front of us.

"This I have a plan for." Thick accent. Joe had a bulbous nose and white hair growing from all kinds of places. Sort of like a koala.

"A *plan*?"

"Is good. I show you," Joe explained. "I go to do it right now."

"Yeah, I can't wait to see that," Eddie answered. "Used to be a motherfucker could just get at one of these cops and they'd hand him a write-up. Till they put them fuckin' J-CAT medders in there. Now everybody and their daddy wants a fuckin' write-up. These cops get reprimanded now for bullshit write-ups when a motherfucker's about to drop. What are your points at Greg?"

"I'm already at level two," Greg said, "but they endorsed me to camp."

"Yeah, you got lucky," Eddie informed him. "What about you kid."

"Thirty points," I told him.

"When's your annual?"

"Four months."

"Well, you might as well get on that sooner rather than later." As we came up to the chow hall Polish Joe broke apart from the group. He walked straight up to the cops who stood in front of the building, grabbed hold of the big, metal trash can next to them, flipped it upside down, and dumped garbage all over the asphalt. Then he hoisted the can over his head and threw it a good twenty feet in front of him. It landed with a clang, and then a clunk, and then it rolled all the way to the dirt.

The rest of us had stopped on the track. We stood there with our mouths open, fairly surprised by what Joe had just done.

The cops hadn't even flinched. One of them stepped forward and spoke to Joe. "Pick it up."

"This I cannot do," Joe answered.

"Pick it up," the cop repeated, reaching for his handcuffs.

Joe shook his head. "I don't tush trash," he said, showing the guard his hands.

"You touch your children, don't you?" the guard smiled.

"What does this mean?" Joe demanded as the cop clicked the handcuffs on. "Do you call my children trash?!"

"No," the cop assured him. "There's a language barrier. You misunderstood me. Let's go, grandpa."

"The trick is to not get taken to the hole," Greg said. We stood in front of the rec gate, waiting to check the softball shit out. "It's easy to get a write-up. But here you have to do something bad enough to get written up, but not so bad that they take you to the hole. How many points will you drop?"

"At least six."

"Then you'll probably need two write-ups. That sucks."

"Tsk. I'll get a write-up." I turned and walked over to the chain link fence that sectioned off the rec area. Two cops were coming toward me along the track. I climbed up the fence, almost high enough to touch the razor wire that ran along the top, sixteen feet off the ground. I hung there like Spiderman, looking over my shoulder at these two guards as they walked by. They looked at me, smiled, and continued on.

I flipped my head to the other side as they walked off and called out, "You guys are assholes!"

Nothing. One cop shook his head, but they never deviated course. I climbed down. "This is gonna be more difficult than we expected, huh?"

"I can't believe they didn't say nothing." Greg was still looking after them. "That's fucking crazy."

I gave him a mean glare. "Com-cast bandit," I spat. I made a gun out of my hands and pointed it at him. "Nobody move! . . . Nobody Fucking Move!"

He tried to walk away, but I followed. "I want all your cable! . . . Now! . . . HBO! . . . Showtime! . . . Titty Movies! . . . Nobody Move!" Greg's fun to pick on.

The next day six of us were playing basketball. The intercom clicked on. "Attention on the A-yard. Clear the track, from Rainier Hall to the Patio. Clear the track, from Rainier Hall to the Patio. All inmates, assume a seated position on the yard."

Everyone else got down; I continued to dribble the ball.

Greg looked at me. "What're you doing?"

"Write-up."

"Oh. Don't get the ball taken."

I began shooting hoops. I was the only guy on the yard not sitting down, and everyone was looking at me. All the inmates, anyway. None of the guards paid me any attention. Of course, with everyone watching, I didn't make very many baskets. I'm really not that terrible a basketball player. I was like, making them all in before everybody started watching.

The cops escorted an inmate from Rainier along the track. As they passed by me I put a finger to my pursed lips and let out a loud "bibidibidibidibi." Nothing. Nobody paid me any attention. I walked over to Greg, set the ball on the ground, and sat on top of it. "This is stupid."

Greg looked up at the rim, then back to me. "You didn't make very many baskets, buddy." Sometimes Greg was a dick.

"I've been goin' about this all wrong," I told Greg when we were back in our cell. "I need a plan. But I figured it out. Look. I go out for work-and-school call, right? Okay, so every time Rainier has yard, I'll walk to the Education gate. Then I'll turn around and walk back to Rainier. I'll sneak in there, and come out to yard with them. They have to catch me. If they don't write me up, then I get double yard every day. Either way, I win."

Greg agreed. It was a good plan. And things went along perfectly. I walked from the gate right back to Rainier. I opened the door to a handful of officers in the sally port.

Just enough hesitation to catch their eye, then I made a move for the A-side.

They stopped me. "Where you going?"

"Pfff. My class is closed. They sent me back." Two of the cops exchanged knowing looks as I continued on to the A-side. I went straight up the stairs and quickly down the third tier to Jimmy Jet's house.

Jimmy was happy to see me. "Hey! D'fuck you doin' in here, kid?"

"Fuckin' up."

"Yeah, this is the old man's department. You don't belong in here."

"Yeah, they're coming to get me right now." The cop had slow trailed me up the stairs.

"Well don't bring 'em here," Jimmy said. "I'm hot."

"All right." I stepped off up the tier, looking up at the cell numbers like I was trying to find someone.

The cop was a mexican. "Where do you live?"

"One forty-eight." That would put me somewhere in the black showers.

"Let's go." He directed me around the tier and down the stairs. Very professional. Once I was down by the sally port he had me strip naked. "Now bend at the waist, spread your cheeks, and cough." I did so. "Bend again . . . . Now spread your ass cheeks . . . . That's not wide enough, inmate." He ordered me to cough again and again. I was young. Maybe he thought I was horribly embarrassed to be standing there bent over with my cheeks held apart. I wasn't.

"What are you hiding up there, inmate?"

"I'm pretty sure nothing, sir."

"You're pretty sure?"

"Well I've been surprised before." Some rainier guys laughed.

"Cough again," he ordered. "That was from your chest. Cough from your belly." I found myself wishing I hadn't shit that morning. This guy deserved for me to simply drop one right in front of him. He leaned over for a not-so-quiet conversation with his partner.

"Look at this. He's got a brown ring around his cheeks, and fuckin' dingleberries hangin' from his ass hair." They both laughed. "Fuckin' *dirty*-ass White boy!" Probably this wasn't true. I generally kept pretty clean. It's just something he said because mexicans hate White people.

The sergeant escorted me back to Lassen. They put me down on the second tier, in an empty cell across from my own. I watched the building cops pull Greg out, talk to him for a minute, then bring him down and put him in with me.

"Wha'd they tell you?" I asked as the cop locked us in.

"Uh . . ." He hesitated, trying to remember the conversation word for word. "He told me he was gonna tear my shit up. And he said the sergeant wanted him to make sure I knew that my shit was getting torn up because of my cellmate's bullshit conduct. Then he nodded at me all slow, like this."

"No fuckin' way!"

Greg smiled. "And then they put me down here with you . . . . I think they want me to toss you up a little."

"Well let's fuckin' *do it!*" I jumped on him and we had ourselves a hearty ruckus. I think I won.

"The fucked up part about it," Eddie explained. "is that if you wasn't trying to get one, you'd have damn three of 'em by now."

"True," I said. "But if I weren't trying to get one, I wouldn't have done any of the stupid shit I just did."

He looked at me. "You bein' a smart ass again?"

"I don't think so." I was.

"Anyway, big dog, the reason I wanted to talk to you is, we got something that come up. Now listen. I know it ain't your turn. I know you done plenty already and a couple times. It's easy somebody else's turn." This was Eddie's way of telling me I could opt out. Usually, saying no is a bit dishonorable.

"But this is a one-on-one," Eddie continued. "Real simple. And it has to be public, so I figger it's a good spot for gettin' your write-up, and still coming right back to the yard."

"Sounds good." Easy decision. "What's the deal?" I asked.

"Well," he said, "let's get Greg, so I don't have to say everything twice." We got Greg. "So I'm inside this morning," Eddie began, "and you know this kid Sean has been coming out and working as a porter. He's not a porter, but he volunteers and what not and helps out out there. Well that indian porter, Joe, is from Modesto too. And I've told that damn kid, I don't know how many times, he was gettin' too damn friendly in his playin' around with that dude. And that fuckin' indian encourages him, so he don't really have too much ground to piss on. But the fact is still there, that the kid was out of line, and it was toward another race, and our answer for that is always a public checking."

"Wait, what the hell did he do?"

"I'm gittin' to that part god dammit."

"Oh. Sorry. I thought you were already past it." Eddie stared at me for thirty seconds, trying not to crack a smile.

"The indian was on my door this morning," Eddie continnered. "He was talking to me about something, nevermind what, and this kid comes walking along down on the second tier across from us. He calls out, 'Hey Joe.' Joe looks, and when Joe looks, the kid pulls his dick out of his pants and shakes it at him. Then the kid walks off smiling. And Joe looks positively offended. He looks at me with his eyebrows all up, and he says, 'Did you see that?' And I say, 'Yeah, I saw it.'

"Anyway, if you don't want to do it, I was just gonna do it. Only I'm worried a punch from me might break his damn jaw. The kid only weighs a buck-sixty. But I already told the indian it would be today."

"No, that's fine. I got it."

"Okay," Eddie said. "It's whatever time you feel like going. That's up to you."

"I think now's probably good." We walked back to the tables. Sean stood at the head of the domino table, watching the guys play. "Hey Sean . . ." He looked. "You remember what happened this morning?"

"What?" He seemed genuinely confused.

"Do you remember this morning, shaking your dick at the indian?"

"Yeah . . ."

"You and I are gonna have a little talk about it." I put my right foot back. "You ready?"

"Yeah . . ." He still looked confused. Definitely not ready.

I brought my hands up. "Are you ready?"

"Yeah" I swung as the word left his mouth. I don't know if, subconsciously, I felt bad about him standing there flatfooted, or if I'm just not as good a fighter as I thought—I short swung my left hook by at least six inches. It was just nowhere near him.

Before he'd reacted I landed a right. Sean backpedaled around the table and I followed him. Hands up, step in, left-right. He dropped, hitting the ground hard and for a second I worried he may have smacked the back of his head on the asphalt. I made a motion to kick him, but stopped myself. Just a checking.

"All right, Seph! You got him!" Brawler was leaning back from his seat at the domino table, his hand out to stop any further violence. "Relax! You got him!"

"Yeah, that's enough, big dog."

I looked over at the two cops standing in front of the chow hall: an older guy, and a female officer. They both stared intently in my direction. The guy held his arm extended across his partner's torso, like he had slammed on the brakes and didn't want her to go flying through the windshield. A glance to my left showed me the Rainier gunner looking down at me, his arms folded in and leaning against the rail. No code. Sean was still on the ground, his sunglasses sitting crooked on his face and his open hands held out in front of him.

I just turned and walked away. As I walked past Eddie he gave me an open-handed thump on my chest. "I can see I'mo hafta watch your little ass!" he said excitedly. He and Greg walked Sean to the sink so he could wash his face.

When they returned I made sure to shake hands with Sean. We were still friends. As he sat down on a bench in front of me, Sean noticed a cut on the top of my left hand.

"God damn, homeboy. That was your left?"

I looked at the cut, oddly shaped like someone's front tooth.

"Well," he continued, "at least it's over."

"Man," I said, "the worst part is, I still didn't get a fuckin' write-up."

"I can't believe you said that shit to him," Greg said, laughing.

"What's wrong with that?"

"Because, Seph. You busted his fuckin' face open, knocked him out on the track, and made him look like a bitch in front of everybody, and the *worst* part is you didn't get written up?"

I joined Greg in laughing. "He didn't look like a bitch."

"He did look like a bitch," Greg said. "Like-a-bitch. The only thing that kept him from another check was he sort of threw a punch at you as he was on his way down. It was just enough that we can say he fought back. But still, 'Awe shucks, I didn't get a write up'? How about 'sorry about your face'."

"You act like he didn't do nothin' wrong," I said. "He knows what he did."

"No, that's true," Greg said more seriously. "You did good. Everybody was real proud."

"I know. Brawler came and apologized for spazzing out. He said he hadn't realized it was a check, that he thought it was just Sean had said something rude. Anyway, he gave me two cigarettes and said thanks for doing the White thing."

"I like Brawler."

"Hey, did me, you, and him—in that riot on B-yard—did we run over and save a guy named Irish from getting stomped out?"

"No," Greg said. "That was me and Rambo."

"Tsk. I knew that wasn't me."

"He was my cellie in the back."

"Who?" I asked. "Rambo?"

"No. Irish."

"Oh. Was he cool?"

Greg smiled. "He talked too much."

"A bunch of ese's gave me handshakes and shit too."

"Yeah," Greg remembered, "there was like six of them on the track when you started. Plus their table is right there."

"So I'm like the hero of the yard now."

"And modest," he smiled. "That's good you're so humble about everything."

I pointed my fingers at him. "Nobody Move! . . . I want the Playboy Channel! . . . Cartoon Network! . . . Nobody Fuckin' Move!"

"Don't start feelin' too tough," he warned.

"What's up?" I joked. "You eye-ballin' me bitch? You know I got knockout power."

"Or maybe you got an easy opponent who made you look good. You miss one on me and I'll make you pay for it."

"Well let's find out, motherfucker!" We wrestled again. I let Greg win that one.

I was discouraged, but not about to give up. First thing the next morning I went to someone's cell on the first tier (Sean's, ironically) and got a cup of pruno. As I walked across the yard I began to sway a little. I wasn't drunk, but I felt I may as well get into character.

The patio cop looked at me as I came through the patio gate. I put my left hand up in a casual wave and cut right, straight for the lieutenant's office. Fat Tony sat at his station. He looked up from his computer and I raised my cup to him as I opened the lieutenant's door. Fuck knocking. The lieutenant and one of his sergeants sat looking over some papers at the far end of the table. They both stared at me as I walked forward, bumped into a chair, and lurched awkwardly over the brown tabletop. I was loud and obnoxious.

"The captain said . . . ernothefucken captain . . . SERGEANT . . . the *sergeant* said . . . that you got, my green ID . . . . That, it's not, in his office . . . he doesn't have it . . . but you have it . . . your green ID . . . *my* green ID."

"What was your name?"

"McCarty!" They actually made a show of looking around. I just stood there blabbering. "Mick-Arty . . . McFarty." I was swaying from side to side, and with each jostle I spilled a dollop of fruity prison wine on the floor, the table, some paperwork, where-the-fuck-ever—I didn't care.

"I don't have it," the lieutenant said. "You're going to have to put in for a new one."

"B'thefuck you wamme do, store and shit, an' I got a visit, on Friday." They were herding me out of the office.

"There are no Friday visits," the sergeant said. "Weekends only."

"Well fuckin', Saturday." The lieutenant put his hand on my shoulder to nudge me forward so he could close the door. As soon as he made contact I dropped my cup. What was left of the pruno spilled out as the plastic mug clacked and bounced across the tile.

I looked at the puddle, then over my shoulder at the lieutenant. "You goosedamn stupma fucker."

He closed the door. Tony and the asian clerk were staring at me, wide-eyed and open-mouthed. I apologized for the mess and left the office.

Officer Alford had relieved the patio cop. I went straight to him. "Hey Alford."

"Yeah."

"Help me out. Look. I just went into the lieutenant's office with a full cup of pruno, spilled it everywhere, dropped it on the floor, and then called the lieutenant a stupid-ass for making me spill it."

Alford laughed. "I wish I could have seen that."

"Man, I need a write-up. I climbed the fence—pulled an escape attempt right in front of your coworkers. They didn't even fuckin' care. Then I went into Rainier. Got caught runnin' around in there. No write-up. Yesterday I knocked somebody out in the middle of the fuckin' yard!"

"I heard about that."

I looked at him in disbelief. "You heard about that? Why the fuck didn't you guys write me up then?"

"You shouldn't have done it so close to shift change."

I dropped my head. "Write me up, Alford."

"Gimme your ID." I handed him my green ID card and he wrote down my information. "Next time there's a code, I'll write you up for not proning out up here at Medical," he said. "You just go in and plead not guilty, like you didn't ask me for this write-up."

"Yeah, I got the convict end covered. Thank you." He never did write me up. Actually, I never saw Alford after that. I heard he got transferred over to South Facility.

CHAPTER TWENTY-ONE

Greg left for camp a month later. Of all the times we ever roughhoused, I won all of them. I want to be very clear on that point. Greg never won. Between the two of us, I am the much better fighter. I only sometimes let him think he had won, so that he wouldn't feel bad.

Two days after he left the cops moved me down to three eleven. I tried to argue my way into keeping my old room, but it was a hard sell. We had four White cells in a row there, and staff rarely lets us get more than two connected. I guess they're worried we'll create little hoods and barrios all over the building. Anyway, I was single-celled now, right in the middle, and I was the newest to the neighborhood. An obvious choice.

They moved me in with Ryan McAlister, a youngster from right there in Salinas. His parents' home was only a few miles from the prison. He had been in the hole while I was back there, but we had never met in person. I just remembered him from the roll call. We got along well, though, and he hung out with Modesto more than anyone else. Besides, when shit cracks, he'll fight. That's all you ever need in a cellmate.

"Well I don't know what the fuck the story is behind it, but he's not on roll call there in the back." Eddie stood with us in the phone line.

"Not for runnin' around with the bullhorn?" I asked. "They're trying to say he pulled some PC move?"

"No," Eddie reckoned. "I don't see how they could work that. We're not supposed to refuse a move to another yard, but all the Fremont guys already have access to all the Lassen Hall fellas. They can't say he's running. Well it's not for sure he's no good, but if he's not on roll call there's at least a question mark."

"That sucks for him," I said. "Still, it seems like we've got enough to deal with amongst our own homeboys."

"Yeah," Eddie grinned, "and the adopted ones." He was looking at Ryan.

Ryan smiled. "What?"

"Ain'tchu got any Monterey County homeboys missin' you?"

"I don't think there are any Monterey guys here," I put in.

"No, there are."

"Where?" Eddie asked.

"Jason" I elbowed him as he pointed his finger at someone in the workout area.

"Don't point," I told Ryan. I was serious, and he looked at me like we were still in high school and I had dissed him.

"I mean it," I said. "Don't ever point your finger at anyone, for any reason. There isn't anything on this whole fuckin' yard you can't describe with words. When you point, people look to see where you're pointing. God forbid the dude you point at has a knife on him, or drugs, and the cops decide to pat him down 'cause you pointed."

Ryan seemed to get it. I wasn't trying to be a dick. Eddie chimed in to help.

"There's even motherfuckers who will come up to you where you're standing like now and ask, 'Hey, which one of these dudes is your homeboy, Jason?' Really, he don't give a rat fuck who Jason is. He just wants to see if you'll point, or if you know better and say, 'Oh, he's the dude in the gray hat, standing to the left of the pull-up bars.' See maybe he's got something hot that's got to get into Lassen, and he wants to see if he can trust you with it."

"Who's this dude over here?" I cut in, pointing my arm across Ryan and Eddie both. I couldn't resist.

"Boy, you's about a stupid motherfucker!" Eddie tried to look mad, but he couldn't help chuckling.

Ryan and I shared a window with our neighbor in three twelve. Apparently one of the blacks in that cell was this famous crip. Every day a new group of black kids would cluster under our window and call him.

"Snowman! Hey, Snowman!"

We'd hear the window clang open. "Who dat callin' up here?" That was his cellie, the hype man. Deep, raspy voice. He always gave a good build-up before Snowman actually came to the window.

"We wanna talk to Snowman!"

"Y'all wanna talk to Snow Man?"

"Yuh!"

"Y'all lookin' fo' Snoooowww Maaannn?!"

"Yuh! Yuh!"

The hype man really built him up. "It's my niiiiiggaaaah!"

"What it do?" Where the hype man's voice was a deep, raspy bass, Snowman's was crisp and nasal. It was Ludacris innerducing Snoop Dogg.

"Snowman," one youngster called up. "This nigga say he know you."

"Nah, nah." The kid in question looked sixteen.

"Hell yeah, nigga!" the first crip argued. "You was just sayin' on the track, 'I know Snowman. I know Snowman.'"

The youngster looked up. "You know my uncle."

"Who yo' uncle?" Snowman asked.

"Shady Mac, Fo'teen Hoover."

Snowman was quiet a second. I could hear the hype man muttering inside their cell, "Oh, no, nigga."

"J-Rock," Snowman called out at last.

"Yuh!" the first crip answered up.

"Have dat nigga run laps . . . . I on't like his uncle."

At first the kid smiled. Maybe he thought Snowman was just joking. The other youngsters made it clear, though, there was no joke. They clustered around him with menacing looks and clenched fists. "Run laps, nigga." "Snowman said run laps." He took off, panic stricken, holding his pants up while he ran.

"His uncle a chump?" J-rock asked, once the kid was gone.

"Nah, his uncle good folks. But I'll teach a nigga to name drop." The youngsters below all chuckled. "Look," my neighbor continued. "Dat nigga's already on the utha side o' da yard."

"God damn that nigga fass!" The hype man always cut in when we least expected him, making it difficult for Ryan and I to check our laughter. We'd even hear him in the middle of a quiet day, when there weren't any kids down below. "Oh, no, nigga! Not my queeen, nigga! You took my queeen, nigga! Butchu stiiilll mmyyy niiiggaaah!"

I only ever spoke directly to them once.

"Hey three eleven."

Ryan turned the CD player down and we exchanged looks of confusion. Was this dude calling us?

"Hey three eleven."

I went to the window. "What's up?"

"Hey. You fuck wit dem thangs?"

I tried to think of what he might mean. After a second I asked, "What are you talkin' about? Drugs?"

He sputtered and spat for a second. "Nah. Dem *thangs.*"

I looked at Ryan. His eyebrows were about even with his hairline as he shrugged his shoulders.

"Cigarettes?"

"Tsst tsst shht tsst!" More sputtering. Evidently I was speaking too loudly. "Nah, man! I'm talkin' 'bout dem *tangs*. Dem saltwater tangs."

If this is really how the blacks communicate, it's no wonder they always get caught up in shit. Still, it's possible another crip would have known exactly what thangs were. "You mean saltwater lighters?"

"Tshht. Yeah," he said quietly. "Them thangs."

"Yeah, I fuck with things. What's up?"

"Mine broke."

"Oh, yeah," I answered. "Shoot it over." He passed his altered roll-on deodorant container through the window. Broke wasn't really the word for it. He'd put way too much salt in the bottle, so the paperclips that extended down into the water had corroded into nothing. I rewired the whole thang and shot it back to him.

"How much I owe you?" he asked.

"No, that's just on being neighborly."

"A'ight, good lookin'." We don't take money from blacks. I usually don't do any business with them, but the lighter is a special circumstance. If Snowman blows the power out trying to smoke a cigarette (or some crack), Ryan and I will spend all night in the dark.

We brought the conversation back into our own cell. "I got a kite from B-yard," Ryan told me.

"Right on. What'd it say?"

"I got an older homeboy over there."

"Oh. Does he want you to move over there?"

"No, he was just saying what's up. He said he wanted to know if I needed anything. He's a little older. Like forty. His name's Taz. Eddie knows him."

Shit. I forgot Taz was from Monterey. I had been rinsing laundry while we held this conversation. Now I stopped and stared at him, trying to think of how best to proceed.

"What?"

"Look," I said. "You know that what's said in here is private, right? If something's said on the yard, then that's a public statement, and anybody who's mentioned should be made aware of what was said. But what's said in our cell is just for you and me. What's said in the cell, stays in the cell."

"Yeah, I know," Ryan answered.

"I don't think you should fuck with that dude, Ryan."

"Why not?"

"He's just one of those dudes, bro. When shit's calm, like now, when there's no tension, he's out there, and in the mix, and about the politics. But when shit starts lookin' dangerous, he's nowhere to be seen.

"He works in the Unit Six office over there. And him and Tracy were in that office when we rushed the blacks. They didn't come out. Later they ran some shit about the door being locked, but it's all bullshit. That door's never locked. Plus there was a black OG named Chocolate Thunder sitting right next to them. They could have got off, but didn't. They let everyone else fight, let everyone else spill their blood, and those two hid in that fuckin' office.

"Anyway, Tracy got smashed for it as soon as we came off lockdown. Taz was supposed to be next, but it never got handled."

"How come?" Ryan was taking it all in.

"Tracy was from Sac, and Sac's got a little more structure than Monterey County. Sac's on top of their shit. Plus there was a lot of shit to deal with when we came up. Taz just kinda got swept under the rug."

I should distinguish here between Taz from Monterey, and Taz from Tulare County. Both men were on B-yard. Taz from Tulare County, Jeffrey Sidelinker, was about his shit.

"But the issue will come up again," I told Ryan. "And the closer you put yourself to Taz, the more likely it is you'll be the one who's asked to deal with it. As soon as somebody owes him money, or doesn't like what he has to say about something, the whole issue will resurface. And if you're close to him, the next thing he does might fuck yours off too. If he's a wreck, why get in the car with him?"

"What should I do?"

"Write dude back," I suggested. "Tell him thanks for the kite. I don't need anything. I'm a short-timer, I'm going home soon, but it was nice to meet you. Then don't ever talk to dude again."

He was quiet a second, thinking it over.

"It sucks for you, too," I continued. "The homeboy connection is an important one, and you don't have a lot of 'em. But any prison you go to, you'll always have friends when you arrive, you know? Even if you don't know them, the other Monterey guys will make sure you don't go hungry."

There was plenty more for us to talk about, but we were interrupted by the building officer opening our door.

"McCarty."

"Yeah."

He handed me three plastic bags while looking down at his sheet of paper. "You're moving to Fremont Dorm."

"No . . ." I was a little surprised. "They didn't even do my annual yet. I'm still level three."

The cop looked down at his paper again, then showed it to me. "That you?" I nodded. "Then you're moving to Fremont Dorm."

I looked over at Ryan, then back to this rookie-ass cop. "Man, I'm sorry to ruin your night, boss," I shook my head, "but I'm not going."

His shoulders sagged a little as he looked at me. "Man, don't make this difficult."

"It's not difficult," I answered. "Just go write me up for refusing a direct order. Problem solved."

"Fine. I will. But you definitely are moving over there for tonight. The only question is whether you want the easy way, or the hard way."

"I prefer the hard way," I nodded.

He let out a frustrated sigh. "We're gonna carry you over there. You realize that, don't you?"

I made a show of looking around behind him. "You plan on doing this yourself?" I asked. "Or do you wanna go get some gooners to help you? 'Cause you are gonna need some help." He closed the door and left.

"Maybe you oughta just go," Ryan said, once the cop was gone. "How bad can it be?"

"I don't know," I said honestly. "Anyway, it's irrelevant now. I already said no."

"Well I'm pretty sure they'd let you change your mind."

"Yeah, for them," I explained. "Not for us."

"Why not?"

"Look, once you say you're going to do something, that's it. That's why I looked back at you before answering. I was trying to figure out if it's really worth all this trouble. But evidently it is, 'cause I said I'm not going.

"Your word and your honor is the most important thing you have. Now that I said I won't go, I have to stick to that. Doesn't matter if they taze you, beat your ass, whatever. Stick to your word."

Ryan had a big smile. "You'd let them taze you?" he said doubtfully.

"Well I kinda hope they don't, but I can't break it down now. Otherwise, anytime they want me to do something they'll just pull out the tazer."

"That's crazy," he laughed.

"Oh that goes for the yard, too," I told him. "Be careful what you say. Doesn't matter if you're drunk when you say it, or if it's some ridiculous shit like 'I'm gonna butt-fuck the next dude who skips yard.' You better find a way to get your dick hard for that man's ass, 'cause you already said it." We both laughed.

"Yeah, but then I'm getting my ass beat for being a fag."

"Shoulda thought about that before you said it."

The cop never did come back, but Ryan and I spent the next two hours sorting out which of my things he should keep and which he should send with me if I did go to the hole. Eventually the dinner bell rang and we headed out.

I sat with Eddie at chow. "Well big dog, if they haven't come back yet, it's possible they're just gonna write you up and let it be. Then again, they might be moving your property out of your cell right now." He was done eating and stopped to wipe his mouth with some toilet paper.

"You know," he continued, looking down at the table, "it might not be so bad livin' in there."

"I already said no."

He looked up and smiled. "Yeah . . . I thought you'd say that. I just want to make sure you know what you're going in for. This one might get rough on you, kid."

"I imagine I'll live," I shrugged. "Polish Joe made it."

"Joe didn't make shit," Eddie corrected. "He's over there right now."

"He is?"

"They wrote him up for throwin' that trash can at the cops. Then they told him they wouldn't assess any points on the write-up, which they can do that. So he'd go right over to the dorm once his SHU term was up. Or, they said, he could just go to the dorm now and they'd throw the write-up away. Joe's been in there since two weeks ago."

Six gooners stood in front of Lassen as we came out of the chow hall. Eddie saw them before I did.

"Probably that's for you, kid." It was. Lassen Hall's sergeant flagged me over as we approached the building. "Just stand over here for a second." He wanted to wait till everyone was back inside the hall. Eddie, Ryan, and everyone else wished me luck and headed in. There was no question of grouping up. This was one I'd have to fight myself.

Once the cons were inside, the sergeant addressed me. "We need you to move over to Fremont Dorm, McCarty."

"Kessler, look," I answered. "I'm still level three. I haven't been to my annual yet."

"We don't have anything to do with that," he explained. "You're on our movement sheet, so we've got to move you."

"Well, I really hate to make your guys' jobs difficult, but what you're asking is unreasonable. That dorm is a disgusting environment, and I haven't done anything wrong to deserve to be thrown in there."

"All right," Sgt. Kessler said. "Cuff up."

I stepped away from the man with the handcuffs as he moved toward me. "Where we goin'?"

"Right now you're going to the patio,"—I let them cuff me.—"but I can almost guarantee you you're going to the hole tonight."

"That's fine. But here's fair warning, Sarge. If you try to throw me in there against my will, you'll wish you hadn't."

"Why? What are you going to do?"

"I don't mean it as a threat. But if you're asking so you can plan ahead, I'll fill you in on my intentions."

"You gonna try to break everything?"

"No," I shook my head. "As soon as you uncuff me I'm going to take off on the first southerner I see." They weren't sure if I was serious, and frankly neither was I. We took three steps toward the patio, though the dorm is along the way, when we were approached by the biggest asshole sergeant Soledad has ever seen.

Sergeant Uppssee (pronounced oopsie, like oopsie-daisy) weighs almost three hundred pounds. Big—ass—samoan. And such an asshole. Even to the samoans.

"What are we doing?" he demanded.

"He's refusing to move to the dorm," Kessler explained.

Uppssee looked at me. "Why don't we just throw the little bitch in there?" Well, that's checkmate then.

"That's an option," Sergeant Kessler conceded. "I was just going to take him over to the cages for now."

"I got it," Oopsie said, seizing me by the arm. Uppssee doesn't outrank Kessler (they're both sergeants), he's just more of an asshole, so Kessler let him take over. "Check this out," he jerked me toward him. "We're gonna put you in this dorm. You've got two options. You can live there peacefully, or you can fuck up. Each time you fuck up, we're gonna break one limb. That's four times you can fuck up. If you fuck up a fifth time, I'm gonna take you to the hole and cell you up with Kirkwood. You know who that is?"

"No."

"He's a big-ass crip who likes to fuck his cellmates." Briefly I wondered if there really was a guy like that living in our Ad Seg. You never know.

"What's it gonna be?" Uppssee demanded.

I made a face like I was thinking things over. "How many times can I fuck up?"

"Let's go." As he jerked my arm I relaxed my legs and sank to the ground.

"GET UP!"

"Nah, I think I'll make you work for it."

Uppssee pulled out his baton. "You wanna do the legs here?" he threatened, holding his club in the air.

"Good," I answered. "It'll give me a good excuse not to walk over there." His baton landed with a surprisingly deep thud, not on my legs, but on my ribs. I grunted loudly. Those might be broken. I could hear people yelling out their windows. "Get off him, you fuckin' pig!" "Hit him again, bitch!" "Galljangit jawhatsit FUCK!"—That last one had to be Eddie.

"Get up!" Uppssee yelled.

"I'm not sure I can," I coughed.

Sgt. Uppssee motioned to the yard cops. "Carry him." They hoisted me, still handcuffed, across their hips like a surfboard and we started to move. Voices still called from the windows.

Oopsie growled, "You look real tough in front of your friends."

"I am tough, motherfucker!" I had had just about enough of Sergeant Uppssee. "You'll find out right now. Tough as fuck! I sneeze with my eyes open!" One of the cops snickered, then went back to being serious.

"Tough as fuck! Tough as fuck! Last night I ate just one Lays potato chip, then put the bag right back in my locker." We passed the first of Fremont's two doors, but Uppssee didn't turn toward it. We moved on. "I killed two stones with one bird." I'd pulled all these clever one-liners out of a magazine. Funny as shit. We passed the second door. No dorm. They were carrying me to the patio.

"Awww . . . . What happened?" I taunted. "You don't want to throw me in the dorm? You get scared?! You get fuckin' scared?! Sergeant *U. Pussy*!" That was enough. He sprayed me.

"What problem do you have living in Fremont Dorm?"

I was sitting in the same chair I'd spilled pruno on when I'd wanted to avoid all this bullshit. Staff had left me unrinsed on the patio for six hours, then put me over in Shasta Hall for the night. The next morning they escorted me up here for a talk. Lieutenant Crane and Sergeant Herrera sat at the other end of the table.

"The living conditions in the dorm are unhealthy. Not only is it overcrowded, but now you've put all those psych medders in there. It's loud, smelly; it's unbearable. Anyway, it's level two housing and I'm not a level two inmate. I'd be breaking the rules to move into Fremont."

"The officers' orders override those rules."

"No way," I argued. "If a cop tells me to punch somebody, I still can't do it. Not if I know his order's asking me to break the rules. That's just like if you guys make a mistake and send me to South Facility. I'm not allowed to take advantage of your slip up. You'd write me up for attempted escape for going over there when I know damn well I'm P-coded."

"You can get an override for level two housing," Crane countered.

"I can, but I didn't."

He picked up the phone. After speaking with my counselor, whom I'd never met, for five minutes, he hung up. "Okay, your annual review took place last Thursday, where you dropped to twenty-two points. You've been level-two for a week."

"I never saw committee, and my review's not for two more months."

"If you sign an absentia waiver, we can conduct your review without you there," the lieutenant explained.

"I never signed any waiver."

"Evidently you did, or we wouldn't have held your review."

"No," I complained. "That's a logical fallacy. That's not how reasoning is supposed to work."

"Either way, you're level two now."

"It's still an unbearable environment," I argued. "You're still punishing me for good behavior. I went to work every day, stayed write-up free for a year, and now as a reward you're forcing me into the worst place imaginable. I would rather catch an A-1 offense—get a year added, a fifteen month SHU, and the twenty-four points—than do what you're asking me to do right now."

"But these are the rules," he said. He turned to Herrera. "Sergeant, how many inmates live in your dorm?"

"Two hundred."

"And how many want to be there?" Crane asked.

"Not a one."

"Then why do you force them to live in there?" I interrupted. "Why do you punish people for doing right?"

"Level three inmates are kept in cells for security reasons." Crane was twirling his pen slowly between his fingers.

"And I'm a level three inmate. That much will become apparent if you force me into Fremont."

He looked at me, still twirling the pen. "What do you plan to do?"

"I explained to Kessler last night exactly what I'll do. Though I'd rather not do it."

"Put the yard officers on stand-by," he said to Herrera. "We're taking you to Fremont."

I leaned toward him. "Look, lieutenant. If you're just looking for somebody your goons can pepper spray and beat up, we can do that on the patio. You don't need to take me to the dorm."

Herrera stood up and came toward me along the table. "Did I hear you correctly?" He tilted his head back and squinted his eyes, looking more mexican than I've ever seen anyone look. He leaned over the table. "Did you just say . . . you want to hit a cop?"

"No," Crane stopped him. "That's not what he said." He threw his pen down on the table. "Put him back in his cell in Lassen Hall. I don't ever want to see him up here again."

CHAPTER TWENTY-TWO

My write-up showed up two days later. The day after that, we were slammed. Nobody knew why. Ryan and I practiced our UFC fighting, which had become daily routine. Around three o'clock one of the asians brought us a kite.

Seph—Hey big dog, just to let you no whats going on. Last nite a norteno cut a White. It happened over in Raineer. Clown shot me a kite saying the dude with keys sent word saying how hes gonna respond. I don't agree with it, but nobody asked my opinon. You know what time it is if you here the bell. Shoes on. White Love + Respect - Eddie

Ryan was up on his bunk. I handed him the note so he could read it as well. Before he had finished with it, the intercom clicked.

"Code three, Fremont Dorm! Code three, Fremont Dorm!" Ryan stopped reading to look out the window. I sat down to put my shoes on, then stood back up and handed my cellie his. He gave me a questioning look.

"Put 'em on," I told him.

"Even while we're in the cell?"

"Sorry, buddy," I explained. "Those are the rules. We're on sight now. And in case you didn't already know, these are not the best dudes to go on sight with."

"Why not?"

"They're dangerous, buddy," I told him. "They're all gonna have knives on them. Plus they're snakes. If you and I get action at one, and we run up to him, he'll put his hands up and say, 'I'm a sureño! I'm a sureño!' Then when we turn around, he'll whack us."

"Fuckin' snnnakes!" Ryan joked.

"Which brings up another point, something you need to think about. Do you want a knife?"

Ryan looked back out the window and I joined him. Whites and busters alike were being pulled out in handcuffs and set in groups on the grass. I saw Cue Ball, and Polish Joe. The numbers were about even, but some of the northerners were in boxers or barefoot, while all our guys wore their state blues. We rushed them.

"Do I need one?"

I thought for a second. "It would suck to fight a couple of them where they have 'em and you don't. But honestly? If you don't make a conscious effort to slip through the cracks, you'll probably go the whole lockdown without shit happening. Anyway, if you do want one, I can make you something decent. Something small, concealable, and fuckin' gnarly."

He continued to watch the sorting, smiling as a caucasian northerner frantically tried to convince the cops he was a norteño, and not a Wood. "Are you gonna have one?"

"Not yet," I told him. "I want to wait till we get all the details. We'll have a better idea then if this shit's gonna go away or continue on. But, eventually, I'll probably have one, depending on exactly what happened."

"When do we get the full story?"

"McCarty." The cop opened our door at seven-thirty. We were both up, with our shoes on, working out.

"Yeah."

"You're going to the patio. Get ready."

"Wait, C.O.!" I yelled as he closed the door. "Is it Medical, or a write-up hearing?" I'd put in for Medical two weeks ago, the day after the riot. The cop just shrugged.

All Whites in handcuffs till we reached the patio's holding cage. Things had escalated. For the first time I had ever seen, Whites outnumbered every race as we waited for Medical. I shook some hands, then headed straight for where the serious conversation was taking place. Some of the B-yard fellas looked at me like maybe I didn't belong in the group, but a heartfelt embrace from EZ cleared up any confusion.

"Seph, this is our homeboy Bones, from B-yard." Shit.

We shook hands. "All right, Seph," he said. ". . . Or Joey."

I smiled. "Should I still call you Boner, then?" He smiled a little too and we unclasped our hands.

"Anyway, the northerners call us for a meeting right in the middle of the yard," Bones addressed the group. Apparently he had been the one talking when I approached.

"They call us to talk on the first day out after this shit happened. A couple of us meet with them, and they say they'd like for whatever happened on A-yard to stay on A-yard. They say it was a mistake anyway, and the youngster who did it just panicked, and even the way the Woods responded sorta suggested that we'd all just like to get through this quickly and with minimal bloodshed.

"Well I don't have keys for the yard," Bones continued. "Dude's at work. But I tell 'em we'll have to talk it over, but most likely we're cool leavin' it over there. Keep in mind, though, this was all their idea.

"So we all lock up for count. Not ten fuckin' minutes later, they call code three Toro Dorm. See they didn't want to fight on the yard, because we outnumbered them. But we only have six guys in Toro, and they're all old-ass men. So thirty norteños fucked up six White dudes. Now there's no northerners in Fremont, and no Whites in Toro."

"I hate them motherfuckers," Easy cut in. "Did we get any more shots in?"

"Yeah," Bones answered. "One of them was down as an other in Shasta. He was getting let out to help serve chow. When the cops opened Robbie and Eric's door to give them trays they ran out on him. Fucked him up."

"Whitney, too," another Wood put in. Apparently he was from Whitney. "One northerner paroled, so the cops pulled him out at four in the morning. But they didn't lock his door. They just threw the bar back down. So when the bars came up for the cops to let out servers, and let us out for Medical, the parolee's cellmate ran out and got busy. I guess he tried to time it so he'd just catch one dude by himself, but Smooth took the buster's knife from him and poked him like eight times before anyone else got to it. Now he's in the infirmary with our guys from Toro. We're waitin' to see if he's gonna die.

"This was two days ago," he finished. "That's why we're handcuffed now."

"Look, I know nothing said here is final," Bones said, "but I want to put the idea out there. This is one of only two mainline pens where these dudes can go. We're on sight with them in Susanville right now too. Why not stay on 'em? Keep working the cracks, and keep catchin' 'em. I have friends who are norteños, and some of them, individually, are all right. But as a group? We're better off without them here."

Easy agreed to carry the idea back to Rainier and we broke apart from the conversation. I was glad Bones had so many things, aside from my arrest, to occupy his thoughts.

"I seen you get carried like a surfboard," Easy said as we sat down at one of the benches. He was smiling at me from under his grizzled beard.

"They gave me a division-D," I explained, showing him the write-up. "Willfully resisting, delaying, or obstructing an officer."

He read the report. "You beat this, homeboy," he said, still reading.

"Why?"

"Read this shit again." He thrust it under my nose. I read the report again.

"What am I looking for?"

He tapped the page with the back of his head. "Look," he said. "It says they ordered you to move, you said no, and they informed you you would be getting a 115. What part of that says you resisted or delayed shit?"

"Well, a lot more shit happened after that."

"It don't matter." Easy spoke quickly. "It don't matter, homeboy. It don't matter if you bit the captain's fuckin' ear off. If it's not written in the report, you didn't do it."

I actually argued with him. "All the cops know what happened."

"Listen to me, homeboy!" He was getting irritated. "When they find you guilty for something, they have to base their decision on what's written on the one-fifteen. And *only* on what's on the one-fifteen. I beat a SBI like that. I fought this dude, and they sprayed us, and took us out. And that's what the write-up said. 'They fought, we sprayed 'em, now they're gone.' Then they found out dude's jaw was broke. They changed it to A-1, but the description was still the same. I beat that shit. They couldn't give me serious bodily injury 'cause the write-up never mentioned any injury.

"All you have to do is plead not guilty, and say that this should be 'refusal to follow direct orders.' You'll get a little thirty-day slap on the wrist."

I thanked him for his advice. "Why'd the buster cut the homeboy in the first place?"

"Oh, yeah," he recalled. "You weren't here for that part, huh?" I shook my head. "Well I didn't see it. This shit happened on the B-side. Some dudes showed up off the bus after night yard had just locked up. Well there's this caucasian norteño who's single-celled up on the third tier, and the cops' movement sheet had this White old man moving in with him. He's like seventy.

"Well the youngster's kinda weirded out. I think he knows he's not supposed to cell up with anyone but other northerners, but he's scared his people will treat it like a PC move if he says no. So he helps the old man bring his property in. And the cop knows the kid's a fuckin' buster. He even says, you know, 'Hey, are you sure this is cool?' And the kid's all 'yeah, yeah, don't trip.'

"According to his people, he didn't get at anyone or ask for advice. He just panicked. Three hours after the old man moves in, the buster cuts him on the back of the head. The old man goes man-down, they take him to the hole, and then we rush them motherfuckers in the dorm the next afternoon."

"Okay," I nodded. "I seen that."

"But get this, homeboy," Easy tapped me. "Get this. Three days later, the old man dies."

"Not from the cut?"

"Heart failure," he said. "The cops say the dude had heart disease and shit, but it's possible the stress of all that brought on his death."

"Still," I argued, "it's not fair for us to say the kid killed him."

"No, but they are, homeboy," EZ tapped me again. "They are. They're all yellin' up to each other's windows and shit. 'We killed a Wood! We killed a Wood!' Bunch of fuckin' little kids runnin' around gettin' stars tattooed on 'em."

"Tsk. Fuckin' punks."

"Yeah, they are fuckin' punks, homeboy. They are fuckin' punks. Homeboy's right. Let's start killin' 'em."

When I got home I relayed the whole story to Ryan. He wanted a knife. I told him I'd make both that night after count. The new developments left us both with some pent up energy. We decided to expel it on some extra UFC ninja training—sadly, the only time I almost didn't win. Ryan didn't win either, though. I didn't want to fall on his head, so I turned to the side and put my arm out to break my fall. I didn't break my wrist, but I definitely fractured it. Now I legitimately needed Medical.

Two days later I took my knife with me to the patio. The word now was that A-yard was on board with B. Fuck a truce. Any treaty they offer was likely to be a ruse anyway. We'd stay on them.

When I finally got in to be seen, I had a little trouble explaining what was wrong. The doctor was this arab who spoke very little English. After twenty minutes, we finally got it narrowed down to pain in my wrist. He had me do some movements, showing by doing rather than trying to speak English.

"It's a sprain," he announced at last.

I was a little surprised. "Really? It looks kind of swollen."

"Yes, yes," he scribbled some notes. "Yes."

"Did you hear me?" I asked. "It's swollen."

"Yes, a high sprain swells," he nodded. "You should drink water."

"Drink water and my wrist will heal?" I said doubtfully.

"Yes, yes. We will give you a wrap. Yes. You should not furl your brow."

I wasn't sure I'd heard the last part correctly.

"Don't furl, don't furl," he continued. I swear I didn't mean to relax my forehead. "That's better," he said. "You have very smooth skin. Very handsome. But you do not smile." Then he smiled at me in a very suggestive manner. "Can you smile?"

Holy fuck. This queer-ass non-licensed arab was tring to bump dicks with me. I needed medical attention, not gay sexual advances, but it had been so long since anyone flirted with me that I smiled in spite of myself. Shit, now I'm all mixed up.

CHAPTER TWENTY-THREE

EZ's trick worked like a charm. They dropped my write-up to a division-F. Then a week later the cop showed up and once more told me to move to Fremont. I refused, but this time they just closed the door and wrote me up again. Thirty days after that, same thing. Three write-ups in sixty days put me on C-status.

Staff moved me over to Rainier-B's first tier. For the next ninety days I could have no appliances, little store, and very little yard (of course, we were on lockdown anyway). I didn't even have a light bulb. I just went to bed when the sun set.

A young man named Brad had come with me. He was my age, but brand new to prison. We moved into cell one 'o-six. One 'o-five was empty, but seven and four were both occupied by northerners.

About a week into this, an asian inmate stopped at our neighbor's door. He had just purchased a large amount of food from the commissary and decided to share some with the hard-timing, C-status northerners.

"Here, look." My neighbor's responses were muffled, so Brad and I could only hear half the conversation. The asian showed the busters a brown paper bag. "There's two bags of chips, some soups, and a jar of coffee . . . . It's like ten dollars, but don't trip . . . . No, don't trip . . . . You don't owe me anything. You guys enjoy that." He set the bag down. "I set it right here by your door. Just ask the cop to let you grab it, or wait till they open your door to give you trays . . . . Don't trip." He gave two downward fist pumps and left.

I'll admit I was a little jealous of the neighbors getting food, what with Brad and me starving next door, and especially with the two groups still at each other's throats. But I didn't hate them enough to enjoy what happened next.

Our neighbors flagged down the building cop, a mexican woman. They asked if she would open their door so they could grab the food. She picked up the bag. "What's in here?" A muffled response. She opened the bag and sifted through its contents. "You're on C-status," she said. "You guys can't have this." A louder muffled response. "Well," she continued, "do you have a receipt showing that you paid for these?"

In his last response I could hear my neighbor yelling, "Get the sergeant!"

"I'll tell him, but you can't have this." She carried the bag out of view.

Ten minutes later Sergeant Villa, a notorious dick, arrived at my neighbor's door eating from an open bag of potato chips—a bag I'm certain had just come from the recently confiscated goods.

"What?!" he asked pleasantly. "That shit ain't yours in the first place . . . . Really? Or did he owe you money 'cause you sold him dope? . . . Show me a receipt and I'll give you this bag right now." He was popping chips into his mouth at every interval. "You'd better hurry!"

By now my neighbor was yelling. Villa walked away and didn't even flinch as a loud pop and the sound of broken glass echoed through the hall. The bangs continued and moments later our neighbors broke out their back window as well. The intercom called a code one. The gooners arrived. The busters next door were cell-extracted, sprayed, insulted, and taken to the hole.

I turned to Brad. "Most of the cops were White guys. Do you think we get credit for this?"

Jokes aside, this was pointless. More unnecessary victimization. We're supposed to be teaching the inmates how to behave, how to treat other human beings decently, respectfully, and with compassion. What part of this was decent?

Toward the end of that month I heard a noisy cart going by outside, and mixed in with the rattle I could have sworn I heard someone call my name. I looked out to see Ryan pushing his janky property along the track. I thought perhaps he was transpacking to be sent to another prison.

"Ryan, where you goin'?"

He pointed at me. "In there."

"You're on C-status?" I asked. He nodded.

They moved him into the vacant one 'o-five. As soon as the cop left his door he came to our shared window. "Zephyr!"

"How'd you get on C-status?" I answered.

"They're doing it for one write-up now. Everybody."

"I know. Brad got it for one. Brad, this is my old cellie, Ryan."

"Hey. What's goin' on?" Brad had a lot of personality.

"All right, Brad.

"After you left," Ryan explained, "I started thinking I should get a write-up, so I wouldn't have to go through all the shit you just went through. I remembered Eddie saying you used to be able to just ask a cop, so I tried. Fuckin', Big John gave me a broken tattoo motor. So I got at this rookie cop while he was passin' out mail. He was actually excited about it. He told me to have it out during count and he'd catch me with it.

"And then his partner's like some trainee. Not even a rookie yet. But when they came up for count, the dude I talked to was on the wrong side. And he looked over and I put my hand up like 'What the fuck?' And he nods and puts one finger up like 'Hold on.'

"Well they both go by for count, and I figure the dude decided he doesn't want to do it. But when I go to set the broken motor back in my locker, my door flies open and that cop's there with his spray out. And he says, 'What've you got?' So I handed him the motor and he closed the door."

"Man, fuck you!"

"Why?"

"Fuck you, Ryan!"

"*Why?*"

"It takes me two years and six ass-whoopin's to stay level three, and you just 'get at the cop'?"

He laughed. "Yeah. Well he had waited till he and his trainee were done counting the third tier, and he told the trainee, 'Come on. I wanna show you something.' Like he was teachin' him not to miss shit. Meanwhile this trainee thinks the rookie, from across the building and through my narrow ass cell window, saw me fuckin' with a tattoo motor, even while he was counting the inmates on that side."

"Oh, he's bad-ass."

"Yeah," Ryan continued. "He told me later the trainee was callin' him supercop."

"Brad got a write-up too. He'll tell you about it." While Brad talked out the window I sat on my bed and wrote a kite.

Hey asshole—If you want me to move over there, you'll have to ask while Brad and I are both at the window. If it's my idea, he'll probably feel like I'm running out on him. I know you may be keen on the idea of staying single-celled, but then maybe tomorrow you get some lame. Either way the move will probably take a couple days to go through, so you still have plenty of time to do weirdo shit and look at your own asshole in the mirror.

I slipped the kite in with a short story I'd written a few days earlier. "Ryan."

"Yeah."

"You wanna read this story I wrote?"

"Is it good? Or are you wasting paper?"

"Brad liked it," I told him.

"Yeah, it was cool," Brad put in. "It's about dreams."

I handed it through the window. "You're in it, and fuckin' Conan is in it."

When he was done reading, he sent it back. "That's cool," he said. "The ending's funny."

"When did you catch on?" I asked.

"Like halfway. I don't get the title, though."

"It's an acronym."

"Oh, shit," he chuckled. "That's cool. Hey, how close are you and Brad?"

". . . We're on separate beds."

"Are you interested in moving over here?"

"Oh."

"You don't have to," Ryan said. "I was just saying, since we're both on C-status now, do you want to still be cellies?"

"I would have to talk to Brad about it. Gimme a second." I got off my bunk so Brad and I could see one another.

"Would you be horribly upset if I went over there?"

"Yes." He sounded like Droopy.

I smiled sympathetically at him. "Man, I don't want to ditch you, buddy, but he's like my best friend. Our families know each other and shit." I don't think any of that was true.

"Tsk. Fuck, man." There was resignation in his voice. "Now you're gonna leave and I'm gonna get some asshole for a cellie."

"Actually, there's a good chance you get the cell to yourself for a while. Look at how long next door was vacant." He'll get over it. "Look," I said. "I've gotta sweet talk the cop to get the move done. So whatever I say, just nod your head."

"'Kay." Brad was moping. Awww. Poor Brad. Poor Brad? Is it poor Bradley boo-boo? Is he sad? Awww. I flagged the cop down.

Officer Navarro stood there with my door open, listening to my honest and truthful dilemma. ". . . but it's been like every day for the last two weeks. We tried to just keep separate, him do his thing and I do mine, but it continuously comes back to us being nose-to-nose, about to fight."

"Why you guys can't get along?" she asked.

"The short version?" I answered. "He doesn't like being told what to do, and I don't like guys who don't shower. But we got at Sergeant Villa a couple days ago, and he said he'd like to help, but he couldn't move us. We're both on C-status, and we're the only two Whites on C-status, and we just have to stay put."

"So why are you asking me to help?"

"'Cause, Navarro, they just moved a White guy in next door. You can move me over there." I pointed over my shoulder at Brad. "Look, he probably just doesn't want the write-up. But I don't want to fight period. He's a little bigger than I am."

"And then what happens when you fight with that guy?"

"No, I know that guy. We've been cellies before, three different times. He showers a lot. He's probably over there naked right now, rinsing off." Navarro glanced at Ryan's door like she might like to see that.

"Let me talk to my sergeant and see what he says."

They moved me over that night.

I put my book down and stood up. "Dinner's coming. Shall we jax a nucka?" Ryan and I had managed to swipe a full canister of Ajax during the move. He stood up in the middle of the cell. We heard doors closing closer and closer to ours.

"Are you ready?" I asked.

"I've got the easy job," he nodded. "Are you ready?"

As the cop opened the door to feed us, Ryan stepped forward and took his tray. "Hey C.O.?" he got the cop's attention and held it while I grabbed my own tray. "It just seems like," Ryan complained, "you got five or six dudes, whether we want 'em to or not! Nobody says nothin'! And then there's third tier! And then there's second tier! Then half the motherfuckers work their way around, and WE'RE ALWAYS LAST!" Then he gobbled like a turkey. "*gobblegobblegobblegobble.*"

While Ryan thus distracted the officer, I grabbed my own dinner and sprinkled a handful of Ajax over the remaining two trays. After wondering what the fuck was wrong with my cellie, the cop continued down the tier. I watched from my window to make sure the norteños next door accepted their medicine unawares. Then I ate my dinner. I'm not sure how much Ajax these two would have to eat before it killed them, but I'm glad they were at least eating some.

We only jaxed a nucka once or twice a week, usually when it was a good meal. C-status was breezing by. I was writing a letter one afternoon while Ryan sat staring out at the open yard.

"Hey, Seph."

"Yeah."

"Come look at this."

I went to the window. "What?"

"Look," he said. "Doesn't it kinda look like the blacks and south-siders are grouped up?"

I looked. "I think you're trippin', buddy. Maybe that can be your prison handle. Tripper."

"You really don't think so?" he asked. "Look at all the blacks in that corner."

"It just looks that way 'cause there's no northerners out there. You really do need a handle though."

"Why?"

"'Cause then you'll be tough. How 'bout Squiggy."

"Who's Squiggy?"

"He's from one of those old-ass TV shows, like *Happy Days*."

"Is he cool?"

"No," I smiled.

Ryan thought for a second. "I could be Mantis."

"Mantis?"

"Yeah. Like praying mantis?"

"Fine," I said. "But you have to move out."

"Why?" he laughed.

"I'm not being cellies with the fuckin' Mantis. People will start calling me Baxter the Fly. Anyway, you don't get to pick your handle."

"I get final say!" he challenged.

"Keep it up and you'll be fuckin' tater-tot," I warned. "Actually, tater's kinda cool. You could be tater."

"I'm not fuckin' tater. If anything, Brad's tater."

"No, Brad could be tater," I agreed.

"He hella looks like Mr. Potato Head," Ryan laughed.

I yelled toward the window from the middle of the cell. "Hey Tater!"

Ryan echoed, closer to the window. "Hey Tater!

I came up to the window and yelled again. "Tater!" Ryan pounded his fist on the wall.

"Tater!"

"Hey Tater!"

"Tater!"

Finally we heard Tater open his window. ". . . Seph?"

"Hey, Tater!"

"What the fuck, Tater!"

"Who's Tater?"

"You're Tater, Tater."

"What?"

"That's your new name."

"Hey, Tate." Ryan experimented with some variations.

"I don't want to be Tater."

"Sorry, buddy. That's the way it goes."

"Can I pick something else?"

"Oh, no Tater, you don't want nothing else," I told him. "It's all down hill from there. Just ask the Flying fuckin' Mantis over here."

A loud yard recall interrupted us. Once the loud speaker was done, we continued.

"How come you don't have a handle, Seph?" Tater asked.

"Seph is his handle, Tater," Ryan answered.

"I thought that was your name?"

"It's kind of both, Tater. I have a yard handle, but it's sort of long and awkward, so no one uses it."

"What is it?"

"Shotgun Killer Outlaw White-Rider . . . Killer. But you'll like Tater. Tater's the kind of dude who stabs motherfuckers in the chow hall for trying to take his sausage patty."

"We have a chow hall?"

Ryan and I both laughed. "Yeah," I said. "Eventually we'll all settle down and stop rioting one another. Then we'll walk to chow."

As the last few inmates were leaving the yard, the intercom clicked. "Code one, Lassen Hall! Code one, Lassen Hall!" Click. Click. "Code three, Lassen Hall! Code three, Lassen Hall!"

Cheers erupted from Rainier. Whites and northerners were still slammed, so we were all pretty sure the blacks and southerners were killing each other inside Lassen. The oh-shit horn roared behind us. A lone officer sprinting along the track from the voc gate toward Lassen dropped his baton and it clattered across the asphalt. As he stopped to pick it up someone yelled, "Yeah, you're gonna need that."

We all stared at the quiet building from our cell windows. "Damn," I said. "You called that one, Squiggy."

"Seph."

"Who's that?"

". . . It's Brad."

"Who?"

"*Who?*"

". . . It's . . . Tater."

"Tater!"

"Hey, Tater!"

"What's up, Tater?"

"*Afternoon* Tate."

". . . What's happening?" he asked.

"They're having a riot over there in Lassen, Tater. Code three means riot. And that big-ass foghorn that blew means the cops are shitting their pants—please bring fresh underwear."

He laughed a little, but still sounded worried. "Are we involved?"

"No, we're on lockdown, buddy," Ryan reminded him.

"And the northerners are slammed too," I added, "so we have a pretty good idea of who's fighting."

". . . The blacks and south-siders?"

"Nooo, hey Tater?"

"Yeah."

"We don't say stuff like that out the window."

"Oh," he said. "Why not?"

"It's just not our business. If you and me are in the shower together or out on the yard, say whatever. But out the window is public. If you're talking out your window, if you're in line somewhere, in a classroom, try and don't mention other races."

"Okay."

"Otherwise you're spreading rumors. I mean it clearly is them, but maybe not. For all we really know the asians took off on the cops."

Ryan laughed, then Tater spoke again. "But you just said 'asians'," he pointed out.

"Yeah, they don't count," I clarified. "There's only like six of them on the whole yard. They don't know what the fuck they're doin'."

Cops had begun carrying the wounded out of Lassen and setting them on the yard. The first inmate stretchered off the yard was a black guy with no shirt on, each cop holding a limb as they carried him toward the stretcher. His intestines skirted the dirty concrete, and his screams were loud even from where we sat. One of the southerners came out hoppig on one foot, pushing medical staff away, insisting he could walk by himself. His foot dragged along behind him.

We watched the procession as more and more CDC officers showed up from further away. Some came all the way from Kern Valley. Eventually, things settled down and program continued, quieter now with all four groups on lockdown. The asians and samoans served us dinner.

Late that night, past midnight, we heard Tater get a new cellie. It was too late to talk though. We'd have to meet him tomorrow.

"Hey Tater!" After a moment I heard the latch on his window pop open.

"Yeah."

"Mornin' Tater!"

"*Mor*nin' Tate." Ryan practiced his backwood drawl.

"Hey."

"You got a cellie?" I asked.

"Yeah."

The new guy interrupted. "Good morning, fellas. My name's Bump, from Modesto Hardcore."

"From Modesto?" I asked.

"Yep."

"And you're a skinhead?"

"Yes sir!"

"Well what's up homeboy and Comrade? I'm Seph McCarty. My cellmate's name is Ryan, from Monterey."

"Right on," he said. "You're from Modesto?"

"Yeah," I told him. "But I'm not a skinhead though."

"That's all right. We can't all be."

"Hey," I asked. "Did Tater introduce himself as Tater when you came in last night?"

"Yeah."

"That's good. He's been tryin' some ol' fake-name bullshit lately. Brad this or that from who-the-fuck-knows where."

"Oh, no, he did," Bump explained. "He said, 'Hey, I'm Brad from San Diego. They call me Tater.'"

"Well, we'll let that slide."

"Yeah," Ryan put in. "That's good enough."

"Oh, is Tater a new handle?" Bump guessed.

"It is," I confirmed.

"Hey, Tate."

Bump was quiet a second. Probably he was looking at Tater. "Yeah," he said finally, "Tater's a good one. You wanna know how I got Bump?" We did. "I was in DVI, and every morning I used to sit up and smack my head on the locker above my bed. My cellmate was my Elder, and he said I hit my head so much they'd have to call me Bump. All I ever do is bump my head."

"Right on," I laughed. "I got mine from an older homeboy who liked to hug me. And Ryan got his from his mommy."

Tater's voice echoed from the back of his cell. He was sitting on the toilet. "I just woke up one morning and Seph and Ryan were calling me Tater!" We all laughed.

"Hey, Comrade. I came in with a package. Do you guys need anything?"

"No, I think we're good," I told him. "But thank you. They said they're gonna let us go to store this week. Course, that was before this shit yesterday."

"Yeah, I was on my way over here from R & R when that happened. We were right under the horn when it went off."

"Yeah, we had poopy-pants jumpin' off for the C.O.'s."

"Well the dude who was bringin' us over here had us all sit down right there on the curb, and he took off runnin' for North. Plus Tater said there's some other shit goin' on. So we're uh . . . we're havin' a good time here, are we?"

"Yeah," I answered. "We got . . . well . . . right now there's . . . for uh . . . I'm just, I'm just gonna get at you on paper, Bump." He laughed, and I continued. "There's just not a whole lot I can say out the window. This yard's crazy." I got at him on paper.

Bump & Tater—Mine to you, fellas. We're on sight with the northerners. They whacked one of ours, a helpless old man, and they're all really happy about it. Fuck 'em. Our plan is to keep killing them until staff removes them, or they all die. Either way, they'll be gone. Your neighbors that way and mine over here are busters. Ryan and I have slowly been trying to kill these ones, though thus far unsuccessfully. Maybe they'll get cancer or some shit when they're older, but for now their insides are just really clean. So boots on. Tell Tater, because he's a first-termer, he can get in the swim class. But he should get at them now. If he waits till we come off, all the new guys will have signed up and the list will be long as fuck. Get at Sergeant Villa to sign you up ahead of time so you're already on the list when we come out. But yeah, fuck a buster. White Love & Respect—Seph & Ryan

"Here you go, fellas." I passed the note through the window along with my 128G. Just seconds after Bump said "All right" to let me know he had both items, Tater called my cellie.

"Ryan."

"Yeah."

"Here ya go." Here you go? That sounded fishy.

Ryan read the note and then passed it up to me. "Check this out."

Ryan,

Can I still borrow your Curves magazine? I won't let Bump see it, if you don't want me to.

-Tater

"Aw, fuck," I said out loud as Ryan laughed. "Do you mind if I answer him?" Ryan didn't mind.

Tater—Since you're all into writing notes and shit, here's a note. First, it is a very bad move to write and send out a kite that you don't let your cellie read. Also, any kite you get, you should hand to your cellmate as soon as you're done reading it. Otherwise, he might think you're getting kites that are telling you to stab him. You and your cellie are a team. Second, you do not touch yourself while your cellie is in the cell with you. I'm not saying you are or you're not but I think you are. Otherwise you wouldn't want the Curves. Wait till Bump goes to Medical. Now in the interest of being teammates,

I want you to hand this kite, and the one you sent to Ryan (that we're returning to you), to Bump so he can read both. And if he wants to punch on you a little, that' just part of being a good team. All Ours—Seph & Ryan.

I passed the response and Tater's note down to Ryan, who read the addition then got Tater's attention.

"Tater."

"Yeah."

"Here ya go."

All was quiet next door for about five minutes. Then Tater called again. He passed more paper to Ryan, who then handed them to me. The collection included my own 128, Bump's 128, and Tater's original kite with some corrections.

Ryan,

    we
Can't still borrow your Curves magazine? I won't let

     to   because he is awesome.
Bump see it, if you don't want me to.

                            –*Tater* & Bump

Three days later the building cops let the blacks out to shower. I was lying in bed, reading from a textbook.

"Hey Seph and Ryan, look out your door window." Ryan got up and went to the door.

"What's up?" I asked.

Tater's response was drowned out by the building buzzer and the intercom. "Code one, Rainier Hall! Code one, Rainier Hall!"

Ryan was peering diagonally out the window, but he shook his head. "The blacks in the shower are lookin' at something by the stairs, but I can't see shit."

"Tater."

"Yeah," he answered in a whisper.

"What's up?"

"Hey, Seph." He spoke quietly. "Hey, can you hear me?"

"Yes, Tater. I read you," I whispered. "Give us your position."

"Hey, they let the blacks out to shower . . ." he cut off, and I could hear Bump talking.

"Come in Tater!" I whispered loudly. "Damn it, man! We're gonna get you out of there!"

"Hey, Seph."

"Tssht! Use my code name."

"Hey, we're gonna get at you guys on paper."

Seph & Ryan—Oi! Oi! Listen to this. I was standing in my window watching the blacks shower, and one of the blacks walked off down the first tier. He walked past one of the cells under the stairs, I think either 141 or 142, and when he walked past, the door flew open and a southerner ran out and stabbed him. Then dude darted back into his house and closed the door. It was like a trapdoor spider. I seen them on Discovery. But trip on this. There's five toads in the shower, and another four sitting at this table in front of my house. They all seen that shit, and none of them went to help. I heard one of the blacks at the table say, while it was happening, "That nigga's his own nigga." Crazy, huh? Sucks to be black. Anyway, that's what happened. WL&R—B8 8mp & Tater

I read the kite out loud to Ryan, but he stopped me halfway through. "They're stretcherin' dude out."

I came to the window to see the victim. He was about thirty-five, yoked up, and wearing only his boxers. We could see the knife still sticking out of his chest. He looked frightened and was clearly in a lot of pain.

With Ryan as my cellie, and the Bump & Tater show jumping off next door, C-status wasn't so bad. A few days after the stabbing, Mag stopped by our door. No handcuffs, no escort. Mag was the MAC rep for the Whites in Rainier.

"Seph. Ryan. How you guys doing?" We were fine. "We squashed the shit with the northerners. Not everyone agrees with it, but they apologized for cutting the old man, and they're over there on B-yard apologizing for snaking us in the dorm. Anyway, some of us would like to go to work, get visits." He sounded like he had pled this same case at thirty different cells.

"Yeah, that's fine," I told him. "We don't care either way. Tell my neighbors we apologize for poisoning them." Mag smiled and shook his head, then he went next door to tell Bump the same thing. I could see the northerner reps out circulating as well. Apparently they weren't on sight with us either.

"Now what do we do with the knives?" Ryan asked.

"We'll break 'em apart and flush 'em down the toilet," I told him.

He shook his head. "They never even saw any action."

"Most never do, buddy." While Mag was still next door we heard a familiar voice outside our window.

"Watchu doin'? Transpackin'?"

"Yeah," Snowman answered, speaking to the cell above ours.

"Where they takin' you?"

"A nigga goin' home," Snowman told him.

"Nah!!"

"Yup."

"How long you been down, Snowman?"

"Fo'teen year."

"And where you goin'? Back to Hoover?"

"Yup."

"Damn. You goin' trip out though, nigga. Hoover change."

"Tsk. Hoover ain't change."

"Hoover change, nigga."

"Nigga, you think Hoover change, you don't know Hoover. I already know. Soon as I get off the bus, some crack-headed bitch goin' run out her house screamin', cross the street, and fall asleep under a tree. Then some nigga goin' steal her flip-flops. Hoover never change. Hoover allus be Hoover."

"He motioned to his property. "I'm fittin' ta throw this shit in a box."

"A'ight, Snowman. Take care yo'self nigga."

Snowman gave a wave and turned to leave. I called out to him. "Snowman."

"Yeah, w'sup? Who dat?"

"This is your old neighbor. I fuck with them things."

"Oh, yeah, f'sho," he laughed. "W'sup wit it?"

"You're goin' home?"

"Yeah."

"Man, good luck."

"Yeah, fo' real." He left.

"How do you think that feels?" I asked Ryan. "That dude's leaving after more than decade inside."

"Crazy," he agreed. "Did I tell you what he said to the new arrivals?"

I shook my head.

"It was late as fuck and four dude's were comin' in off the bus. Three blacks and an asian. Well they cross under the window, and Snowman calls down to the blacks. He says, "Hey. Any y'all niggas from Smoot?"' Ryan did a good Snowman impersonation. "And they all freak out. Nobody answers, and it's dark, so all you really see is three big-ass sets of eyeballs. They don't stop walking, but they all look up."

"Then, 'cause they don't answer, he yells, 'Hey! I'm talkin' to y'all!' But they keep going. They're like three cells down and he yells out, 'Hey y'all niggas ain't got to be scared to talk!' Then he calls out, 'Scared-ass bitches!' He's all pissed off, and dude I'm just crackin' the fuck up."

We laughed. Sometimes shit's funny.

"Tsk. I'm tired of being stuck in here," I complained to Ryan. "With *you*. Fucking black people out walkin' around, transpackin' and shit. I'm goin' outside." I got up and stuck my ID card face-out in the door window, then began putting on my blues.

"How're you gonna get out?" Ryan taunted.

I looked at him blankly, then pointed at my ID card. "We're gonna start with that, and then go from there. We're gonna wing it, buddy."

I couldn't get any cop's attention for the first hour, not until the building officer came around to let out servers. I called him over. When he approached the door, I didn't talk to him, just grabbed my ID card and buttoned up my blue shirt. Then I turned and just about walked into the door, like I expected it to be open already.

The cop just looked at me. "What?" He wasn't going to let me out.

"Oh, they didn't call?" I asked.

"Who?"

"Nothin'," I shook my head. "I'm waitin' on Medical. They're supposed to call for me."

"Hey Bosques," he called over to the sallyport.

I knocked on the door to get his attention before the sallyport officer could answer. "It's cool," I told him. "I'll just wait. They'll call." I was still nodding my head as he walked away.

"That was brilliant," Ryan said. "I'm surprised no one's ever thought of doing that." Shut up, Mantis.

I got another chance as they came around to serve us dinner. When the door opened I grabbed my ID and stepped out.

"Where you goin'?"

"Medical called for me," I told the cop.

"Uh," he looked toward the cage.

"Sally already knows about it," I explained. "Bosques is the one who told me to get dressed." I put my ID in my pocket as Ryan grabbed trays for both of us. "I go up there every day at this time. I have herpes, and it's been flaring up." I waved my hands upward when I said 'flaring' and he took a step back.

"I tried to get the nurse to apply the herpes ointment for me, but they make me medicate my own herpes." Every time I said 'herpes' he retreated a little. I finished by saying herpes three times together, then I took off down the tier.

I borrowed an empty blue tray from the servers to get me through the sallyport, then headed straight for the back of Rainier-A. I wanted to visit with friends, but I didn't really know where anyone lived. I found Bird in one thirty-two. We made it halfway through the A's starting lineup when a cop spotted me from the second tier. I gave bird's door a hearty shake, then stepped off up the tier, shaking each door as I went.

The cop intercepted me. "Where do you live?"

I barely looked at him. "I'm doing something right now."

"*Where* do you *live*, inmate? You're locking up."

I turned to face him with my hand palm-up, then glanced down toward the cage and back to him. "Man, Sergeant Villa told me to shake every door, to make sure none were left unlocked during chow."

"He did?" he asked doubtfully. Always the skeptic.

"He said for security or whatever, but honestly, I think he's just checking up on you guys, 'cause of the slip up this week." He glanced over at the sallyport.

"Look." He was young. Easy to hoodwink. "Obviously they're all locked. But *if* one's not, I'll just tell you and you go lock it. Either way I'll tell Villa they were all locked." Thankfully some idiot on the second tier started banging on his door to get the cop's attention. When the officer turned to see who it was, I went back to shaking doors. He left me alone.

Villa stopped me as I tried to cross back through the sallyport. "What are you doing? The Whites can't come out to help serve yet."

"I'm not," I answered. "I'm supposed to go to Medical."

"Oh, did they finally call?" The cop who originally wouldn't let me out stood next to the sergeant.

"Yeah."

"Do they still need an escort?" he asked Villa.

"Nah. Just send him." I tried not to look surprised as they unlocked the door and let me outside.

The yard was empty, with the exception of Captain Roberts who was just seconds away from leaving through the patio gate. I really had nothing better to do than to walk ten feet over and talk to Bump and Tater. "Tater!"

"Seph, what are you doing out?"

"You out for a stroll, Comrade?"

"Yeah, but don't worry," I told Bump. "I'm on my toes." Then I looked around for would-be challengers.

"Seph," Tater said quietly. "You know we're not on sight anymore, right?"

"Who told you that?"

"Mag."

"Don't listen to it, Tater. Them dudes paid that guy to go around sayin' that shit. They're trying to catch you slippin'. Don't be the one, Tater."

"They paid him?"

"Heroin, Tater! What else? Shit, I'd do it too. I'd sell you to these motherfuckers for half a gram. You and your cellie both. If I work it right I can get half a gram for each of you. That's almost a full gram."

I stepped over toward my own window. "What's this fuckin' idiot doin'? Squiggy! Quit fuckin' touchin' yourself!"

The latch on our window popped open. "Zephyr!"

"Get off my bed, you freak! Get on your own bed and do that shit."

"My bed doesn't smell like you."

The door to Rainier opened up and out stepped the poor bastard who let me out of my cell. He had come outside to throw something in the hot trash. He saw me. "What are you doin'? Did you go?"

"Yeah, but I was comin' back"

"Well get back inside then."

"Boss, listen. Roberts pulled me over on the track as I was coming back. He said they're doing a walk-through tomorrow, and could I go by each cell and ask the inmates to take shit out of their windows: paper, sodas, whatever looks like trash."

"Well then do that."

"No, I was," I insisted. "I was honestly just askin' these dudes to take the stuff out of their windows." I turned to Tater. "Thank you, fellas." Then I moved on. I had to actually ask four cells to take things out of their windows, because the officer had trouble unlocking the hot trash lid. Once he'd gone back inside I came back to Tater. "Take that shit outta your window!" They laughed.

The next cop who came out hadn't spoken to me yet. He was opening the door so the servers could bring out the food carts.

"Hey," he called me.

"Yeah," I answered.

"Help push carts." . . . Okay.

Together the servers and I brought the food carts back into the kitchen. I ran into an indian named Irv whom I knew from Lassen. He gave me a burrito and we bullshitted. I came out of the chow hall twenty minutes later—all of the servers had returned long ago.

When I came outside, Sergeant Villa and several officers were lounging at the cop table by the chowhall door. I tried to spin around and dart back in, but Villa called me.

"What are you doin' in there?" he demanded.

"I was helping bring the carts back."

"Carts came back twenty minutes ago."

"Yeah, I know," I agreed. "We got 'em back on time."

"Weren't you supposed to go to Medical?"

I looked down toward the patio. "Uh . . ."

Another officer spoke up. "Nah, he's supposed to stop at each cell, and ask the inmates . . ." he trailed off, apparently catching how stupid that sounded.

"Why are you out of your cell, inmate?" Villa demanded.

"Uh," I squinted. "Because I have herpes?" They escorted me home.

CHAPTER TWENTY-FOUR

C-status ended abruptly. Staff simply opened the door one day and told us to pack up. They split me and Ryan up again, sending him in with Lifer Bobby and putting me with my homeboy Brandon Morgan, whom everyone called Mad Dog. At least we were both back on Lassen-A's third tier.

". . . and they took Eddie for this out-of-state bullshit. He said he'll write. Anyway, everything I got, you got. Just do your part so we can both keep the cell clean." Brandon was a good cellie.

"Look," he said. "I got to go to work at work call. When you come out for yard, can you set this shit by our neighbor's door?"

"Sure," I told him.

"I got some food from them while we were on lockdown. So now we're up and they're not, I'm getting' 'em back." Sounds simple enough.

The southerners had been declared the aggressors in the Lassen riot. Blacks were down as victims. Staff had begun an age release with the blacks, so we had forty-and-olders out moving around, but the two groups were still on sight. When I came out my neighbors were asleep—way against the southerner code, but I wasn't going to tattle on them. I slid a few of the narrower items under their door and set the rest of the bag next to it. They'd be pleasantly surprised when they got up.

I had planned to hang my shower bag by the showers and head outside, but when I passed the shower I caught glimpse of a wrinkly, pruny old body I just had to get next to.

"Hey, youngster," I greeted him as I stepped into the shower.

"Hey, Seph," Mac answered. "Oh, good! You're back. I wanted to talk to you about something. You're unassigned now, right?"

"Yeah," I told him. "'Cause of C-status."

"I'd like to make you the PLU clerk. Do you want to do that?"

"What's that?"

"He coordinates the law library," Mac told me while shampooing his sixty-five-year-old balls. "You'd make all the legal ducats and keep track of who has active cases going. With you there and me still in Unit Five, we'd be able to do all kinds of shit."

"Yeah. Sounds good. But I'm still on the GED list."

"Don't worry about that," he said. "We'll bypass all that. I process all job assignments anyway. I'll put you down, you show up for work, that's the end of it. You'll find out, buddy. Package ducats, cell moves, everything: clerks run this whole prison."

"Right on," I said. "It's good to see you again."

"You too, buddy, I tell ya. I've been stuck playing chess with Junior. He's a good player, but so irritating. Oh, you've got a new homeboy on the B-side named Woody. He says he knows you."

"Younger guy?" I asked. I was rinsing my hair with my eyes open. I don't like closing my eyes in the shower. Every time I do I hear this thunking crack like someone is punching me in the temple.

"No. He's like thirty-five."

I thought for a second. "The only Woody I know from Modesto was on B-yard. He's my age. He was there three months, beat up a different guy each month, then he left."

"Well, this guy was over thirty. But he told me, 'Oh, yeah, I know Seph.' It sounded like you guys were old friends."

I thought of Snowman making the youngster run laps. The custodian from my high school was named Woody, but he definitely didn't know me as Seph. When I went upstairs to hang my shower bag by my door, the neighbors were awake.

"Hey, that was you who slid that shit under?" I nodded. "How much was that?"

"It was from Mad Dog," I told him. "It's whatever he owed you guys from a while back."

He looked at me with a purposefully confused expression. "That was only like six dollars." In his hands he was holding the few things I'd slid under the door.

"No, that, plus I put a bag right here next to your door with some mackerel and coffee and shit in it."

He put his face up to his window to look downward. "Oh, there's a bag?"

"No, there's no bag now. You didn't grab it?"

The mood changed instantly. We stared at each other through the window as both of us quickly tried to figure out if the other party was just joking, or really attempting to pull some shady bullshit. I could tell this ese would swing a knife over a few cans of mackerel and I don't doubt he got the same impression from me.

After a solid minute of just staring, I backed up and put one finger up. "Gimme a second," I said, then took off up the tier. I wasn't really going anywhere, just trying to think.

Why would this dude lie? He'd originally given Brandon this food on the strength. And if he needed more, he could just ask and any one of us would come through.

But if he wasn't lying, then it was stolen. How could that happen on a three yard? It doesn't. I could set ninety-dollars worth of store in the middle of the softball field, go to work, a visit, whatever, and when I come back not one soup would be missing. People don't steal shit on three yards because people get stabbed for stealing shit on three yards. Plus I was only in the shower twenty minutes. Where could that shit have gone?

I finished my lap back at the southerner's house. "How much is all that right there?"

"Six."

"How much did he owe you?"

"Twenty. He didn't really owe me, but he said he was gettin' me back."

I pointed toward my own door. "I've got the rest in my locker," I told him. "I'll grab it when they unlock at recall." He nodded. I left.

I reasoned it was my fault for not waking him up and letting him see the bag. But where the fuck could the bag have gone?

"What's on your mind, Seph?" Curt asked as I reached the table by the showers.

"I'm missing a bag."

"Did it have coffee and mackerel in it?"

I turned quickly. "Yes."

"The blacks at the top of the stairs have it, on the fence side."

"Why do they have it?"

"I'm sorry, bro. I didn't know it was yours. I was passing out toilet paper, and the cop opened their 'door. That bag was sitting there on the fire-hose box by their cell. I asked if it was theirs, and they said, "Oh, yeah, yeah.' So I handed it to them."

"How the fuck did it get there from cell three 'o-seven?"

"I don't know, Seph. The first time I saw it was . . ." I actually ran up the stairs to knock on their door. One of the two inhabitants came to the window.

"I need the bag of mackerel and coffee," I told him.

"Oh, was that shit yours? I thought that was from my folks'."

"Check this out, friend. I don't want this to be a big issue. But that bag needs to come out of your cell immediately. I'm gonna get the cop to open your door."

"Man, I ain't even gonna lie to you, Wood. That shit's already in traffic." I didn't doubt it. If I had just peeled another convict's shit, I'd want to get it out of my cell quickly too.

"Look. I know you guys still have some issues with these southerners, and maybe dude thought he was gettin' over on them, but that shit wasn't theirs. It was mine. I need you to pay it back."

"How much was it?" he asked.

"Fourteen dollars."

"Yeah, don't trip, Wood. We gotchu. Make a list up, and when we come out we'll go to sto'."

"Thank you." I walked away. Thank God that was over. Of course I'd never really make a list or bother them for the money. Like I said, we don't take money from blacks. I just needed him to accept blame and offer to pay it back. Crisis averted.

When my door opened I grabbed some things for the neighbor. I didn't bother relaying the whole fiasco to my cellie, even though it was his money. It was just too much to deal with. Anyway, if it came up later on I had my bases covered.

"We got a new homeboy on the B-side," Mad Dog said.

"Yeah, Mac told me."

"Well, he's a fuckin' idiot."

"What happened?" I asked.

"He was out there serving and some black ran over his foot with the cart. And the black said, 'Watch out, now.' And the kid told him, 'No, motherfucker, you say excuse me.' So the black got offended, and our homeboy told him to meet him behind the stairs and he'd beat his ass."

"Ah, shit."

"Yeah, well," Mad Dog continued, "an hour before that, Rain was trying to explain something to him about the dayroom and he called Rain out." Rain was big. "Anyway, we're gonna go have a talk with him tomorrow. He says he knows you."

"How old is he?" I asked.

"Your age."

"Yeah, I know him."

On my way out to yard the next day the blacks called me to their door. "Hey, Wood. We doin' what we cans, ya feel me? But my cellie don't wanna pay his half. So I'ma getchu seven, ya feel me, and y'all gots to speak wiff my cellie fo' his half." You can always tell when the blacks are trying to hustle you because their grammar goes to shit. I turned away and tried to stay calm.

"Listen," I said, turning back to him. "Work with me on this. The group I run with, we don't take food from you guys. We don't take anything from you. I don't want you to pay me back. I just want you to say you'll pay me. That's it. Then we'll never talk again. Make sense?"

He looked confused, but he nodded. I looked past him to his cellie and gave a thumbs up. He nodded too. What a fuckin' headache.

Mac was in the shower again. I couldn't join him this morning, because I had to go meet Woody, but I stopped by to flirt a little.

"Hey, Seph, you start Monday."

"The LSU thing?"

"Yeah," he chuckled. "Just show up in the morning at work and school call and show the librarian your ID card. She knows all about it." Thumbs up for Mac, and we continue.

EZ had made it out with us. I joined him and Big Dave at the bleachers. "Where's dude?"

"He's over there with Brandon at the fuckin' phone line," Dave explained.

"I thought we were all gonna talk to him together?"

"Yeah, well, I tried to talk to the motherfucker this morning about what happened with the blacks and he got all bowed up. Now he wants me to meet him behind the stairs when we go in."

I threw my head back. "Whadda-fuckin'-idiot!" Easy laughed, but Dave was still pissed off. Minutes later the man in question arrived alongside Mad Dog.

"What's up, Woody?"

"Oh, now you know me?" I just looked at him. "You told the old man you didn't know any Woody from Modesto."

"Why don't you quit name droppin' a motherfucker and shit like that won't happen." I dare this idiot to call me behind the stairs. I swear to God it'll be the last thing he does.

He came forward and handed me his paperwork. I gave him my own. Since I knew him from another yard, I was technically the one who should check his 128G.

"Your last name is Birch?" I asked.

"Yeah."

"That's funny."

"Why?"

I asked him, "You know what's unique about Birch trees?"

"What?"

"They have really short life spans." Everyone laughed. The joke helped ease things.

Brandon looked at EZ. "Will you come with me to talk to the blacks?"

"What's up?" Easy asked.

"They said they want to talk," Brandon shrugged. "Some shit about food that went missing in Lassen."

"Mother fucker," I put in. That's why we don't do business with them.

"What?" Mad Dog asked.

"I need to go with you, bro. In fact, do you care if I speak for us? I'm the one they're talking about."

"Well, do you want to fill the rest of us in?"

"Don't even trip, Brandon," Easy urged. "Homeboy's got it. Let's go."

The five of us walked along the track till we reached the black table in front of Lassen. The blacks noticed us and I stepped forward away from the group. One black OG waved me toward them. I stepped just two feet into their dirt—enough to acknowledge the invitation. The OG approached me along with another older cat holding a bag.

"W'sup wit it, youngster?" he aksed, looking past me to some of the most dangerous guys on the yard. "You the dude?"

"I'm the dude. What's up?"

"Man, look. You know the one gentleman wants to make it right. He good for his seven. But his cellie didn't have no part in it. As his own person, he does not feel responsible to the point where his payment would come to fruition. So you've got seven, and you're owed fourteen. We got about nine-fifty in this bag."

"What's in the bag?" I asked him.

"We got some tuna . . ."

"I'll settle for one can of tuna."

". . . some beans . . . a toothpaste . . ."

"Partner? Did you hear me?"

"hmmm?" He looked up from the bag he'd been rummaging through.

"For one can of tuna, I'll call it even."

He looked puzzled. "You don't want the whole bag?"

"Just one can. Please."

He handed me a single can of tuna. I left without shaking hands. The fellas made to follow but I put my hand up, asking them to hold tight. As I walked along the track toward the voc gate, I dug the little P-38 can opener out of my wallet and began wrenching on the can. Once the lid was off I clacked the fucking thing upside down on the curb. There. Let the fucking cats eat it.

As the fellas caught up with me Easy put his hand on my shoulder. "I like that shit, youngster. We'll kill all them motherfuckers over some shit we won't even eat."

CHAPTER TWENTY-FIVE

The sprain in my wrist never did go away. I put in to go to Medical again, but before I could even see the doctor a nurse sent me over to Central for X-rays. I came straight back, and had another four-hour wait until I could finally be seen.

"That's nothing," Kahuna told me. "You oughta try asking Mental Health for help sometime. One of my cellies, Chuck, hung hisself two years ago."

"You let your cellie hang himself?" I couldn't believe it.

"No. He did it in the hole," Kahuna clarified. "But we were cellmates the whole time he was begging these assholes for help. Chuck put in a request to Mental Health about once a week. He came up here a dozen times, telling them he had really bad anxiety and that he suffered from panic attacks. They wouldn't help him. They were convinced he was trying to hustle them for pills.

"He told me after the fourth time he met with them they finally just told him straight up, 'There's nothing wrong with you. You're just trying to work us for medication.' So he tells them, 'Don't give me pills then. What else can you do?' And he said the doctors were more like cops than psychiatrists. He said they were grilling him, pointing their fingers in his face and shit, saying 'What do you want us to do?' So he told them, 'I don't know the options. What can you do?' And they just kept repeating, '*No.* What do you *want* us to do?'

"He had explained his problem a dozen different times, but they just told him, 'You know, inmate, when you say things like 'can't take it' or 'it's just too much,' that concerns us that maybe you're thinking about hurting yourself. It might be a good idea for us to put you on suicide watch.' And you know what that's like," Kahuna continued. "They strip you naked and leave you in the rubber room over night."

By now Kahuna had an audience of five. "So Chuck tells 'em, 'No, nevermind. I don't need help,' and he goes home—which is what they want. These prison guards' salaries are so high now that every other department is under pressure to come in under budget. They won't prescribe anybody shit. Even if you have broken ribs or something, you'll have to 602 for two months before anyone approves your Tylenol.

"Meanwhile my cellie is having full-blown panic attacks twice a week. I had to give him the bottom bunk, because out of nowhere he would just turn and throw up over the side of his bed. He said he wanted to go to the toilet, but it was all he could do not to throw up on his own bedding. He said when he gets fucked up, his limbs don't respond to what he's trying to make 'em do, and the toilet just seems miles away.

"So we get this system going where I help him to the toilet. This one time he's over there, and he's resting in between rounds of throwing up, and he shits his pants. Not a lot, but he shit 'em. I mean Chuck was seriously, clinically fucked up. His back is all blown out, 'cause when he has panic attacks his back spasms out, jerking this way and that. He wakes up with pulled muscles all over his back and he can't hardly move.

"Well, I tell him he's gotta go up to Medical. I tell him, 'Don't even change your pants. Just go up there. If Mental Health won't help, ask Medical to give you something for your back. Can't they physically check to see that your back is fucked up?' And he said, 'I think they *can*, but I don't think they will. I honestly don't think they want to help.'

"He went up there and told them the same shit he always told them. He demanded they help him. Then they took him up to suicide watch.

"After one day they came back and asked, 'Do you feel better?' And he said, 'No. I still have anxiety, and I know I'm gonna have more panic attacks, please help me.' And they told him, 'You're not having panic attacks.' So as they're leaving he asks to use the toilet. And they point to the shower drain and say, 'You'll need to use that.' That drain, I mean you can piss into it okay, but if you shit it's not going down. Your shit will just hang out there with you.

"Chuck said he held it for like three days, but in the end he just told 'em he was okay now. He came back to our cell, drank some coffee, and shit. He changed clothes while he told me all this shit about what happened, then he went straight up to Medical.

"That was the last time I ever saw him. The cops called me in off the yard and asked me to pack up his property. They said he knocked one of the doctors out cold. One punch. Anyway, a few weeks later we got word he was dead—hung hisself from his air vent with half a bedsheet."

"That's insane, Kahuna," I said. Bump was one of my fellow listeners and he nodded his head in agreement.

"No, Seph. That's not the crazy part," Kahuna continued. "The crazy part is, both those Mental Health doctors still work here. Nobody asked why an inmate was on suicide watch for three days and never got any treatment.

And nobody wondered if that inmate's suicide could have been prevented. I honestly feel they just look at it as, 'Well, now we definitely don't have to prescribe him anything.' This whole prison is fucked up."

"Tell me about it," I agreed. "Last time I was up here the doctor made a fuckin' pass at me." Kahuna nodded his head, but Bump chuckled like he didn't believe me.

"I'm not fuckin' around," I told him. "The dude put his hand on my knee and told me I was handsome. Then he asked me to smile for him."

"What?" Bump wrinkled his nose.

"I wasn't even trippin'," I explained. "I told dude, prescribe me a shitload of Vicodin and I'd let him touch it."

"Fuck," Bump laughed. "How'd that all work out? Do you still have to see the same doctor?"

He tapped me. I hadn't really heard what he had asked.

"What was the end result?" he repeated.

I mumbled some shit while looking away from him.

"What, Comrade?"

". . . about a year," I said, turning my head toward him.

"What was about a year?"

I looked directly at him. "I was on Vicodin about a year." A few guys laughed. Some groaned. That *is* gross.

The doctor took his time looking at the X-rays. His English had improved a little. "hmm . . ."

I didn't know if he was waiting for me to ask a question or what. I just sat there.

"You broke your wrist, maybe three months ago. You should have come in."

I couldn't believe what he just said. "I did come in," I argued. "Four months ago. It was in November. You remember that? You said it was a sprain."

He looked at his chart. "Yes, yes," he nodded. "You had a sprain in November. This would be after that." He showed me the X-ray. "See? Fracture. Clean through." I want to kill this dude.

"What are my options?" I asked. He raised his eyebrows. "What can we do?" I repeated. I was trying not to shout.

He shook his head. "It is not such a break as we should break again. Just a fracture. So it healed wrong. It will hurt you sometimes. There is nothing to do."

"Should I drink some water then, doc?" I wasn't even angry anymore. It's just stupid.

"Yes, yes. Always drink as much water as you can."

"How 'bout jackin' off?" I asked him. "Should I not use that wrist anymore?"

He didn't know what to make of that.

I took the rest of the day off, since the librarian thought I was at Medical anyway. I shook some hands and got tally on a game of chess. The two dumbasses who were already playing liked to take five minutes a move. When I finally did sit down I only had time to touch two or three of my pieces. Brandon interrupted the game.

"C'mon. Our car's having a meeting."

Sure. Fuck what I'm doing.

You never notice how many homeboys you have until they all get together. I counted twelve, and a few of the Rainier guys hadn't made it out. Bump wasn't there, but skinheads are usually skinhead first, hometown kinda. Robert, an older homeboy with a cane, did most of the talking.

"The way I see it is there's two issues that ought to be looked at separate from one another. Yesterday the skinhead Ruckus pulled a couple of our youngsters aside"—he indicated Spider and Skillet—and told them they had to jump on Tex. He said Tex owes the paisas five hundred dollars, and he told these two that if they didn't beat up seventy-year-old Tex, all the skinheads were gonna rush the Modesto car.

"We'll talk about the Tex thing, but I want to get this skinhead issue out of the way first. White-on-White violence is supposed to be against their creed. I don't know what kind of skinhead this dude Ruckus is—maybe he's just a skinhead 'cause he thinks the skinhead tattoos are really cool—I've never met the dude. But he needs a good ass whoopin'. His comrades are saying he was drunk, and he didn't mean it, and they say he'll get checked in the cell.

"There's a good chance it's just a little sissy scuffle anyway, 'cause they like that dude, but even that's good enough for me. It's just the point of humbling a motherfucker, of them saying he got checked. Evidently he fancies himself some kind of shotcaller. He just needs a reminder that he's not. If the rest of you are satisfied with that, I am as well."

We all nodded our assent.

"Next is Tex," Robert continued. "Tex does owe the paisas five hundred dollars. He agreed to bring in some dope for one of them through visiting. He had already swallowed the balloon, and his visitor was in the process of passing him a bill, and they got caught. So fuckin' Tex is in the hole for the hundred dollars.

"A few days later that balloon come out the other end, and Tex is stuck in Ad Seg with a good issue. He doesn't think he's coming back to the yard, he doesn't want to get caught with it in the hole, and most important, Tex is a dope fiend. He does about half of it, he shoots some to the fellas, and he even sent some to the paisas, since it was theirs originally.

"But this is all two years ago. Tex did come back. By the time he got back, though, that paisa had already been sent to another prison. The dude who's claiming the debt now was the original guy's cellie, which is sort of an insipid claim anyway." What did he just say? "True, it was paisa dope, but how do we know dude left the debt to his cellie? How do we know that guy won't show up here in a year and want the money hisself? We don't.

"I've got fifty dollars I can put in. I figure if we come up with half, they'll settle for that. If we smash Tex, they won't get shit."

"Nobody's touchin' Tex," EZ said. "And fuck Ruckus for even sayin' that shit."

Robert nodded. "Right. Well what I need is four more homeboys with fifty dollars, or some calculation thereof that can get us halfway up the ladder."

"I've got fifty." Mad Dog was first. My own hand was right behind. Eric, Easy's cellmate, threw in as well.

"Perfect," Robert nodded. "We just need one more."

After hesitating for a minute, Brawler spoke up. I've got a hundred I was ordering a package with. I can cancel the package and send that."

"If you want to send the whole hundred," I told him, "I can get you seventy in store in two weeks." He was happy with that. After a few formalities and thank-you's the meeting ended. Good. I went back to playing chess.

CHAPTER TWENTY-SIX

The PLU job was great. Mac was right, clerks did everything. Most days I did nine things at once. I organized the ducat schedule, I kept the department's supplies current so guys could type their motions. In my *free* time I learned software programming. I ducated guys from both yards for meetings, I let the fellas here speak by phone to the fellas at Central. I made copies of pictures and tattoo patterns for everybody.

The law library is used mostly by black lifers, some of whom can't read or write. One of my chief duties was to photocopy each motion typed in our library. I was supposed to make four copies: one for the county clerk, one for the court, one for the respondent, and one for the inmate. But if any particular motion was exceptional, I make a copy for myself.

Mac was well versed in law—there was even a rumor he had been a practicing defense attorney in another life. I used to bring my copies of these motions out and read them to him, impersonating the voice of its author. I loved making that old man laugh.

MOTION TO IMBIBE JUDGMENT

This motion, filed forthwith in due process and duress, doth declare certain actions of the state erroneous, as pertains to the above mentioned criminal proceedings. It is in the opinion of this appellant, as expressed in this motion, written in this the language of the courts, that the sentence rewarded in this case was erroneously based on factors other than those which the courts should declare relevance in the announcement of aggravation, namely racism.

POINTS AND AUTHORITY

The alleged defendant in this case, without conceding that any crime has in fact taken place, points to the erroneous sentencing which occured on the date of August 17, 1987. Upon the date their mentioned, the defense was sentenced to an aggravated term for robbery, as well as a five-year gang enhancement, a ten-year gun enhancement, and further enhancements for prior prison convictions.

The Merriam-Webster Dictionary defines aggravation as "formed by the gathering of units into one mass." The appendix to this motion, attached in lieu of a codicil, lists a number of selected cases, chosen to illustrate this fact, whereof the predominance is of white males who did not receive the aggregate. Even many African American Citizens have received middle-term or even mitigated sentences for robbery.

We must ask, what criminal is not a member of a gang? We must ask, what robbery shall be performed without a gun? The aforementioned circumstantial evidence exact to double taxation, which dates as far back as to Thomas Jefferson. A maximum sentence are therefore imposed in this case indiscrimination.

These things carry on for sometimes thirty pages and often include photocopied sections of irrelevant rulings on ancient cases. The motions are a horrible waste of time, a waste of the law library's time; they're a waste of paper, honestly. Our library alone pumped out four a day.

I kept copies of the most ridiculous motions in a binder and I labeled the spine, "People vs. Spooty 'n 'em." I and some of the other clerks found them amusing, but some appellate judge actually has to sit and read through these things. Meanwhile some guy who perhaps did get an unfair shake gets swamped in an overcrowded appellate court.

Still, they were good for Mac. Nothing made him laugh more.

"That's the most ridiculous shit I've ever heard," he told me once he'd caught his breath. "I would love to be in the room with some judge when he reads this. I mean, I'm dying to know if he manages to scrape through with his professionalism intact, or is he just crackin' up and sharing different parts with his staff."

"Why do you assume it's a man?"

"Who?"

"The judge. You said 'he' reads, 'he' stays professional. That's sexism."

"Oh, yeah. How are your college studies coming?" he asked.

"Great," I told him. "I study for finals when I'm supposed to be working."

"Well, I'm a true liberal, Seph, not some freak of political nature like most of your professors. I will tell you: sexism is mistreatment or bias based on a person being a man or a woman. It has nothing to do with pronouns, or assumptions, or words like manhole cover."

"That's not what my textbook says, Thadius."

"Yeah, well, your textbook was written by a very ridiculous *person* who has had no adversity in *his or her* life, and so has no way to distinguish what matters from what is simply unimportant. If *he or she* had ever had anyone die in front of *her or him* (God forbid), *he or she* might finally realize there are more important things to worry about."

I nodded. "That's a good point. But I'm gonna keep doing what the professor tells me to, or he or she will fail my ass."

"Well, that's good, buddy. That's exactly the right attitude to take. Do what you have to do to pass the course. Just don't let it fuck with your head too much. Take it all in, regurgitate it out onto the final exam, and then leave it all there on the desk when you exit the room." Together we set up the chessboard.

"I might have to beat up Shithead," Mac told me without looking up.

For a second I was too shocked to answer. "Why?"

"He did some stupid shit on the B-side"

"No I get that. Shithead's a shithead. But why you? You're like sixty-five."

"Yeah, well, so is Shithead. We've all got to do our part."

I made a few moves in silence. "It just seems like your part should be done by now."

"No, look at me, kid." I looked. "No one's part is ever done. There's always more work to put in, more bullshit to deal with. It never ends." Well that's depressing. We played a second game after I lost the first.

"What's up with Shithead?" I asked him. "He's been doing a lot of stupid shit lately, even for Shithead."

"He's about to go home," Mac answered. "I'd have thought you would have learned that one by now." I just looked at him. "Shithead's been down eighteen years," Mac went on. "He has no family, no money. His parole papers had to fill the space for paroling address with a homeless shelter in the county he got arrested in.

"The extra drama you're noticing around him is his subconscious fucking with him. Somewhere inside his head, Shithead knows that prison has more to offer him than the real world. They feed him here. He has a bed and a television. He has friends to irritate. It's not about being institutionalized, Seph. Prison is the better option. So now his mind is revolting against him, trying to get him in trouble so he won't parole. He doesn't even know he's doing it.

"I tell ya," he continued, "I've seen this a thousand times. And nine times out of ten the asshole in it ends up getting himself hurt. Basically, Shithead's got three months to get himself killed or this place is gonna dump him out onto the streets."

Mac's gloomy conversation reminded me to call my own family and tell them how much I missed them. I got a hold of my parents while they were driving down to visit my younger brother. Halfway through the twenty-minute phone call I noticed Wacko standing at the phone next to mine. His last name was Grier.

"G-R-I-E-R. Yeah. Just a full background check, whatever you can find off the internet." I smiled at Wacko. I was only fucking with him, and the real-world couple on the other end of the phone certainly had no idea what I was talking about, but the reaction I got from Wacko was not at all what I had expected. He was truly scared. He had honesty smeared across his face and fear dancing in his pupils.

Ah, shit.

I continued with the joke. "Nothing," I told my mom. "I was just messing with the dude next to me. We play around a lot." Once Wacko was certain it was in jest, he laughed it off. Too late, I'm afraid.

I shared what I'd seen with just one other person. "Don't fuck with Wacko anymore."

"Why not?" Ryan asked. "Did he burn somebody?"

"He's got smut on his." I relayed what had taken place at the phones.

"That's it?" Ryan asked.

"Yeah, buddy. That's it."

"That could be all kinds of shit," he argued.

"It's not anything good," I told him. Ryan didn't seem to appreciate the severity of what was happening. "Listen to me, Squig. I am one-hundred percent certain about this. Wacko has shit on his jacket. He's going to end up getting hurt. Unless you want to be the dude who hurts him, you ought to stay the fuck away from him."

Squiggy reflected. "Have you told anyone else?"

"No. I'm not out to get the dude hurt. I'm telling you because we're friends, and because I know you and he are friends. But you need to shake him. If he's playing pinochle, go work out. If he comes to work out, get in the phone line. If he gets in the phone line with you, ask him to hold your place while you take a piss, and don't come back."

"No, but what I'm saying is, if you don't say anything, and I don't say anything, how will anyone else know?" He put his hand up, like this was a good point. I wondered if I had ever been that naïve.

"He's got no poker face," I shook my head. "I mean it's not really about having the best poker face, but it is about keeping your poker face on at all times. For two seconds that dude let me see straight through him. And now he's freaked out about it. With both of us not speaking to him, he's gonna have question marks painted all over his body.

"You'll notice it yourself, if you pay attention," I continued. "Dude's are gonna wonder why Wacko's standing like that. Why's he keep lookin' around when I'm trying to talk to him? How come Wacko doesn't ever sit down to play pinochle anymore? This shit happened less than an hour ago. I'm willing to bet someone else already knows what time it is."

CHAPTER TWENTY-SEVEN

Ryan and I stood in the cluster of inmates waiting in front of the commissary. I was trying to get a place in the store line, so I could buy Brawler his seventy dollar list, but the last of the southerners had come off lockdown. The yard was heavily crowded now, and store was a crapshoot. A southerner named Spooky kept us company.

"The corner of the window is all a bust now," he told us. "The cops hit like four houses yesterday, and the corners of the window grate is the first place they looked. Tell your people: that shit's blown up."

I nodded. "We've been using the Nescafé coffee containers. You know, with the black lids that pop open? The inside peels away and you can stick shit in there."

"Yeah, commissary shit's cool," he agreed. "If something happens, they'll transpack that shit with you. Some of the homies pull out the bottom part of their Speed Stick, after they use most the deodorant. But some things won't fit inside a deodorant." He meant knives.

"An older homey was tellin' me," he continued, "that all these hiding places go in and out of style. He said like ten years ago, all the homies were unhinging their light fixtures, and stashing shit up there. Then the juras figured it out, so the spot was no good. But by now all the cops that used to check there either retired or have forgotten, you know? I'm back to stashing shit in mine."

"What happened to your foot?" Ryan asked after a pause. Spooky was wearing an elaborate leg brace.

"I had to have surgery," He confessed. "The morenos threw me off the second tier."

"That was you?" Realization dawned on Ryan. "We saw you coming out of Lassen, pushing the nurses away, trying to walk by yourself."

Spooky nodded. "Yeah, it was crazy. I didn't know it was about to kick. I was up by my cell. So when it cracked, it was just me and five blacks right there. I'm glad I got thrown off, though. It could have been worse. After I landed, the homies threw one of them off the third tier. He hit his head on the table.

"But it's different fighting inside a building. There's less room to move around. At first it was disorganized. But we regrouped. Some of the Woods slid their knives out to us. It got better. We cornered most of 'um in the back of the hall and just kept pulling one after another out of their group. Some of them were fucked up."

"Yeah, we seen that shit," I nodded.

Brandon interrupted us. "Hey," he asked me. "Are you going into work today?"

"Yeah, if I can ever get Brawler's shit to him."

"I need to talk to you about something." Brandon looked at me when he said this, but the words were for someone else to hear. Spooky gave a little wave and turned to speak with another southerner. Call it professional courtesy. Once Spooky was out of earshot, Mad Dog continued. "Wacko just got taken to the hole."

Ryan did a good job of staying quiet.

"What for?"

"We don't know. There was no code or anything. He's been all skitzed out for like the last week. I figured he was high, but his cellie says he don't owe any money. Just follow him on the system and see where they take him. And we need his lockup order."

"You'll have to get at Mac or Casper for the 114," I reminded him. "I can't get it. But Mac's probably at work right now."

"He's not. He's in his cell transpacking."

"What?"

"They're sending him to Avenal. Your cellie too," he nodded to Ryan. "They're taking like thirty lifers out of here. Just get what you can on Wacko." He was gone before I could think of anything to say.

"Damn. You called that one, Seph."

I wasn't even sure what Ryan was talking about. Half a dozen things had just happened, and I certainly had not seen any of them coming. Lifer Bobby was leaving, which meant Ryan was now single-celled. We needed to act before CDC could give him some lame-ass cellmate. We needed to move him in with someone solid. But we'd just lost our Unit Five connection. Mac was leaving."

. . . Mac was leaving. Somewhere inside I felt a faint imitation of emotion. The arrogant old bastard who wouldn't play chess with me had been my longest, most consistent, and most valued companion. Just like that he was gone. He was transpacking for Avenal, as good as dead to me. I would never see him again.

Why were they sending all the lifers to Avenal? What change was staff about to make that they felt the lifers would oppose? The lifers are who hold us within reason, who keep the violence from getting out of hand. They are also the ones who give us the strongest protection against integrated housing and other ridiculous bullshit.

For his part, Wacko did more than I expected of him. Some might call it the right thing. If you're no good, and you know you're no good, roll your ass up. Don't wait around, clinging to some skewed sense of honor, so that somebody else has to fuck his program off, and get sprayed, and lose more time just to deal with you. And the fact that Wacko left without running up any debt raised him a good three points in my estimation.

That night I brought news back to my cellmate that Wacko was in O-Wing, 116L. He had locked it up. Two days later, Mad Dog sat at the bleachers reading Shifty and me the lock-up order Casper had just given him.

". . . stepped into the unit sergeant's office and stated, 'I have to go. The other inmates found out I have a rape on my juvenile record. They're going to stab me.' The inmate was removed from general population." Brandon looked at us. "I didn't know about any rape."

"I couldn't wait to agree. "No, but that explains why he was acting all twitchy."

"Well who the fuck knew about this shit, and why didn't they say nothin'?"

"Well he's gone now, either way," I said. "I doubt he's coming back."

"Fuck either way. You wouldn't say either way if you had keys for the yard." He backhanded the piece of paper angrily. "This shit makes it look like we had a rapist here and didn't do nothin'."

Ryan joined us, looking forlorn. "Bobby gone?" I asked him.

"Yeah. He left this morning. Mac too."

"I know," I answered. "He didn't even say goodbye."

"Awww . . ." Brandon teased. "Wha'd you want him to do? Hold your fuckin' hand?"

"At least I don't let rape-o's walk the line," I muttered.

"Here," Ryan handed me a letter. "Read this."

"What is it?" I asked, unfolding the paper.

"Bobby left it taped above the bottom rack."

Listen to me Ryan,

> *There's a lot a human being stands to gain by coming here. You now have things in you that most people don't understand. Courage, determination, you have an unshakable iron will any time you choose to enact it. You're now the kind of man who can be tortured and not break. Someone could tie you down and chop your arm off, and you have it in you to write the arm off as a sunk cost, to look at the guy holding the axe and say, 'Fuck you.'*

> *These things come at a price. You bleed, you ache, you give up your freedom months at a time. You have paid, and you will continue to pay as long as you're here. But while the cost is constant and indefinite, the benefit you receive comes mostly in the first three years. You've heard advice from the old and the wise, you've had time to put theory into practice; any further sacrifice from you will be for naught—like pumping quarters into an arcade machine that's not even plugged in.*

> *Leave this place, Ryan, and never come back. Never let a criminal thought cross your mind. Remember that Superman would only be a regular guy on his planet, and he only*

became great because he came to Earth, where no one else was like him. You have an advantage over every adversary you meet, whether it's in contract negotiation, a bar fight, or just picking teams in a fantasy football league. They won't understand why you're beating them.

Prison has tempered your core into fine steel, but it has left its stamp on you as well. Even when you're home, you'll catch yourself reminiscing. You may be miserable now, but later you'll remember what it felt like to hold the knife, to walk up for a removal, or to plunge fist-first into a crowd of mexicans. Shake it off. Understand that these thoughts are side effects of a poison you ingested. If you come back, you'll end up an old man with squiggly indiscernible tattoos, writing a letter to some kid, wishing to God the note could somehow travel back in time and end up in your own twenty-three-year-old hands.

All My Love, Young Man,

⚡obby

"I hate they took them motherfuckers from us," I complained, handing Ryan back his letter. "If they were getting out I'd be happy. But taking 'em just to take 'em? And they wonder why cops get stabbed."

Brandon smiled. "I think you were butt-fuckin' that old man." He turned to Shifty. "Can you take care of the runaway when you go in?"

Shifty shook his head. "I gotta go to work, Brandon."

"*I* gotta go to work," Mad Dog echoed.

255

Shifty gestured in my direction. "Give it to Seph."

My cellie looked at me. "You hear about the new kid?"
I shook my head. "He was on B-yard and was single-celled.
They tried to move him in with another White dude, and
the kid refused. So, they took him to the hole. Now they
brought him back on our side."

"You want me to check him?" I asked.

"No. Do you have to check every motherfucker who
comes through? Are you like fuckin' Woody now?" I waited
calmly for him to get to the point. "Just grab some youngster
who hasn't done nothin' yet, and tell him to take the kid
behind the stairs."

"Where'm I gonna find a youngster who hasn't done
nothin'?" I smiled at Ryan. He flipped me off.

"The kid's name is Ronnie," Brandon finished. "He
lives right there under the stairs, in one forty-four."

I came out to shower after the lunchtime lockup.
Ronnie was there, sitting at the table, shaking hands and
smiling and clearly unaware he'd done anything wrong.
The shower's ceiling blocked most of the second tier from
my view. I could see feet, and the edge of the tier itself. It
reminded me of stagehands running around between scenes
when the curtain was pulled most of the way down. That
fits. These tiers are very much like the set of some eternal
and fucked-up dramatic production, with a new cast every
year but always the same plot. One guy tells another guy to
beat up a third guy, and the second guy does it. The same
mistakes, the same corrections, the same fucking story.

I got dressed, then turned to the kid at the table. "Hey
Ronnie, come with me. You and I are gonna have a talk." I
took him to the back, behind the stairs.

"When you were on B-yard," I told Ronnie, "the cops
asked you to move in with another White man, and you

said no. We don't do that. That makes him look bad, like he's not fit to live with, and it makes you look scared. Next time, you say yes. Then the next day you can go about getting a cell move."

He nodded.

"Now put your hands up," I said. "We're gonna fight about it, then we can be friends."

He turned to look down toward the rest of the Whites.

"Hey!" I shouted. He quickly turned back. "I just told you we're gonna fight and you look away from me? How smart is that? Put your hands up." He did.

He went down after three shots—three light shots—and he hadn't even swung back. He wasn't trying to win. "Get up," I said. "We're not done."

Once he was back on his feet with his fists raised, I told him to fight back and stepped in again. I decided to eat some punches, but I didn't want him to knock me out. I slipped his right, ate a left, dodged a right, took a left. Then I remembered my left was his right. Damn this dude hits like a bitch.

He fell again and I helped him to his feet. We shook hands. The last thing I told him was, "Always fight back. No matter what."

CHAPTER TWENTY-EIGHT

I don't remember what reason staff had for splitting me and Mad Dog apart, I just remember it was stupid. These asshole prison officials make as much money as doctors or lawyers, but they're nowhere near as intelligent. Imagine someone else being put in charge of your own home. This random idiot decides what you eat for each meal and who cooks it. He creates an unnecessarily elaborate shower schedule. Then he announces a new policy. On the first Tuesday of every month, the residents of your home are going to rotate bedrooms, moving all their furniture and belongings one bedroom to the left.

This policy, Regulation 3316(b), is being implemented to provide fair treatment for all family members. Some bedrooms have their own bathrooms, some are next to the noisy air conditioning unit. Two bedrooms have windows that face the sunrise, a privilege residents of other rooms do not have access to.

When you point out that all that furniture moving is surely more trouble than it's worth, the crazy asshole reminds you that you are entitled to file a grievance. You should fill out form CDC 602(a) (which we don't have, we're out of stock right now) and send it to the F.U. Board for cursory review. You can expect to receive their denial somewhere between 90 and 180 days after the board's receipt of your complaint. You then have ten days, upon receiving said denial, to forward your gripe—refiled on form CDC 1671(j)—to Sacramento for second-level denial.

In the meantime, you will move your furniture, or you will be pepper sprayed and taken to the hole. They moved Brandon in with Conan—a large biker who used to be even bigger. I went in with Big John.

John Allicotta, from San Gabriel Valley. Big John was the biggest dope fiend I've ever known. He was always high. Unusual for a dope fiend, though: he almost always paid his debts. I don't know where he got all the money.

John had been with us in the B-yard riot. Of course, I hadn't had time to meet and shake hands with everyone out there. Since then he had lived on A-yard. I had seen him before, standing in the shower, rubbing his face and grunting for an hour straight. Really, really high. His cell was dirty, his underwear were dirty, even the sound of his voice was dirty, like a truck tire rolling over gravel. My first action, upon moving in, was to scrub everything.

"mmmm . . . uhh . . . I got, forty-five days left . . . Seph."

"Really?" I asked. "How long you been down?"

"Fuckin', ten years." He sat down on his bunk and lit a cigarette. "Anyway, I wanna clean up. You know? I'd like to go these last six weeks without using, so that when I get out I don't immediately run for the bag. So I figure, mmmm, if you and I are cellies, we could make a pact, that neither of us will do any drugs till I parole. That would really help me out."

"Fuck yeah, let's do it," I told him. "No crank, weed, heroin; none of that shit."

"mmmm . . . I don't even want to drink."

"What about tobacco?" I asked.

"What about it?" he smiled, before taking another drag.

Big John was much easier to live with than I had anticipated. In fact, he was one of my favorite cellmates. I was reclined on my bunk one day, studying for a final exam in yet another finance course. John stood at the sink, gazing thoughtfully at a cup he was washing.

"I was at Avenal . . . mmm . . . maround, ninety-eight, I think." No way. Story time?

"You ever been to Avenal?" he asked me.

I shook my head expectantly.

"They got these, squirrels. Everywhere. They're all over the fuckin' place. Thousands of 'em. They even got little fuckin' signs, that say, you know, 'Don't feed the fuckin' squirrels.'

"So I'm at Avenal. And I'm eatin' this fuckin' ice cream . . . that I got at the store. It's a fuckin' . . . mmmm pint, or half-quart. Whatever. So I'm eatin' this ice cream, and watchin' the squirrels, . . . and I get this idea." John's a heavy, pot-bellied man with a bulbous shaved head. The mischievous smile he gave when he said "idea" was reason enough to laugh.

"Well, mmm, I finish this ice cream, and I go rinse out the container. And I take my knife, and I cut little rectangle holes around the lid. Then I cut the bottom out of it.

"And I go over . . . . I got these, fuckin' carrots, they used to give us in the lunches. You remember, the baby carrots? Or carrot chips? I don't know why they quit giving 'em to us. Fuckin' carrots are too expensive, I guess. But I got these little fuckin' carrots.

"And I go over, to the tables. I'm sitting on one of the tables with my feet on the bench. And I open my fly and pull my shit out, and stuff it into the bottom of this container.

So I'm sittin' there . . . mmmm with my dick and balls in this fuckin' thing, and I'm tippin' the lid up, just a little bit at a time. And I'm playin' with these fuckin' carrots, to where it looks like I'm slipping carrots into this container.

"And it never failed. I would do this, while we were out at yard, and within ten or fifteen minutes of doing it some hapless, nutless, fuckin' youngster . . . mmmwould come up and say, 'What're you doin'?

"And I'd look up . . . and tell him, 'I caught a baby squirrel, homes.'

"And this fuckin' idiot, . . . he'd put his fuckin' head down, right over the container, and peek through those holes. I mean his eyeball, is less than an inch away from the lid. And he's staring at my fuckin' testicle, trying to figure out, which end of the baby squirrel that is.

"And every time, the kid would ask, 'Can I feed him?' And I'd tell him, 'Yeah. Fuck . . . . I've been trying to feed him these carrots . . . . Squirrels eat carrots, right?' And he'd say, 'I don't know.' So I'd tell him, . . . 'Well, try and give him a carrot. We'll see if he eats it.'

"But I'd let the kid work the lid. You know? I'd tell him, 'mmm . . . don't let him jump out.' So the dude lifts the lid up just enough, to slide a carrot in, and then he clamps the lid back down. And we're both lookin' in there to see if he's eatin' it or not. And he'd ask, 'Is he eatin' it?' And I'd say, 'I don't know . . . . mmmm, I think he's asleep.' And I'd give the container a good shake, and you'd hear my ding-a-ling rattle around in there. Then while he's down there peeking through these holes, I'd just take the lid off."

John looked up at the ceiling in thoughtful reflection. "It would take him a second, usually, to figure out exactly what he was lookin' at.

"But I'd mix up the punch line. You know? There'd usually be a dozen or so guys watchin' this. And they all know what's really in the container. Sometimes I would just remove the lid. Other times, I would jerk the lid away and yell, 'Don't let him get away!' You know? See if I couldn't get him to clap his hands down over my shit.

"This one fuckin' idiot, . . . mmm he puts the carrot in there, and I just lift the whole container up to my face. And I lift the lid off a little, . . . and look in there, to see if he's eatin' it. And everyone else is laughin' their asses off, because they can all see my dick and balls down there on my lap. But the kid, he's lookin' up at me, and the container.

"So I tell the kid, 'I think he's sleepin',' and when I bring the container back down I use my other hand to tuck my shit back into it . . . . The fellas are all laughin', but this kid didn't catch none of it. He's back peekin' in the holes, and he asks me, 'Can I feed him another carrot?' . . . And I tell him, 'Yeah, fuck. I don't care. Throw another one on there."

I laughed my hardest when he said this, which made John laugh too. "Hey!" he shouted through the laughter. "Hey! He went right back to feedin' my dick some carrots!"

A few days later some of us got together during Lassen yard for a picnic at the bleachers. We had to get together anyway, to talk about the ridiculous shit that needs be talked about, so we might as well make it a picnic.

There were seven or us: Shifty, Haywire, Big John, Mad Dog, Conan, myself, and Big Dave. We discussed a variety of subjects, like who might be fucking up and who had yet to put in work. We talked about who owed money for dope, and how far into debt they had gone. Someone suggested imposing a credit limit, a restriction Big John heartily opposed. "I think that sorta takes all the fun out of it. Don't you?"

Brandon sat mixing a bag of ramen, sausage, jalapeños, and chips. Someone else opened up some tortillas. Along the way Rick, a nineteen-year-old from Shasta County, joined the group. He was too new to realize he was interrupting a private party. No one bothered telling him to leave. We couldn't discuss yard politics with Rick standing there, but it was about time to break for burritos anyway. We even gave the kid one.

Apparently Rick decided that, since no one else was talking, it must be his turn to speak. He enthralled us all with gripping tales from Shasta's county jail. " . . . and we were waiting for court, and the cops brought a child molester into the room with us. He's just sitting there with one deputy between him and the rest of us.

"When they uncuffed me so I could change into my jury-trial clothes, I smashed the child molester. There was six deputies and bailiffs trying to get me off him, but they couldn't." Rick weighs a hundred and thirty-one pounds. "I stayed on him. I broke his jaw, his eye socket. They couldn't stop me."

And he continued. "My older homeboys approved me getting my letters, because of the work I put in. I was thinking of getting them in an arch over my belly button." Sex offenders fall under a no-hands policy, and county work doesn't earn you prison letters. You're off to a great start, kid.

A few of us exchanged smiles, fully confident that we had never been like that. "When I was in reception," Rick went on, "in DVI, they considered putting me in the SHU. The classification officer assigned to my case thought I was AB."

Big John had heard enough. "Uh . . . kid . . . . Shut the fuck up . . . . You know? . . . Just shut the fuck up. Nobody gives a fuck about anything you're talking about. Nobody cares."

Rick was stunned. John continued the lesson. "Everybody here, has spilled more blood than you've had drip, in all your periods combined. Way back, from when you first started havin' 'em. Nobody's impressed with anything you have to say."

The burritos were really good.

"Look who you're standing here with," John said. "These are the fellas. And nobody's told you to leave yet. So just shut up. Don't talk. You know? Then when you're over doin' pull-ups with the other dipshit youngsters, then talk. They already think you're cool, 'cause you get to hang out with the fellas. Tell *them* your stories. Go tell *them* you're AB."

"I'm *not* AB," Rick clarified. "It's just that the cops *thought* I was"

"Yeah I don't care," John cut him off. "The only way the cops ever had you down as AB is if you told 'em you were. No one else is gonna tell 'em that, 'cause we all know how ridiculously fuckin' stupid that sounds. Yeah, fuckin', Skinny Ricky from Shasta is a member of the most dangerous and well-respected prison gang in the world. That adds up.

"And as far your letters, mmmm, you can have 'em. I'll put 'em on you myself. I don't care. Plenty of dudes who aren't about shit have letters on their stomach, so why should anyone ask you to prove yourself before getting yours?"

Rick tried to speak, but John wouldn't let him. "Yeah I don't care. Nobody cares what you've done or haven't done. I'll tattoo all kinds of shit on you. Bolts, Swastikas. I'll give you a War Bird holding a Swastika with . . . fuckin' bolts for eyebrows. I'll put all that shit on you. 'Cause the way I see it, if you don't deserve it, we'll find out pretty quick. Motherfuckers are gonna test you. So you'll either prove your merit, or you'll get fucked off and end up on a PC yard. Then you'll just be another lame with a paint job. God knows there's plenty of them in the world."

John went back to eating his burritos. Poor Rick. I'm not sure if he caught what Big John was trying to tell him, but at least he stayed quiet for the rest of the picnic.

CHAPTER TWENTY-NINE

When it rains, it pours. And when bullshit springs up, it rolls across the yard in massive waves, stagnating all movement and leaving everyone with an offended sense of smell. Breakfast found me sitting at a very serious table of four—me, Mad Dog, Big John, and Bob, a big, older lifer who worked in the voc textiles shop.

"The shop supervisor found some things—material and sewing needles and stuff—stashed inside one of the machines," Bob explained. "It was a vacant machine, but David's machine is right next to it. And you know how David is: just as square as it gets." I stole a glance at David, who had his shirt tucked into his pants.

"The manager doesn't like David, so he immediately accuses David of stealing. But David hasn't had a write-up in like twenty years. He's convinced that if he can stay write-up free, he'll get out some day, and he's like terrified of write-ups. He tells the shop manager, 'Well, I didn't put that in there. Those black inmates put those things in that machine.' And he pointed over to the two black guys at the next table." I was trying really hard not to laugh.

"I don't see what's so fuckin' funny," Mad Dog growled at me.

"Really, Brandon?" I challenged. "You don't see how this is funny? 'Cause I'm barely holding it together here, buddy."

"Well," Bob continued, "the shop manager thought it was pretty funny too. He's not gonna write it up. He just took the stuff he found and laughed for half an hour. So nobody actually got in trouble. But this is the second time David's done this. Last time he told on an asian guy. Somehow it was reasoned down to David just not being with it, and it got blown over. Everyone just let it go."

"Well," Mad Dog said, "nobody's letting shit go this time."

"Textiles is closed today," Bob explained. "He'll be out at yard this morning. I don't want to get him hurt, but he's gonna end up getting all of us hurt."

"It's just gonna be a two-on-one," Brandon told him.

"You don't think we should have him stabbed, Brandon?" Big John suggested.

"What for?"

"'Cause he told on another race."

"On blacks," Mad Dog scoffed. "If it was southerners, yeah, we'd have to stab him—'cause southerners stab their own snitches. But all the blacks tattle their-damn-selves. Since when do they care about snitches? Plus nobody got a write-up. As far as I'm concerned, we're not even beatin' him up for telling on the blacks. We're just getting him off the yard so he doesn't tell on anyone else tomorrow."

"All right," John concluded. "Who goes then?"

"Billy and Millhouse are both on deck."

"Voc's closed; not maintenance," I reminded him. "Billy's electrical; Millhouse is a plumber."

"They can skip work for this," Mad Dog said.

"That complicates shit," I argued. "How much time will you have before they start paging these dudes over the intercom? What if David gets into the phone line or store line? You won't have the luxury of waiting for him to come out of that crowded area."

He shook his head. "I'm tired of motherfuckers bitching that those two haven't done theirs yet."

"Yeah, but this isn't serious work, homeboy. This is fuckin' No-Trouble Dave, who couldn't beat a girl scout in a fair fight. Billy and Millhouse are on deck because they fucked up. Motherfuckers will bitch more if you let those two off the hook on some minor task."

Mad Dog thought for a second, then begrudgingly nodded his head. "Fine," he said. "We'll put two youngsters on it. Any suggestions?"

Big John had one. "mmm, myeah. I nominate, fuckin', AB Rick." I couldn't agree more.

"Young Gunz, too," I put in. "He said something a while ago about wanting to put in work."

"Fine," Brandon concluded. Breakfast was over. We exited the chow hall.

Mad dog and I took the long way home, stopping at the pill window so we could return to Lassen late, after everyone was already locked back up. That way we would be able to circulate, to speak with Rick and Young Gunz. Along the way we crossed paths with the guys from Lassen-B, who were just heading into the chow hall.

Big Dave called Mad Dog. "Come with me. We gotta talk."

"I can't," Brandon answered. "I got some shit to take care of."

"*I* got some shit to take care of," Dave countered.

"I got it," I told Mad Dog. I traded my coat and glasses for Brandon's blue beanie and went to the chow hall for a second breakfast.

Dave got right to the point. "Chuck got a new cellie two days ago. Well the fuckin' new dude just came to my door as we're getting ready for chow. He says last night he woke up 'cause he heard his cellie movin' around. So he looks, and Chuck is standing at the toilet jacking off, penetrating himself with a shampoo bottle."

That's it. I'm done. Fuck this shit.

Dave kept right on talking. "And dude says he told Chuck they'd talk about it in the morning, and then went right back to sleep. Which, if it's me, I'm fuckin' dude off right there. I don't know what the fuck they have to talk about in the morning, or why the fuck dude would go back to sleep with that still in the cell with him.

"But Chuck's a fuckin' creep," Dave continued. "He's fishing on his cellie. And even if he's not, he's still doing some weirdo shit. He's gotta go."

"That's perfect," I told him. "Put Billy and Millhouse on him."

He frowned at me. "Well, it's gonna go through your cellie no matter what." Big Dave was not a big fan of youngsters making decisions.

"Yeah, that's fine," I answered. "I'm just saying it coincides well with a conversation we had earlier this morning."

"Make sure you let Brandon know that some of the dudes on our side feel like Chuck's cellie should be one of the two to deal with it, since he really should've took flight on the dude right then."

Brandon was at the first table when I returned to Lassen-A. I relayed everything Dave and I had discussed. Then I repeated most of it. Then I promised Brandon I wasn't lying or making it all up.

269

"That's fuckin' creepo shit," Brandon said. "You might have to miss work today."

"If it was work, I'd miss it," I told him. "I have a test this morning."

"What test?" he scowled.

"I've got a final exam for one of my business classes."

"What I'm sayin' is," he clarified, "you might have to stay out on the yard to help deal with this shit."

"And what *I'm* sayin' is, no, homeboy. These courses cost me nine hundred dollars apiece. I don't give a fuck if we're rushin' the cops at eight-thirty, I'm taking my exam at eight o'clock."

He left. I stopped by my cell to grab a calculator and a pen and was about to head out as well when Time Bomb got my attention.

"Check this out, Seph. This dude Bizzy has like three extra TV's he says are his and he shoots around to whoever to let use. One was in Gator's house when Gator left, so I got it from Gator's cellie and gave it to the youngsters in 251 to use 'cause they didn't have one. Fuckin' Bizzy told the youngsters to come off it 'cause he'd rented it to someone else, so I told the youngsters to tell Bizzy I've got his TV, and to come get it if he wants it. Well he fuckin' went snivelin' to this cop and told the cop I wouldn't give his TV back"

"Time Bomb," I stopped him. "This is too much right now, buddy. We have all kinds of shit going on today."

"Oh, no, don't trip," he reassured me. "I'm gonna go take care of this myself right now. I just want someone else to know why dude got his ass beat."

I looked to where Bizzy was busy sweeping the tiers. "You're gonna beat dude's ass right now?" He nodded. "Give me twenty minutes," I asked. "Let me get into Education before they call any code."

Time Bomb looked toward Bizzy as well, then back to me. "I'll give you ten."

"Fine. I'll jog." I walked quickly.

I made it into Education and received my exam from Mr. Williamson, the prison's vice principal. A number of other inmates sat in the room with me, also beginning tests. Some were TABE testing, some trying for their GED's. A few were taking college exams. I put my name on the first page, but before I could cross the "t" a code sounded for Lassen Hall.

I raced through the multiple choice section, while I was still fresh, saving most of the time allotted for essay questions.

1. Assuming the firm has full monopsony power, depict graphically an input supplier's decision for price and quantity supplied.

Dave and the other guys on the B-side have a good point. If dude was in the cell when this happened, he should have a hand in its resolution. That's exactly the sort of structural balance built into our way of doing shit that keeps motherfuckers on their toes. Otherwise we're rewarding the guy for not taking action. And that sends a bad message: if you see something wrong, just ignore it and someone else will clean it up.

Do monopsonies have marginal revenue curves that are separate from their demand curves?

Okay if dude didn't know, then he didn't know. He's not in trouble for not jumping on Chuck. But next time he will know. This is how you learn. Why pass it off on someone else? Of course Billy and Millhouse have both been on deck for some time, and comments have been made about how long they've been allowed to slide. Each of them needs to get his part over and done with.

My graph is terrible. This isn't an input monopsony, it's an output monopoly, laid on its side with its ass sticking up in the air. Did I even read this fucking chapter?

And Chuck is a fucking creep. I can't believe I used to do pull-ups with that dude, and I really hate when shit like this comes out about dudes we already know. If somebody shows up off the bus and is no good, then fuck him, it's no big deal. But when it's somebody we know, everybody wonders how they didn't see it. Everybody looks at everybody like we're not certain we really know one another.

I need some coffee. Or crank. These amortization schedules would make a lot more sense if I were spun out. I wonder if anyone here has any. Shifty looks high. But if he is and I ask him, he'll panic and find a reason to leave the room.

Another thing to consider: dude's not really with it. He's just starting out in prison, and already he has a negative stigma strapped onto him. He's the guy who caught his cellie with a shampoo bottle. The other cons will probably nickname him The Watcher. Why not put him on it? Why not send him to the hole on a battery, and let CDC send him to a new yard? Wouldn't he have a better go of things somewhere he can keep his own name? And if corporate loan interest is tax deductible, why the fuck does its presence lower an investor's ROA? Interest shouldn't affect ROA.

"Code one, A-yard! Code one, A-yard! All inmates prone out! Get down on the yard!"

So okay, put dude on it, and pair him with either Billy or Millhouse. Then the guys who are complaining about Billy and Millhouse will have less to complain about. But which one? Billy's been on deck longer, but Millhouse's fuck up was kind of bad. He was lucky not to be the guy getting attacked.

Eventually the exam ended. I wouldn't say I finished it. Mad Dog stood waiting for me as I stepped back onto the yard. "'Bout fuckin' time," he growled. "Come on." We started walking.

"Look, Bubba," I told him, "just put Billy and Millhouse on Chuck. Set dude up to be on deck for whatever comes next. But let's get the Billy and Millhouse bullshit over and done with."

"What?" he asked. "No. We already worked all that out. This is something different. We gotta have a meeting." We were walking faster than usual.

"What's up?" I asked.

"Rick and them are gone."

"Yeah, I heard the code." Damn! Interest is only a percentage deductible. I wonder if I can sneak in there and change my answer before Williamson sends that shit out.

"Well, there was another code before that," Mad Dog said.

"I know," I told him. "Bizzy and Time Bomb."

He rounded on me. "You knew about that?"

"Yeah. Time Bomb wanted to make sure somebody knew his reasons for beatin' dude's ass."

"And you told him it was okay to jump?"

"I didn't see how it would jeopardize anything," I argued. "Anyway, Time Bomb wasn't in any sort of mood to be told no."

"Well, congratulations," he said. "You probably just got one of our homeboys killed."

Homeboys came from several directions and we made a circle in left field. It was still raining. Everyone stood. Bump and two non-Modesto skinheads joined us.

"Short and sweet, gentlemen," Jimmy began. "Brawler and I were up at Medical after breakfast. It was raining pretty good. There was a code in Lassen. Two southerners, instead of proning out in the rain there on the patio, they darted into Dental.

"Now me, I don't give a fuck. I'll prone out anywheres. But Brawler seen them two southerners dart in there, and he thinks, 'Oh, yeah, what a good idea.' He goes too. Only the patio cop sees him. He shouts at him and comes runnin' over and basically throws Brawler to the ground. And the cop yells, 'What the fuck were you thinkin'?'

"Well Brawler, he stutters and bumbles and tries to talk his way out of trouble. He says to the cop, 'I don't know. I seen them go, and I thought I could go too. I just didn't want to lay in the rain.'

"And the cop says, 'You seen who go?' and he goes to check inside Dental. And sure enough, he finds two wet sureños sittin' in chairs they're not supposed to be in. He gives all three of them write-ups."

I felt the ground go diagnal underneath me. Thoughts zoomed in and out of focus but the only one I could decipher with any clarity was, "You can't stop this from happening."

"Now I spoke with Brawler about this," Jimmy continued. "He is determined not to leave this or any yard of his own free will. He knows it's either a two-on-one, or a stabbing. He said to tell you all he'll be at the dip bars when we reach our decision."

One of the non-Modesto skinheads spoke up. "This is pretty straight forward. Dude fucked up, and he's got shit coming." I'd be lying if I said the words *I hate skinheads* didn't flash through my mind.

"When one of their own rats on somebody, the southerners stab him." *The southerners stab each other for anything.* I fought back words that seemed hell-bent on coming out, words so hot I could feel steam coming off the back of my neck. I wanted to call them cowards, to say they were pandering to the mexicans. If it were any other group, they wouldn't want him stabbed. What kind of skinhead stabs White men on behalf of some wetback? What kind of anybody thinks he can stab my Homeboy in front of me and not lose his fucking neck over it?

"Dude needs to be hit, and it needs to be done where the mexicans can see it. They do the same for us." I swallowed my thoughts, reminding myself that they were irrational. I know these points are reasonable. Still, it had been so long since I was at the mercy of my own emotions that I felt like I was high on some unfamiliar drug.

"Bump is from your town. Skinheads are front line. We feel it should be done by a Comrade."

"You're not fuckin' touchin' him." Everyone looked at me.

". . . Well, Seph, this is a very serious conversation we're having," Jimmy said. "What exactly do you mean by that?"

"I mean exactly what I said. None of these skinheads is layin' a finger on Brawler. That's on my fuckin' skin, Jimmy."

". . . Are you sayin', you want to do it, Seph?"

"Yeah, Jimmy. I'm doin' it." I left.

CHAPTER THIRTY

You want to know why prison doesn't work? It's because the motherfuckers who operate prisons don't want it to work. If CDCR actually corrected criminal behavior, if it actually rehabilitated inmates, guards and staff would be out of a fucking job.

But not just on a broad scale. Individually. The individual prison guard needs prison a hell of a lot more than anyone else does. He needs to come in and give orders. He needs to invade some guy's room, cut down his clotheslines, and confiscate his radio because it has a missing button. That makes him feel powerful. Without that he'd be forced to live in the real world, where his brother still owes him money, his best friend is fucking his wife, and nobody listens to a god damn word he says.

Inmates are job security, and the more the better. Why would the administration want to turn a single one of them straight? We've given every member of the Prison Worker's Union a vested financial interest in keeping prisons full. None of the officials making decisions gives a second thought to curing criminality or reducing recidivism. Decisions are made according to what will make the Union stronger, and what looks good on paper. If these same decision makers actually wanted to correct and rehabilitate, the process would not be difficult.

Step One: Each inmate should be issued a non-removable RFID wristwatch that gauges his position with pinpoint accuracy. If a stabbing occurs, a computer should be able to tell us who was swinging his right arm, whose pulse was up, and who walked to the toilet immediately after. The watch would save the money spent on random drug testing, since heart rates would tell us who was getting loaded. And if the watches sound expensive, consider the money they would save you in step two.

Step Two: Fire half your fucking staff. It doesn't even matter which half. Trust and believe the half you fired were assholes, and the half you keep will now take their duties a little more seriously now they see you're not above chopping motherfuckers' heads off. I'm sorry, but it does not take nine fucking officers to run a three-man building.

By percentage, prisons are more overcrowded with fucking CO's than they are with inmates. And if the Union strikes, fire all of them and replace them with National Guardsmen. Good. More money saved. CDC should not be allowed to strong arm the fuck out of the state government. And they do. They file these whining-ass reports about an officer getting stabbed, then use that to justify asking for more money to hire more cops.

But they don't tell you the full story. First, that cop was an asshole. (Trust me, I know. That cop was an asshole.) Second, that stabbing occurred in the level-four, maximum-security SHU. But all these new cops they're hiring are going onto two yards. Somewhere, right now, there's a chain link fence going up dividing a yard in half. That way we can justify hiring three new sergeants and twelve new CO's. Gotta have a sergeant for every section, you know.

Also, while your in the process of firing people, replace all of CDCR's higher officials. Your duties are to correct and rehabilitate. After several decades of proving yourselves incapable of either of those two tasks, how do you still have jobs? Why has no one held you accountable for this immense failure? Or are they all to worried your incredibly powerful union will vote them out of office?

That's the idea, of course. The Union demands more money, so they can hire more officers, which bolsters there union, so they can demand more money. CDC's union, by a wide margin, exerts more influence against a state government than any other union in the country, and it fights only against state lawmakers. Most unions pit labor against management. This one includes all employees, united to bully the governor.

How about replacing your counselors with people who actually counsel. I've never even met my fucking counselor. I just received notices in the mail that my visiting application was denied because of an INS hold, or that I couldn't work in welding because I had yet to earn my fucking GED. In five years at Soledad, you know how many cops, or counselors, or anybody asked me about my arrest, or tried to talk to me about drugs, or crime? Not a fucking one! But rest assured plenty of old convicts taught me how to cook dope, or where to get guns. Thanks for the advice, counselors. What fucking step are we on? Four? Fine.

Step Four: Give the inmates a fucking choice. I've earned one hundred and sixty-eight college units while at Soledad. They didn't even have anybody to coordinate when I started; I had to 602 just so someone would proctor my exams. Then I had to suck some dick at the package-room window 'cause the officer didn't want to give me a textbook that had a hardback cover. And I went through hell trying to keep the classes going. Imagine trying to study for a midterm when you're on site with the mexicans nextdoor, and every time you hear a key jingle you're convinced the cops are coming to carry you to the dorm. I once had three hundred pages of financial data confiscated because my professor had printed it out off the internet, and we're not allowed to have shit printed off the internet.

The point is, you would think staff would want inmates to better themselves, since a degree might offer an alternative to armed robbery as a profession. But they don't. Most cops seemed offended that an inmate was even taking college courses, especially while the officer's own son was too busy smoking weed and fucking sorority chicks to pass any of his classes.

Tie educational progress to release and let the inmates earn an early trip home. And fix your yard structure. There are two types of yards in California: sex-offender yards, and violent yards. So either you go hang out with a bunch of child molesters and rapists, or you go to Soledad and stab somebody.

We should change that. First, leave the sex offenders where their at, fuck them. But for GP, create programmer yards and fuck-up yards. Then let the inmates choose where they'll go. I know that's dificult for CDC to swallow, but let the inmates choose. Don't just make the decision for them, because you can and you don't give a shit.

Tell them if they like to fight, or shoot dope, or play fucking pinochle all day, they should go to the fuck-up yard. Fighting there is a little thirty-day offense, and nobody ever gets drug tested. Or they can go to the programmer yard. Fighting gets you in a lot of trouble, and you drug test once a week, but you actually have a shot at becomming a normal human being.

Another Fucking Step: Fuck yourself. I say that ahead of time because I know none of you asshole CDC officials are going to listen to one fucking word of this. You don't care what I have to say. If you cared, you wouldn't have tried to move me to the dorm. If you cared, I wouldn't still be on the fucking GED waiting list.

You don't care, and it's because you don't care that your prisons make criminals worse rather than better. From the top policy makers to the lowest building officer, you motherfuckers prod and poke us with sticks, irritating us for what seems like no reason other than to see how angry you can get us. Well congratulations, I'm fucking pissed off.

You poke motherfuckers until they bite you, then you document the teeth marks and whine about how you need more officers. And we've been doing it for years. Solano is GP, and it's violent. Folsom is PC, and its not so violent. So we report all the violence at Solano until the state approves us hiring more guards there. Then we switch all the inmates from Folsom to Solano, and Solano to Folsom. Now Folsom is GP. So for the next to years we will document all the violence there and complain until the state approves us hiring more officers for Folsom. We use these and other deceitful reporting methods to feed the enormous green dragon that CDCR has become.

The biggest lie we push is the idea that more guards mean safer prisons, or that we do not already have the means to reduce our inmate population. We should further classify and segregate the prisoners, separating the salvagable from the lost. Many life-sentence inmates should be released.

For those who cannot be released, who unofficially do not have any chance for parole, we should remove them from the equation. Two of our state's thirty-six prisons could be designated as lifer-only. Rather than on rehabilitation, these penitentiaries could focus separately on budgetary independence. Inmates work for seventeen cents an hour. Many could be trained in computer operation and maintenance, and CDCR could then contract that labor to companies who now outsource tech suport overseas. Old men who rarely fight and need little supervision would actually be reducing the department's budgetary problems, providing income for California in a very real sense. And rather than be located in areas of moderate weather, as is done for inmates on psychological medications, these facilities could be located in the hotest or coldest parts of the state, thereby naturally reducing the average inmate's length of occupancy.

For those inmates we deem salvageable, effort must be made to change that person's views, opinions, and behavioral patterns. We are not the California Department of Babysitting, and if we expect to correct or rehabilitate anyone, every employee.

Must make helping the inmates a personal priority. for too long have we viewed confinement as punishment, rather than as a chance for recovery. Understandably, these men deserve to be punished, but simply punishing and then releasing them does very little good for society. Anyway, trust me, spending any number of years without access to pussy and swiming pools is punishment enough. If a guy is simply hell-bent on being a pirate, best course is often just let him be and soon enough he'll end up in the SHU.

Some assholes are just born for this shit. What kills me are the cops who think their so fucking smart because they caught somebody's line, because they cracked Aaron's binary code or figured out how we ghost messages onto paper. You're not smart. Smart is the motherfucker who thought that shit up in the first place. You only even know about it 'cause some fucking rat gave up game—sorta the way I do throughout this whole fuckin' book. So go on ahead thinking you're smart. Meanwhile the assholes you're supposed to be keeping tabs on are running circles around you. And you want to look to me for help understanding this shit? You've got nothing coming. Fuck you.

CHAPTER THIRTY-ONE

I got the large razor blade from one of the textiles guys, the same model Wingnut had fallen victim to. That one had a handle. I didn't bother putting a handle on this. For a riot or something, yeah, you'd want a handle, but this was just a single task and then it would need to disappear. This was just one slice.

The mexicans differentiate between a cut and a stabbing. If it were their trip, they'd stab. But we're not mexicans. Anyway, better me cutting than Bump stabbing. Bump might kill him.

I came out for yard. John and I lived all the way in the back, 228, so I took the back stairs to get off the tier. Somebody stopped me.

"Seph, you gonna play softball?"

"No, I can't," I shook my head. "I gotta make a phone call."

"Well come over when you're done. We'll pick you up. Do you know, is Ryan gonna play?"

I shook my head again. "I don't know."

"Man, are you all right? You look sick or some shit."

"No," I answered. "I'm good."

"You sure? You don't need allergy pills or nothin'?"

I shook dude off. I just needed to get out of the building. Once outside I joined up with the first group of Whites I saw moving along the track. We walked. Someone was talking to me, I think Wacko.

". . . for whatever reason, by the first of September. Did you hear about that?"

I shook my head.

"They said all of North Facility. However they're gonna do it, I don't know. Some dudes here have been through it before. They say they'll move us out in big waves, all in the same week."

"Wait," I stopped him. "What's happening?"

"They're making both yards SNY," he said. "Soledad North is gonna be fuckin' PC."

I couldn't believe it. After more than forty years as one of the most violent yards in the state, Soledad would be turned into a punk-ass dick-sucking festival.

Good riddance.

Someone bumped into me heading in the opposite direction. I apologized. My friend spoke again.

"Are you all right, Seph?"

"I'm fine."

"You're high, huh?"

I shook my head.

"If you're high, you're high. You don't gotta lie about it."

"Fine, I'm high." I broke away from the group at the phone line so I could meet up with Woody. "Walk laps with me," I said as we shook hands.

"Dude's doin' dips."

"Let him do 'em. Walk laps with me."

"You're not ready?" Woody asked, squinting at me.

"Evidently I have shit on my face," I told him. "Walk laps with me so I can get my head on strait." We walked laps.

I couldn't help but notice what a nice fuckin' day it was, puffy clouds and shit but mostly blue sky. Plus I had my

Homeboy with me. Brawler was our Homeboy too, and we weren't going to let anything happen to him. We would talk it out with the mexicans. We would find a way to keep him here and we would never wash a good Wood for nothing. Brawler would do the same for either of us.

We peeled off at the workout area. Brawler was doing dips facing the yard. He came down off the bars as we approached. I shook his hand. No hug. He wouldn't feel much like hugging, given the circumstances.

"Anyone talk to you yet?" I asked him.

Brawler shook his head, almost imperceptibly. He was watching our hands on the sly. If I didn't already know, I wouldn't have noticed him doing it. I kept mine in front of me and out of my pockets. Woody did the same.

"Well you're still here," I commented. "That's a good sign."

"How'd the talk go yesterday?"

I shrugged. "A surprisingly large number of dudes had nothing to say, one way or the other. I think most of us were just shocked. I put my piece in, and so did Brandon, sayin' basically that shit was accidental and could have happened to any one of us. Last I heard, no decision had been reached." Brawler clung to every word.

"Jimmy and one of the skinheads are supposed to talk with the southerners this morning," Woody put in. I gave him my full attention. "They're tryin' to work it so you can still come back to the yard."

"If it were my call," I told Brawler, "I'd say two-on-one in front of them, and you come back to B-yard. Then it's over. If they don't like that, they can get theirs." Woody jumped up to do a set of pull-ups. "Are you getting' in the phone line with me or not?" I demanded.

"Yeah," he answered. "I'm just doin' one set."

"Tsk. That's like half a workout for you anyway," I joked.

Before he went back to doing dips, Brawler gave me a hug. "Love your life, kid." He hugged Woody too.

We joined the tail end of the phone line. Brawler's cellmate was Mitch. They were doing dips together. Brawler would do a set facing one way, and Mitch would stand facing the other. Then they would switch. Mitch was the only man on the whole yard Brawler really had any trust in.

The phone line moved and so did we. I was supposed to be laughing and joking with Woody, but honestly none of the shit he said was that funny.

Before the line could move again, Brawler and Mitch strolled off toward the pisser. Mitch approached the toilet, facing away from us. Brawler stood at his back, facing toward us. I laughed as Woody motioned toward something at the basketball court. Once Mitch was done, the cellmates switched places.

The second Brawler's back was to me I hopped over the phone line railing. I made my way quickly toward the toilet, muttering the words to a song every White convict has heard at least once.

> My name is Imp, the gimp, the Peckerwood
>   pimp
> Sellin' my bitches 'cause my dick's gone limp

I hurried across the horseshoe pits. The same plot, the same story; a new cast every year.

> I run, I hide, I jump behind a tree
> Po-Po's comin' but they can't catch me

There's more to the song, but I was already at the pisser. If Mitch had really been standing post, he would have let Brawler know one of his Homeboys was approaching. But we had spoken with Mitch. He had needed few words to see the wisdom of siding with the group over siding with the cellmate. He let me pass.

Brawler had taken the stall all the way to the left. Anyone coming at him from a neighboring stall would have to use his left hand. I stepped into the stall to his right and reached over the short divider, setting the blade to Brawler's neck just below the jawbone. I slid it forward with enough pressure to convince myself I wasn't taking it easy on him. His body jolted in response to the cut and I heard his piss stream cut off as I leaned forward to flush the blade.

He lifted his hand toward the wound but stopped halfway. He shook his dick and pulled up his pants. He pushed the button to flush the toilet. Then he looked at me.

If I still had a heart, if prison hadn't taken mine from me, that look would have broken it.